Praise for
Entitled

"The inside story of a rich fam's succession that's more gripping than *Succession*."

—Peter Carry, writer, editor

"The twisted plot of this surprising whodunnit is a hunt for who didn't do it—who it was that tried but failed to kill the rich and ruthless old patriarch. From the start, however, those suspects include even the old man's loved ones. Set among the strivers and connivers of New York's upper 1%, Orr's engaging tale is a feast of family disfunction, privilege, and secrets."

—William C. Rempel, bestselling author of *The Gambler* and *At the Devil's Table*

"This is an intelligent, strong, intricate narrative, carried along by characters who are well drawn and complete, at least for the purposes they play in this narrative. While Benjamin claims much of the spotlight, Charlie Cantling's presence is remarkable in its various roles—catalyst, antagonist, egomaniacal patriarch, with personal traits that all point to meanness and manipulation. Beyond that, four distinctive sisters, a woebegone brother, and Benjamin's own brother come across as the various components of a complex mélange, each with his or her own psychological damage stemming from Charlie's machinations. There's a sophistication to all this that is quite refreshing, and very well done."

—Greg Fields, author

Entitled
by Leonard H. Orr

© Copyright 2024 Leonard H. Orr

ISBN 979-8-88824-530-9

All rights reserved. No part of this publication may be reproduced, stored in a retrieval system, or transmitted in any form or by any means—electronic, mechanical, photocopy, recording, or any other—except for brief quotations in printed reviews, without the prior written permission of the author.

This is a work of fiction. All the characters in this book are fictitious, and any resemblance to actual persons, living or dead, is purely coincidental. The names, incidents, dialogue, and opinions expressed are products of the author's imagination and are not to be construed as real.

Published by

3705 Shore Drive
Virginia Beach, VA 23455
800-435-4811
www.koehlerbooks.com

Entitled

Leonard H. Orr

VIRGINIA BEACH
CAPE CHARLES

With love for my real-life family.

PROLOGUE

He lies in a hospital bed, bandaged to the nines and attached to the latest instruments of artificial life. Images flicker before him, and fluttery lines on a monitor vouch for brain activity, but few would call it thinking. In his fractured world, he doesn't hear the beep of machines nor feel the stab of needles. He doesn't remember instructing his driver to stay ahead of the Friday-night traffic before it peaked. He doesn't recall the rise in the road that hid the jam ahead, doesn't recall his driver's cursing when the car reached the crest, the scream of the brakes, the veering off, the tumbling.

The police have measured tire marks, a coroner examined the driver's body, and chemists have parsed the dead man's blood. They found a routine case of too much velocity and not enough time and redirected to more opaque disasters.

Visitors to the hospital are where the murk sets in. Men Charlie Cantling hired for the corporation—and a few women—arrive, look grim, and muse aloud about his chances and in silence about their jobs. They'd love to redo the pyramid of who reports to whom, each with a different design, but ancient arrangements leave them neutered and send them to lunch with headhunters. Real power resides with Cantling's children, who arrive with a minimum of tears and some aptitude for scheming. With Charlie likely dying, they'll need cold blood for decisions to come, and over the years, with their father's help, they've acquired it. Some have seen the family lawyer, who advises inaction and waiting for further advice. Some, whom Cantling would call ungrateful, have lawyers of their own.

When he's little changed day to day, the flow of visitors thins, for this protracted dying is somewhere between nuisance and tragedy, and doctors still can't restore the dead. Then the surprises begin. His bones mend, his limbs and organs start to function, he has moments of near lucidity. The doctors admit he has chances, but early progress is crucial, and his may have been too slow. He's in his late sixties, and his health was good, but setbacks or stagnation are still major risks. The most reasonable hope is he'll stabilize, neither paralyzed nor mobile, not numb and not alert, sometimes sensible, often not, born to command and commanding nothing.

In his lucid moments, the doctors warn him: because of drugs and trauma, you can't trust what you think you know, can't tell the real from the imagined. About his brain's wilder renderings—wingless flying, jumps in time, cameos of the dead—he agrees. One scene from the present is too coherent to shrug off and so vivid that in druggy variation it repeats again and again. He's on his back in his hospital bed and half-awake. Suddenly, there's a pillow on his face, a strangely heavy heap of fluff pressing on nose and mouth. He fights. The weight feels huge, relentless. He struggles to breathe but sucks in fabric and stuffing. He's suffocating. His hands rip at forearms above him. He won't let these bastards win. He writhes and swings his head, finds a pocket of air—and breathes and steels himself for further struggle.

The weight lifts. "Tough old guy," whispers a voice he can't identify. "The man's mind doesn't work, but his body keeps fighting. We'll have to find another way." "It would be the right thing," someone whispers, "for him." "Yeah," the first voice whispers, "for him and everybody else."

As his strength returns and his drug-induced delirium subsides, he notifies the authorities and calls for guards and cameras. He exults and he rages. Phantoms or not, the whisperers have lost. Their chances have died, and he hasn't.

It takes him weeks to fully recognize his mistake.

CHAPTER ONE

BENJAMIN

BANG! Asleep, I dreamed of flying.
BANG!
A second explosion woke me. A shelf must have fallen.
BANG!

A chain reaction, shelf after shelf? Or maybe the extremely noisy engine outside was backfiring.

BANG!

I sat up on the edge of the mattress and pressed a palm to each ear to muffle the noise.

I tried to ground myself. It was a Friday night in June. I was here for the weekend in the old, mortgaged house near the Sound. Was it gunfire? Sometimes our neighbors, the Cantlings, shot at raccoons. Local kids practiced with targets. But not in the middle of the night.

I lifted my hands from my ears and again heard the full throb of the engine. BANG! The point of origin seemed to be on the south side of our property. Then I remembered my brother, Jody, had arrived home earlier than usual—and Jody, at thirty-one, three consequential years younger than me, had a penchant for trouble.

In my light pajamas, I stumbled to a window and saw that a mist had settled in, blocking out the stars and moon and creating a gauzy darkness around the scene. Near the Cantling property and a few hundred yards away from our house, a small helicopter hovered above the beams of its landing lights. Near it, an emergency flare settled toward the ground, its slow descent the only calming note amid the uproar. BANG! A muzzle flash on our patio. Another red flare floating down from on high.

The helicopter, outlined in lights front and rear, with a relentless strobe on its tail, retreated into the sky. I ran downstairs to the patio door and reached outside to flip a wall-mounted switch. In the patio lights, I glimpsed my brother in a barefoot dash to the six-foot-tall rhododendron at the patio's edge. He crouched behind the bush and motioned toward me, appearing to shout, but I couldn't hear him over the pulsing engine and beating blades. His waving hand held an orange pistol.

I stepped onto the patio.

"For God's sake, Benjamin. Turn off the lights! They'll see us!"

"Have you been shooting flares?" I shouted back.

"Turn the lights off!"

"Has someone been shooting at you?"

"They might start if you leave lights on," Jody said.

I imagined the general reaction of former Apache pilot Charlie Cantling and his helicopter passengers. After a late-night flight from the city, the travelers would yearn to be in their seaside beds, the lapping wavelets lulling them to sleep. This delay would vex them, and I assumed each was at this moment searching a quadrant of the dark perimeter for the source of the flares. Though they were unlikely to spot me through the mist, I wondered how my addressing a rhododendron might appear to them.

I turned my back to the bush and said, "So it was you who fired the flares. What's the emergency?"

"The guy flies right on top of us. Wakes us up over and over. He's harassing us so we'll sell out to him. Tonight he got a warning."

"About what? How you'll shoot him out of the sky?"

"With a flare gun? And I didn't aim anywhere near him."

"Flares could start a fire."

"Everything's wet," Jody said, ready with answers. "It's been drizzling half the night."

My brother had a point about Cantling's designs on our house. Over the years, the man had bought two properties adjacent to his own, and we'd heard rumors he wanted to buy us out.

"That car crash!" Jody said. "That fucking hospital! He should have died when he had the chance. You'd think he'd learn a lesson about safety. No, he flies around like a crazy man in the fog."

"Might there be a better way to deal with him?"

"Like what? A box of cookies with a request? Some chocolates? Turn the lights off. We don't want him to pin this on us."

"Us? Us?"

"We need him to think it could have been anybody in the neighborhood."

I tried to stay calm. More than most jobs, mine required that I avoid legally dicey situations. Jody was right. I flipped the switch and darkened the patio, expecting the helicopter would depart to deposit its passengers at the Cantling house.

BOOM! A fiery blast rose behind the rhododendron. The red emergency flare drifted downward in the sky.

"Will you stop it!" I shouted. "He might see the muzzle flash."

"No way. He'd have to be looking right at us."

As if to mock Jody's reassurance, the helicopter's engine revved, and the machine came toward us like a noisy metal monster on the prowl. A branch snapped in the rhododendron as Jody crawled in. "Run, Benjamin! If they don't see us, they can't do anything!"

"That's your plan?"

"I'm out of flares," he said, as if this were a negative. "I'll wait here. Run!"

"What good is that? He knows who fired the flares. He could call the cops. Don't we have enough trouble with them already?"

I stood my ground. The helicopter stopped and hovered before it reached our patio, its spotlight directed at me.

"Give me the gun," I said, looking away from the rhododendron.

"Why?"

"Just give it to me."

"Deny everything," Jody said. "Just wave at them and go inside. I'll stay in the bush. They'll go away soon."

As usual, I tried to be patient with Jody's behavior. At birth he'd been adopted by our parents, who were eager for another child after learning Mom couldn't have any more children naturally. Then, a dozen years ago, our mother died of breast cancer. Jody had to deal with two mothers leaving him when I could scarcely reconcile myself to losing just one. And three years ago, our father succumbed to heart disease, leaving only me and Jody. How many wounds was Jody supposed to endure? I wondered if he could ever grow up.

"You got me into this," I said. "Give me the gun."

"You'll mess up."

"Give me the gun."

"Okay, genius. You might have had a scholarship to Yale, but you don't know shit about Charlie Cantling."

A long arm extended from the rhododendron and slid the pistol across the flagstone, a move those inside the helicopter were likely too distant to observe. I picked up the flare gun, a single-shot pistol of hardened Walmart plastic. I had purchased it for the small motorboat Jody used for spearfishing after his many misadventures with rocks and weather and darkness.

Turning on the patio lights, I held the pistol above my head and rather ceremoniously paced a few feet toward the floating helicopter.

I bent over and set the flare gun down. Then I straightened and backed away.

As if to acknowledge my surrender, the nose of the helicopter dipped. I hoped for a pivot and flyaway, followed by an awkward call tomorrow, but the machine resumed its flight toward us. Its engine churned, its propellers thumped. A hundred feet overhead and looming very large, it oppressed us with noise and downdraft. Its spotlight found the pistol and stopped moving.

Glittering droplets of mist, stirred by the huge blades, swirled within the cone of light. Then the spotlight glided away from the pistol and scoured the patio, the rhododendron, and a portion of the lawn before settling its otherworldly beam on me.

"Benjamin, this isn't like you," Charlie Cantling's amplified voice boomed from the sky. "Where's your brother?"

I raised my arms and shoulders in an exaggerated shrug.

"I know he's down there."

"He can harass us all he wants," Jody shouted for my benefit only. "We're not selling our house. You and me are in this together."

Unfortunately, we were. When our father died, Jody announced he'd move in for eight months a year and contribute to the upkeep. In warmer weather I joined him for weekends, commuting from my apartment in the city. It was rather bold of Jody to insist we not sell when his cash contribution was slim and erratic. As a result, my responsibilities felt oppressive, with the inherited mortgage gobbling money and the deferred maintenance piling up: unpainted trim, a large, leaky window, a score of nagging failures. But Jody held firm to the house, as I did to him.

"I know you're down there, Jody," Cantling called from the sky. "You shoot flares at a helicopter in a residential neighborhood? You're supposed to know something about real estate. If I report you to the cops, you'll lose your license." Cantling was referencing Jody's fledgling career as a real-estate salesman specializing in the low end during the seven months when folks in Stonefield tended to look. "How would you like that?"

Jody emerged from the bush in his jeans and polo. When the spotlight swung around to light him up, I noticed that the front of his shirt was badly torn. He pulled it off and tried to brush away the mud and dirt covering the front of his body. He was lightly bleeding from a cut on his chest. I expected he'd heal before daylight. His physical health was magnificent.

Halfway cleaned up, Jody extended both middle fingers toward the sky. The disrespect was startling, as Charlie Cantling believed those around him had been placed there to take dictation.

"A classy look," I shouted over the noise of the chopper. "Soon to go viral if someone's recording. When the clients Google you, it will sell a lot of houses."

"Wrong," Jody shouted back. "I'm doing this for the market. Who'd buy anything with helicopters buzzing everywhere?"

The chopper settled further toward us, its spotlight now fixed on Jody.

"Sorry to break the news." Ann Cantling's voice from the helicopter's loudspeaker seemed to fill the sky. "Jody, you're putting on weight."

The intervention of Jody's ex-girlfriend yielded some rare chagrin. Jody retracted his middle fingers and dropped his hands.

"Same old, same old," my brother said to me, still shouting above the din. He waved at the copter. "Great girl. Keeps it together—and with a father like that. But can't she cut a guy some slack? Teach skiing three months a year and see what happens to your body," Jody said. Jody was tall for a skier but was such an athlete that it didn't hold him back. "What she saw was muscle."

"I was hoping I'd run into the Gould boys," Ann announced. "It's been a while."

It had been ten months except for the two cameos in New York. But who was counting? In recent summers, Ann Cantling had scarcely been in Stonefield. With her father nearly recovered from last September's accident, I hadn't expected her now.

"Dad's having his June bash," she said. "I'm inviting both of you. Tomorrow at six."

"Not the Early Fourth," I groaned.

"We can't say no," Jody replied, suddenly the obliging neighbor. "She's celebrating her father's recovery. And she's not here that much." He aimed a big thumbs-up at the sky.

"Jody, I need you an hour early," Ann announced. "I'm having people for tennis. What do you say?"

Another thumbs-up from Jody. The disconnect of a friendly conversation booming from a loudspeaker was disorienting.

"Benjamin, is there a chance you'll come to the party?" Ann said. "Four of the five sibs will be there. Humor us."

Ann knew my opinion of the Early Fourth, where every year the Cantlings erupted into squabbles without warning, despite the grandeur most of them sought to project. Drink loosened tongues, and hunger inflamed the spats, for cocktails were plentiful and food was sparse. There could be accusations, rants, tears, and sulking. Yet in spite of the event's history, nothing would stop Charlie from holding it. That so many showed up attested to his power and charisma—and perhaps to a desire to watch.

I made an exaggerated eating motion, lifting one hand repeatedly to my mouth.

"Really, Benjamin?" Ann said. "Yes, there will be plenty of food." Negotiating with a helicopter might normally feel bizarre, but these were Cantlings.

I raised two thumbs to her, though I had no intention of attending.

"Benjamin. Jody. Wait," Cantling said. "After we land, I need to talk to both of you."

Jody pointed his thumbs down.

"It's either that or the police," Cantling said. "Do you want me to tell them the truth about the flares?" He aimed the helicopter straight up.

After Jody retrieved the flare gun, we watched the helicopter settle onto the Cantling lawn. Soon the only reminder of the thunderous nightmare was the stunned silence of birds, the only noise the soft crackle of waves, little more than ripples, against the stony Cantling beach. A few lights tripped on in the Cantling house. My fear and irritation toward Ann's father were nothing new, but I resented Ann's presence. Why? Because I liked being around her so much.

It's possible I was already half in love with Ann the day she started her dalliance with Jody. Cantlings and Goulds had grown up spending summers next door to each other, and Ann was almost exactly between us in age. She and I had skipped pebbles across the water, hung out at the local beaches, started to drink when we were teens. The books and songs say love's an up-and-down thing, hot and cold, on and off. With apologies to the poets and professors, my affection for Ann has been a near constant ever since we started to trade observations of our families and made a secret place from which to view our relatives and the world beyond. That's how I learned that the main role for Ann, the middle of five siblings, the most reliable and grounded, was to try to keep them all from one another's throats.

Though Jody and Ann acted as if it weren't happening, they had a different kind of summer a couple of years ago. There followed a few months of commuting between New York, where Ann worked, and Colorado, where Jody sort of did. Only after they'd broken up did they admit to what had happened. And all that time, I struggled with my feelings for Ann—struggled to play the friend and confidant in our increasingly infrequent contacts, to pose as clever and content when much of the time I was no such thing. The posing strained our relations almost as much as her sleeping with my brother did.

On our patio, Jody gestured toward an eye-level pinprick of light on the field that sloped up toward our house. Only the light's steadiness distinguished it from the dancing fireflies, darts of yellow in the blackness. The glow grew brighter until it nearly reached us. I imagined Charlie, still limping after the accident, moving slow.

"Are you there, fellows?" he called. "I can't see you."

"I wish I had another cartridge," Jody whispered to me.

"Behave," I whispered back.

"Wimp."

"Jody? Is that you?" Cantling said.

"Move a little closer. Widen my target," Jody said.

Charlie's light switched off, sending us back into darkness.

"Enough of that," Cantling said. "If you're coming to the house tomorrow, we need to talk now—as old friends and neighbors."

"I should shoot you," Jody said.

My brother is a person of spirit and contradictions. At the time, I believed him destined for greatness or self-immolation or both. His gig selling houses was acceptable, but the market had slowed, and sales were seasonal. Because Jody knew the job would never be enough for him, he didn't work hard or well. But what would satisfy him? Nothing could turn him into a lawyer or an accountant or civil servant. Nothing seemed to divert him from bars or brawls or women.

"I'm carrying a pistol, too," Cantling said. "And people think I'm crazy."

"If you're crazy," Jody said, "how do you manage to fly over our house?"

"The wind bounces around up there. It's my only safe approach."

"It bounces around because you planted too many trees."

"I have property rights. I'm not gonna down trees to suit you. Plus I have a business to run. I can't land at the airport and sit in traffic forever on the highway."

"Didn't you use to drive from the city all the time?" Jody said.

"Have you forgotten? That drive almost killed me."

"Next time don't race up a truck's ass. Now get off our property."

It seemed preposterous that these two, almost forty years apart in age and sparring since Jody was three, could be so at odds over a bit of noise in the night. But neither of them could back down.

I supplied the sanity. "Jody, you have no more flares. Charlie, you're not carrying a gun. I'm going to turn the lights on. If I'm wrong, fire away."

"Don't!" Jody said.

With the lights came the night's first glimpse of Charlie, dressed in suit pants and a white shirt with rolled-up sleeves. He was tall and broad chested, with buzz-cut white hair and a gritty set to his jaw. The fold-up cane he wielded at full extension attested to his diminished strength. How humiliating his weakness must have felt! I knew that as long as he needed that cane, he'd be a lion in rehab and a bastard at home.

It seemed he'd been bluffing about a pistol. The only weapon in sight was Jody's orange flare gun.

"Bro, you don't get anything, do you?" Jody said. "You've made everything worse."

Cantling waved the cane at me. "Your brother and I were having a disagreement. Nobody was shooting anybody."

I said, "What are you doing here, Charlie?"

"Benjamin, I want to make sure I see you tomorrow. I'm counting on you for a reasonable evaluation of my offer for the house."

"Told you so," Jody said to me. "Charlie, we're not selling."

"What offer?" I said.

"It's late. Come talk to me before the party."

"I look forward to it," I said to Cantling. I was already planning excuses when a red light began to pulse from behind our house and whirl and flash across our patio, followed by a crunch of stones on our derelict driveway. It had to be cops, no doubt summoned by neighbors. I assumed Jody would hide the flare gun from our new guests, maybe slide it back under the rhododendron, but he set it down in the open on a flagstone.

Jody had some unpleasant history with the Stonefield cops, who had detained and released him a couple of times as the result of bar fights. But our real problem was drugs. Though I hadn't used since college, and back then nothing hard, as luck would have it my brother kept a smidgeon of cocaine around the house. If the arriving cops conjured exigent circumstances and charged inside, we'd be at risk. Normally, given a chance to snag one of the second-home owners that the community depends on, the Stonefield Police drug net would be reliably porous. But Jody's history with the cops might have turned us into targets.

As the police car approached, I fancied rushing upstairs to grab the dope from Jody's sock drawer, after which I'd flush it into septic oblivion—but my dash might create those dreaded exigent circumstances, and the only thing flushed away would be my claim to not know about the cocaine. I let Jody, an excellent dodger, take the lead. He didn't budge. Neither did I.

The cruiser stopped beside our house. The flasher stayed on. I steeled myself for confrontation, but I noticed Jody and Charlie grinning like happy ghouls in red stroboscopic hell. Charlie had reason to be smug. But why was my brother filled with goofy confidence?

Two cops ambled toward us, their flashlights blinding Jody and me. The summer night felt cold.

"Charlie Cantling here. How can I help?"

The flashlights swung to Cantling.

"I haven't seen you out here since the accident, Mr. Cantling," the cop said. The flashlights aimed at Charlie's feet, lest the bright beams inconvenience the great man. "We've been meaning to thank you for your gift to the softball team. With all you were going through, you didn't forget us."

"Forget you guys? Never."

"Sir, you should come to a game." When police of any stripe seem deferential, it's often laced with rage. But this slobber was real. "Mr. Cantling, isn't it late to be visiting your neighbors?"

"I just flew in. I saw the Goulds on the lawn and wanted to talk to them."

"Officer, I gave money to the softball team too," I said.

The two flashlights redirected toward me. "We're so grateful," the first cop said.

The cops switched off their flashlights. As my eyes readjusted, I saw the cop behind the spokesman standing at the ready, his right elbow bent and his palm resting on the handle of his holstered pistol.

"We had a call from a neighbor," the lead cop said. "He heard shots. Saw flares. I assume it had something to do with you three. What kind of weaponry we looking at?"

"I've got a flare gun. It's on the ground. See?" Jody pointed toward the Walmart Special. "It's empty."

"I have a pistol in an ankle holster," Cantling volunteered, reaching toward his shin. "It's licensed." Our neighbor had been armed!

"Did you fire it tonight, Mr. Cantling?" the cop asked.

"No."

The cop turned back to me. "What about you? Any weapons?"

I was dumbfounded. Jody had been bluffing an empty flare gun against our armed neighbor. "No weapons," I mumbled.

"So, Jody, it's you we need to talk to. I understand some folks around here don't like helicopters. Was that you shooting at Mr. Cantling's aircraft?"

"Look, Charlie's flyovers bug the hell out of me. But him being an asshole doesn't mean I'd let him crash in the fog. I heard him flying around in the soup. I did what I could to help him locate the shore."

Okay, Jody had a story ready. But he still needed Charlie to back him up.

"Mr. Cantling?" the cop said.

"As long as I've known him, Jody Gould's been a pain in the ass," Charlie said.

"Fuck you," Jody said. "The next time you're ready to crash, I'll let you."

"Please don't," Cantling said. "The helicopter's radar isn't good enough for tight spots. The flares were helpful. They marked our angle of approach. Jody, I owe you."

I watched in wonder. Decades of antagonism between Charlie and my brother had somehow created a basis for spontaneous cooperation.

"It seems you're in the clear," the cop told Jody. "But no more flares unless there's very real trouble."

"Count on it."

Our guests departed in opposite directions. I switched off the patio lights, and Jody and I retreated to our living room.

In the years since our father died, our budget squeeze hadn't let us correct Dad's misallied furnishings: musty and faded couches, antique chairs, cheap landscapes on the walls, and print curtains with thinning colors. Under the paired light of unmatched lamps, we flopped down to decompress. The adrenaline burn had left us hungry, and we popped chocolate squares into our mouths from a selection of bars I'd brought from the city.

"I love you, bro," Jody said. "But a lot of times, you just don't get it. Lucky for us, I figured Charlie wouldn't press charges about the flares. It would hurt the Cantling brand on social media. I know you don't like the Early Fourth and the Cantlings usually act like morons at the party, but you've gotta follow up and see him. We don't want to piss him off more. Let him make an offer on the house. They say he's got plenty of cash. His company made a big score before the accident. Show some interest until tonight blows over. Then we tell him we're not selling."

Jody had turned sensible, but I wouldn't admit it. I said, "I didn't cause this mess, and I don't feel obliged to clean it up."

He stood, stretched, and yawned. "Eventually, you'll realize you need to go. But don't make any deals. Charlie Cantling is dangerous."

He switched off the closest lamp and went to the stairs, then paused after several steps. Light from the still-lit lamp barely found him. With an arm on the railing, he seemed a frozen shadow. "What was that all about?" he said.

"What was what?"

"Hasn't it occurred to you? Charlie used to shoot a shotgun now and then, but I've never seen him with a pistol. Not once. What the hell is he afraid of? Charlie Cantling doesn't like to be afraid."

CHAPTER TWO

BENJAMIN

B y the next afternoon, I'd capitulated and agreed to humor our neighbor, so Jody and I retraced the path Charlie had round-tripped the night before. It had never been explicit, but Charlie and his wife tended to think of us as scruffy Jews with no class. Accordingly, despite the still and sunny weather, I had opted for a blazer, gray slacks, and a tie. I hoped the costume would make me feel comfortable among the dressy Stonefield elite, and as we weaved through the trees separating the properties, sweat beaded on my forehead and lips. I made for a sorry comparison with my racket-bearing brother, who looked quite the lithe young hunk in dark shorts, a red polo shirt, and a tattered black baseball cap.

We heard the rhythmic thumping of a tennis ball and saw flashes of blue and green through the maples Charlie had installed as a windbreak. As my brother shambled toward the court, I lingered behind the surrounding chain-link fence to observe. Jody began stretching out his long muscles. Ann, in blue shorts and a white top, was warming up opposite a young couple I didn't recognize.

Ann was dark haired and pretty, albeit not as slim and beautiful as her sisters, but who was? She was the most independent of the Cantling sibs, the one who seemed to have her wits about her. She'd lived in Paris and worked at a bank—her French was that good. Now she was a paralegal and had started courses in clinical psychology.

Since her father's accident, I'd been trying to connect with her. My texts had been thank-you'd, my unanswered calls briefly appreciated in texted replies. Beyond that, all I'd managed were one or two drive-bys at New York City events. At the first, I'd munched on party food while she brought me up to date on her schedule. I'd sighed in sympathy at her father's slow improvement. The second meetup had been an uninspired repeat. I'd always hoped she was immune to the troubles that plagued her sibs. Now I worried. Was Ann Cantling, Vassar cum laude and Cantling escapee, in a depressive rut? Or was it simply that with her family in more extremis than usual, she had little time for me?

Not being chosen for tennis was even more humiliating because I, though shorter than Jody and less athletic, with my hairline already receding and stomach tending toward a paunch, was the steadier and better tennis player. Ann's avoidance of me and her pursuit of Jody for tennis were reason enough to hang around and observe the match.

WHOMP. An Ann forehand, the weight shifting nicely, the swing smooth from low to high, the stroke fluid and measured as if she were caressing the ball. WHOMP. An Ann overhead, a swift whack to speed the ball beyond the reach of others. I was on Cantling property, longing again. I, who detested mistakes, whose work required daily feats of finding and correcting them, had plainly made a big one. Everything I had done to rid myself of Ann—all the self-lectures about futility, the dead-end romances, the resolve to forget—had failed.

It occurred to me I should take the chance and declare myself. But if I wasn't even Ann's choice for partner within our family, in a world population of eight billion, how low on her list was my name?

If I spoke up, all the apparatus of Cantling condescension might accompany my rejection.

My cell phone chimed. A message from Al "Twenty-Four Seven" Byrne popped onto the screen. I was surprised to hear from him. Like every Byrne missive, this one declared it was encrypted end to end.

"Meet set w Cantling? Important." Byrne's texting style had been adapted between divorces to appeal to younger women.

I was surprised. As far as I knew, Cantling wanted to see me about buying our house. Why would my boss weigh in, my boss with whom I was on somewhat shaky ground? I pondered Al's text while Jody sauntered onto the court. The others halted the warm-up and approached him. The woman visitor, dressed like her partner in safe guest whites, tugged at the dyed-blond ponytail jutting through her cap, redirected it down her back, and smoothed it there. Through handshakes, recitals of schools attended, and a gaggle of do-you-knows, the four combatants never dropped their smiles. With his roguish knack for seeming acceptable, my brother easily passed inspection.

I bent to my phone and poked out in elliptical Byrnese, "U know about meet w Cantling?" I'd have asked precisely how he knew, but disposable underlings like me didn't interrogate Byrne.

On court, the ponytailed opponent directed a warm-up ball toward Jody. My brother whirled his racket back and, in a swooping C-shaped motion, uncorked a mighty swing. The ball careened skyward off the racket frame, soared over the awestruck opponents, and rattled chain link on the fly. Adjusting, Jody hammered the next two into the net.

Byrne's reply: "Cantling didn't tell u? He contacted me. Wants u. Poss big new client. Poss matter life and death. Keep me informed."

Possibly a matter of life and death? If that was true, would Byrne trust me to handle it? Was I to be engulfed in Cantling chaos?

Only one thing was certain: I had to follow through and try to meet Cantling.

The tennis match began. Ann played smartly, but the opponents kept hitting to Jody, whose exaggerated ambitions lost him and Ann the first two games. When Jody was about to serve the third, Ann approached him. I saw her exasperation as she brushed a speck of yellow ball fluff from Jody's cheek. Then Jody tolerated what I assumed was a whispered lecture on shot selection. As they separated, he tapped the strings of his racket on Ann's derriere. This was not a normal move with Ann Cantling, whose dignity and self-possession were constants. What did Jody's tap mean? Was it his friendly acknowledgment of Ann's advice—or a reminder of last week's fuck?

Tennis resumed. With nary a wild attempt, Jody won the first three points of his service game. When his angled volley gained the final point, he bowed. Ann strolled over, stood on tiptoes, and kissed him lightly on the cheek. When she turned from him, Jody swung his racket and again tapped her ass. She aimed a quick glance at—good Lord!—me. Did I detect some Ann alarm? Did I spot a flicker of exasperation? If so, was she angry at Jody for ass-tapping, or me for what I might be seeing about the two of them?

It was always difficult to assess one Cantling sister without referencing the other three. With the exception of Ann, their looks were similar, in a long, bright-skinned, narrow way. Ann was wider and darker, with fuller muscles and, as Jody's racket reminded me, a more rounded derriere. The ass-tapping raised the possibility that Ann and Jody had secretly restarted their old duet. Which might help explain her distance from me this winter. Of course, if Ann and Jody were at it again, I couldn't declare myself to her. Jody and I were all each other had. I couldn't risk an estrangement to pursue the Ann mirage.

A game had ended on court, and the teams were changing sides. I waved goodbye to Ann and Jody, turned away, and started toward the Cantling house.

"Benjamin. Wait," Ann called. She trotted over. With a hand stretched high on the chain link and her lips nearly touching metal, she said quietly, "It's good to see you."

"Always."

"I couldn't see more of you in New York. I was too upset about my father," she said, answering a question I hadn't asked. It seemed our mutual mind reading lived on. "You were good about it."

"Ann, there's nothing to apologize for."

"Do you understand why I didn't ask you to play today? You're too good. It would have been a mismatch."

That was one excuse I had missed. I struggled with an old enemy: hope. I told myself: Find a way. Declare yourself. Soon.

"It might be a mismatch anyway," I said, "if Jody plays smart."

"Can he? You're never sure how he'll hit the next ball. Just what I want, another unpredictable man. Like my father isn't enough."

Quickly, cruelly, my hope subsided. She was confiding in an old pal.

I said, "Jody makes it interesting out there."

"If you like suspense."

"Do you?"

"Less and less," she said, wrong-footing me.

"There wouldn't have been much suspense with me. I'm steady."

"If I'd have asked, would you have played?"

"Of course."

"Then next time, you and me," she said.

"Okay, you two, that's enough," Jody called from the baseline. "Time to play."

It had long been evident that Jody didn't know I had feelings for Ann. But I wondered whether Ann had sensed something.

"You're seeing Charlie?" she said quietly. "Why?"

"I assume he wants to buy our house."

"That's what he's told us, that he's going to make an offer. But he's not the same these days. He's brooding about something. None of us understand what's going on."

"Almost dying is a big deal."

"Promise me we'll talk afterward. I'd like to hear how you think he's doing—and what's on his mind."

"I'll tell you whatever I can."

"Good," she said. "This conversation, let it stay between us."

I headed toward the Cantling house, where Ann's parents and sibs would be receiving.

Beside the entrance drive, Charlie's helicopter was parked on a flat, open area of mown grass. Placed for all arrivals to see, with the family cars relegated to a parking area some distance away, it seemed to proclaim Charlie's power and revived my resentment about the need to make peace with its owner. Closer to the house, several young men in magpie dress of black pants and short-sleeved white shirts lifted boxed supplies from the back of a van and lugged them indoors.

I circled the house, which faced north toward the rippling Long Island Sound. Party prep consumed the area around the patio while a recorded string quartet supplied tasteful soothing. A pair of lengthy folding tables were set up, and floral arrangements burst from shapely vases along knee walls and ledges. On the main property, which sloped modestly seaward, decorative plantings were in decent form despite the Cantlings' recent long absences. The expanse of lawn was clipped and green, and the pair of flanking cottages looked fit for guests. Down by the water, a large American flag hung high and still on a fifteen-foot pole.

Charlie couldn't have cared less about lawns and gardens, which were the domain of his wife, Tessa. I spotted the model turned habitué of benefits and balls and charity boards—and the occasionally photographed "flavor of the week" at SocietyLately.com—in a white blouse and styled lime-green work pants. She brandished a pair of gardening gloves and held a nearly empty tumbler of white wine. The elegant hausfrau was a trim, still-attractive woman in her late fifties whose delicate bone structure warred with her husband's strength in the design of their children. She was fit and smooth skinned. Ann had told me that Tessa's straight hair was gray but she dyed it black and had the dye stripped from a few strands for authenticity's sake. She and a groundskeeper hovered over a small, unimpressed azalea bush.

Her stubby son, Theo, who was shaped more like his father and, in jeans and a fitted work shirt, bulkier than I remembered, stood nearby with an empty cocktail glass in his hand and nodded gravely. When he was drunk, Theo could turn mean, and he seemed at least halfway there. With the other two not watching, he lifted a middle finger toward me and grinned as if he were joking. This Early Fourth already promised trouble. I fixed my gaze on the faint scar on Theo's left cheek, where at age fifteen he'd caught himself with his fishhook while demonstrating a proper cast.

"I know my azaleas," Tessa was telling the groundskeeper. Her accusatory finger angled downward from her thin, bent wrist. She had yet to notice me. "As I keep explaining, there's a right way and a wrong way to prune them. Last year you left them too stringy. Well, this year there's a new regime. You can't slip things by and hope I'll say nothing."

"I understand, ma'am. But an azalea will grow the way it wants to." The groundskeeper was about six inches taller than Tessa, which made deference problematic. He managed it with slow talk, few words, and an averted gaze.

"What an azalea wants is one thing. What we make it do is something else," she said. The subject of the debate, the ordinary-looking plant in a row of similar plants, sported a smattering of late blossoms above a carpet of fallen petals. Tessa continued, "Don't try to tell me that with proper use of pruning tools and precision cuts, these branches couldn't have been angled better."

"We did our best."

Theo glared at me and dragged an imaginary knife across his throat.

"We've been doing this a long time," Tessa said to her employee. She glanced at Theo, who nodded gravely. "I can read your mind. You tell yourself, 'This lady is a bird of summer. She peeps and flutters. When she's gone, I'll decide how the azalea gets pruned.' Well, this year is different. This year, I'm going to watch closely. Let's call this our test azalea."

"I don't want to get it wrong," the groundskeeper said, seeming to note this more assertive avatar of Tessa, even if the issue seemed trivial. "I can email pictures, before and after."

"Good idea."

"We need those pictures," Theo said. "Don't fuck up."

Finally, Tessa saw me. "Benjamin Gould! The old wise man himself!" She lifted the wine glass to draw me forward. There was something posed in her gesture, which was not unusual. Tessa and a majority of her daughters seemed to regard many a humdrum activity as a photo op. She waved a hand to dispatch the groundskeeper, who backed up and shuffled away.

"Fuck you, Gould," Theo muttered. He turned and ambled toward the house.

Tessa downed the rest of her wine to free the hand that held it. Then she hugged me longer and tighter than I'd expected. She stepped back and studied my face with apparent pleasure. I noticed that her lips had turned down somewhat and her face was more lined than it had been last year. She hadn't abandoned fashion. The sunglasses on the chain at her neck were wide, round, and stylish. Her petite sneakers were a flashy orange and gray.

"Benjamin, I love the jacket and tie. We don't see enough of that anymore. Your generation needs to understand what occasions are. Well now, what a fine young man you've become. Nothing in the way of a girlfriend, I hear," she said, using the license that her airhead routine allowed her.

As usual, it was hard to tell to what extent she was toying with me. Which, of course, was part of the toying.

"I don't get it," she said. "You're intelligent. You have a certain awkward charm. Lose a little weight, more style to the hair, better clothes, and who knows? Never mind. Who wants to hear an old lady rattle on? Here's some advice: Now that you're back in the picture, stay away from my daughters. Your brother's already done enough damage there. That boy would flirt with anybody. There were times I thought he was eyeing me. For practice, I suppose. Like it's a game. My daughters have had enough of the Goulds. Stay away."

"How can I? You have so many of them."

"Yes, I was busy for those eight years, wasn't I? Let's go through the list. Vivian's too old for you and not interested, I imagine. Though maybe if you were a horse. I suppose a horse is the most interesting thing in the world. Ann's the next, except you two have been friends forever. Not much there, I assume. Nicole is far away and out of reach. Which leaves Melanie."

"Melanie?"

"Admit it. You've been ogling her for years."

"Melanie?" I repeated, trying to contain my surprise. "I hear she's off-limits."

"You mean she's gone over to the other side? Doesn't everyone know Melanie is just testing, pretending to change what can't be changed?"

"I'm not sure I understand, Mrs. Cantling. Are you encouraging me with Melanie?"

"No. I keep out of my daughters' lives. But my husband's another matter. What are you up to with him? Why is Charlie talking to a

Byrne and Company operative? I don't see any corpses. There's been no thieving I know of."

I had never experienced the full Tessa treatment. I felt off-balance. "I'm not a Byrne and Company operative," I said. "As far as I know, Charlie wants to make an offer on our house."

"I wonder. Something else might be going on. My husband is closer to the vest than ever. He gets like that when he's cooking up a big deal. Recently, he's been worked up about something for the first time since the accident. But I can see the crash is still on his mind. Weakness. Suffering. Uncertainty. They gnaw at him. Maybe he wants to prove he's back. Every once in a while, this darkness passes across his face. This is Charlie, after all. When he gets notions, he sticks to them."

"What notions?"

"He doesn't tell us. The mood is like yesterday's storm. It passes. Until the next storm comes, you don't remember what it was like. Maybe he's just worried. Because he's not out of danger. He's at risk of infections. And embolisms, whatever they are. Eventually, the surgeons will have to take the pins out of the leg. We've had a taste of what it's like without him and can't help but wonder if it might happen again. If Charlie's thinking seriously about possible futures, you getting involved could be a positive."

"As far as I know, I'm not involved in possible futures," I said. "Neither is Byrne and Company."

"Whatever you say. But I must tell you, I don't understand him these days." She waved her hand as if to shoo away the impression that she was being indiscreet. "To think of how he always tempted death—daredevil skiing, stunt flying, scuba diving. He liked anything that could kill him. He kept getting away with it, only to almost die in a car crash. How cruel that would have been. A horrible death for an adventurer."

I thought I detected tears in her eyes.

"But then what?" she said. "He stared death directly in the eye, rose up, and won. It's just like Charlie to do that. Except the experience changed him. You've got to tell me what happens between you and him—what your impressions are, what's said, what isn't. You would do it as an old friend, of course. Without violating confidences."

"I keep telling people, I'm here to listen to an offer about our house."

"Who have you been telling?"

I'd already slipped. Ann wanted to keep her interest a secret. "My brother," I said.

Tessa tilted her head to one side, exposing a fine clavicle on the other side. She studied me. "Don't be coy. I hate that. Do I really need to spell it out? Some of the issues are all over the internet."

"Like what?"

"Like before the accident, Charlie sold part of Cantling Market Research. What's he going to do with the proceeds?"

"How would I know?"

"In a half hour, you might. You must feel so central, so powerful. Something's on the great Charlie Cantling's mind, and you might get the first hint. It's just like Charlie to sit on four hundred million dollars, do nothing, and then, boom! Whatever he wants from you, promise me you won't commit to anything before you talk to me."

"Mrs. Cantling, I don't know anything about that money."

"How could I forget? You know nothing about anything. But someday, my friend, you might."

Tessa had unsettled me. I tried to recover on my approach toward the house. Cedar shingled and with a gabled roof, it was large but not ungainly as it spilled from its central rooms to either flank. Stone walkways extended from the wings, giving easy access to the outdoors from several parts of the house.

Past the patio, where party setup proceeded apace, Theo strode toward me. Old questions arose again: did he dislike me because I'm Jewish or because I'm smart? His sensitivity on the matter was odd because Theo, a Dartmouth grad, might have been the smartest of Charlie's five children.

"I hear you've got something going with my father," he said, his voice already slurred.

"We're just talking about our house."

"Bullshit. Here's the thing," he said with an acid smile. "Don't mess with me or Charlie or anybody else in this family. Stick your nose into our business, play the know-it-all, and no question about it, I will kill you. A worm like you! I'll slice you into little pieces and use you for bait."

"Theo, what's this all about?"

"Don't play games, Gould." He poked a finger at my chest. "You cannot fuck with us and get away with it. You and your brother have been hanging around for too long, pulling shit. Well, I'm the one to stop it. I'll have the best lawyers money can rent. 'Self-defense.' 'Did the world a favor.' It won't even go to trial."

"This is not funny, Theo. Cut it out."

"It's not supposed to be funny. Maybe I'll just burn your house down, with you and the king of flares inside. It'll be his fucking fault."

"So you'll kill both of us?"

"Push me far enough, and there's no telling what I'll do. By the way, this little talk? It never happened. In fact, it was you who threatened me."

"Theo, you're not a gangster," I said, summoning my nerve. "You're a spoiled kid doing a bad imitation."

"Am I? We'll see."

Although I tried to hide it, the threats had the desired effect. It now seemed that Theo on his own might have turned the party into what Al Byrne had called a matter of "life and death." Theo drunk was capable of terrible mischief. Except for Ann, I wanted nothing to do with Cantlings. But I was stuck. Byrne wouldn't let me drop out before I even started.

I usually grow hungry in the afternoons, and in my hurry to leave our house, I'd forgotten to fortify with a snack. Now, with the stress, I was ravenous. I hoped a snack might ease my growing alarm. On the patio tables, plastic cups and bowls of ice were positioned in front of a long queue of bottled booze, but there was a glaring absence of food. Cantling women, Ann excluded, lived in mortal dread of calories. With their narrow feet evolved to fit on a bathroom scale, they had learned to subsist on extract of lettuce and weak tea, and they didn't keep food in the house nor leave it on tables for guests.

Eventually, servers would emerge from the kitchen with miniature trays of hors d'oeuvres, but even those meager morsels were not in evidence. Fearing cucumber sandwiches, I entered the house, where air-conditioning replaced the seaside ambiance with a cool, lifeless calm. I shivered at the clammy chill of my evaporating sweat. My route took me through the large living room and dining room, newly redecorated in the hypermodern minimal fashion. I found my way to the dim and windowless white corridor that led to the kitchen.

When I reached the end, I smelled food and felt warmth, this time dry and from ovens, and discovered counters stacked with trays of uncooked chicken slivers, cold little pigs awaiting toasty blankets, and inscrutable flecks of white vegetables on trays. A squat female chef in black presided, seconded by a hefty male assistant.

"Here's a place where a hungry man can eat," I said, straining for jovial.

"You like trichinosis?" the chef said. "We just started to cook."

"Anything in the refrigerators?" I edged toward one of the Cantlings' twin cooling colossi.

"That one's ours," she said. "Nothing in there, either."

"The food's not ready? Or you won't let me have any?"

"Both."

"Come on. You don't prepare cold appetizers in advance?"

"Our contract says we start serving in a half an hour. Until then, we can't feed everybody who comes begging. We don't have time." Her smile was daggerlike.

"You're not using the other refrigerator. Can I check it?"

She shrugged.

I opened the fridge. Empty containers and a pitcher of water populated the upper shelves, and on the twin doors were dregs of condiments and old jelly jars. A multitude of limes mocked me from a drawer named COLDER. In another, a pair of ravaged carrots, limp with age, begged to be left alone. An unopened glass of store-bought yogurt brought unexpected hope, but a turn of the jar exposed an expiration date from the French and Indian War. I was about to close up in despair when I noticed—easy to miss in the back of the lowest shelf, white against the white of the interior—a sizable cardboard box. A ribbon in pale silver resolved in a bow on top. Amazed, I slid the box out of the fridge and felt its encouraging weight. Dessert in Cantlingland. A waterfall in the Sahara.

Hugging the box to hide it from the chef and assistant, I lifted a long knife from a counter and edged into another corridor off the kitchen. Steps away, I reached a small door to what I remembered was a storage closet. I shut myself in total blackness and pulled a dangling cord. The naked bulb on the ceiling revealed a cramped space filled with mops, brooms, buckets, bags, and copious cleaning supplies. Because the air-conditioning hadn't penetrated here, it was, strangely enough, a last redoubt of sea air.

The walls of the house were thin, the floors reverberant, and in the stillness of the closet, I heard the thud of footsteps and the murmur of voices all around. The cacophony lent urgency to my hope, since I might be found out at any moment. I examined the cardboard box and noticed that in one of the quadrants created by the ribbon crisscrossing its top, someone had scribbled a two-line message:

Do Not Eat
Melanie

    I was stunned. In my world of written communication, with life and property in the balance, proper punctuation is absolutely essential. Its absence here compelled me to imagine some. A comma between "Eat" and "Melanie" (Do Not Eat, Melanie) might be warning Melanie to avoid eating the cake or possibly anything else. A period in that spot (Do Not Eat. Melanie) would have created an instruction from Melanie to not eat the contents of the box or perhaps anything else. A period at the end (Do Not Eat Melanie.) would have created two options. The first: someone with gaps in her education, such that she was unaware of the decline in flesh eating, might be trying to save Melanie from cannibals. The second: a sexual prohibition.

    Forced to choose, I decided that the ever-dieting Melanie must have scribbled the message to save the box's contents for her own unknowable purposes. Since no true chocolate cake had recently touched those thin, lovely lips, the box seemed likely to contain something low calorie, like vegan cheesecake. Which would mean I'd find nothing inside that I could stomach. Hastily, I untied the ribbon, pulled open the top, peeled back the sides, and discovered a large round cake with dark-brown icing, sitting on a cardboard plate.

    Was I encouraged? Yes. Convinced? No. I had to be wary of a baked carob outrage or some other low-cal obscenity masquerading as true cake. I probed with the knife and licked the blade—and was delighted. The cake was unmistakably chocolate and nicely sugar sweetened. And it was fresh! And in my power!

    Footsteps in the corridor reminded me of the risk. If someone on a cleaning jag suddenly opened the closet door, my present circumstance would be terrifically embarrassing. I removed a wedge of cake and stuffed chunks of it into my mouth. It was immensely satisfying, and although a hint of unknown spice dulled the sweet explosion, my sizable slice was sure to stave off hunger during my tête-à-tête with Charlie.

I'm no psychopath. Even as I chewed and swallowed, I regretted that, frightened by Theo and frantic to raise my blood sugar, I had been forced to turn thief and ruin a fine cake's perfection. As hungry as I was, I nevertheless limited the damage to one wedge.

I finished my wedge and licked knife and lips to remove incriminating remnants, then reconstituted the box and arranged the violated cake inside. I retied the ribbon. Switching off the light, I cautiously opened the door and skulked to the kitchen, where the chef and assistant were leaning over the stove and oblivious to me. I restored knife to counter and box to bottom of fridge.

High on sugar and derring-do, proud to have used the Cantling lion's resources to bulk up in his den, I returned to the hallway to the blast of inner trumpets. I told myself Jody wasn't the only family member with magic on the high wire.

As I passed the storage closet, another door opened at the end of the hall, and Melanie appeared. She blended into the white hallway in her gray pants and white blouse, her head tilted lovingly toward the cell phone she pressed to her ear. She saw me and ended the call, stuffing the phone into a black pocketbook with unfamiliar designer markings. I stood and gaped while she floated toward me.

Long and lean and fine boned, Melanie was indisputably beautiful and carried herself accordingly. She would have looked even better without the rouge and lipstick and other assorted add-ons she'd applied for the party.

"Benjamin, what are you doing here?" she asked. In white heels, she was an inch or two taller than me. "You weren't looking for food, were you?"

"Why would I look for food?"

"Because you always do when you visit."

This was offensive. "Hang me," I said. "I stole a glass of water."

"By the way, I like the blazer. Dull but sober. Right for the occasion."

She spoke like most Cantlings, with sharp words masked by droll delivery and playing to the crowd, as if using phrases without experiencing their meaning or impact. I felt unlucky. It wasn't unreasonable to run into Melanie in her own house, but did it have to be here, in this hall? I told myself to relax. As far as Melanie knew, this place and this door had no special meaning.

"What's wrong, Benjamin? I'm worried about you. You look pale."

"It must be the lighting."

"If it was bad lighting, I'd look pale, too," she said. "Do I? Be honest. We're old friends."

"You look great," I said.

"Thank you."

Just in time, I'd remembered that the Cantling women's condescension didn't immunize them against compliments.

"How have you been?" she said, a likely introduction to talking more about herself.

"I've been good. What about you?"

"There have been some changes. Positive, I think. Do you know what I'm talking about?" The reference to intimate secrets was surprising and gave me no choice but to nod.

"Thanks for not judging," she said. "A lot of people do. It comes in all sorts of shapes. Mostly, they tell me it doesn't seem right because I've always liked boys. Homophobia, plain and simple. What's happening is I'm meeting interesting people in a new and different way. I suppose it's also a good career move. You know what they say in show business? A little lesbo goes a long way. Crude, but that's men for you, the poor dears. They see you and they get ideas."

Melanie Cantling had the looks of a star actress but not much chance to be one. Her career to date had shown that beauty, ambition, connections, and scheming didn't guarantee stardom. Throw in no need for a day job, a rotation of outfits shuttled to a hundred auditions, and a bland YouTube show featuring designer clothes, and it still wasn't enough. She was attractive and, though indecisive in most matters, determined to be an actress. It was cruel that she could command a room but not a stage and had only landed background roles in clothes commercials and a petulant "Goddess of Love" in an Off-Off-Broadway pretension too loud to sleep through.

"So the lesbian thing isn't real?" I said.

"I wouldn't go that far. Everybody knows sexuality is on a continuum. Each of us is some of this and some of that. Makes it interesting, doesn't it? Lately, I've leaned a bit in one direction. I want to be clear: it wouldn't take much to lean me the other way."

"Okay. Whatever works."

"Don't you get it? I could call off the experiment today. For you."

"Me?"

"How many years have we been friends, and you still don't know? Are you making me come right out with it? Okay. Think of it this way: I've had a crush on you since I was six years old."

I was amazed. Melanie Cantling had offered herself to me! Even if there was something self-consciously theatrical and mocking in the performance, it was succeeding. Like her sisters, Melanie was exceptional in manner, looks, style, carriage. Forget the failures of the Cantling sibs: two college dropouts never to be reversed, careers not started, two flash marriages, and unpromising ventures enabled by youth and money. Most of the Cantlings seemed to assume the world had been arranged for their benefit, and they managed to bear unexpected misfortunes as if they were triumphs. A Cantling sister could spend a night in a dumpster and leave it looking photogenic and upbeat.

Though it was unlikely that Melanie believed today's rewrite of reality, the key fact was not in dispute: no Cantling sister had ever shown interest in me, phony or otherwise.

I said, "I don't believe you. Weren't you and Jody an item for a while?"

"If I was with Jody, and I'm not saying I was, it was my way of getting close to you."

"You might have tried me direct."

"I guess I was afraid," she said.

I was glimpsing a clever, devious side of Melanie that I'd never seen before. Of course it would show up in matters of sex, where she had power and had to know it. I realized she had been working the lesbian angle, had teased me by confiding.

"You?" I said. "Afraid of me?"

"Fuck you! You never noticed how I felt?"

"I've offended you?"

"What a question! What planet are you on?"

Before I could reply, she leaned toward me and gave me a medium-intensity kiss on the lips. All Cantling women, with one painful exception, were by instinct flirtatious. They could give directions to a taxi driver or order a meal by phone, and their tone would be inviting. I, for the first time an object of what might be a Cantling advance, was frightened by the attention. I was in awe. The hint of progress with Ann at the tennis court started to fade away.

I pulled back from Melanie and said, "I suppose you want me to tell you what happens between me and your father."

"I don't know anything about you and my father. Can't you understand? You are what matters. You."

She wrapped me in her arms and kissed me harder. I tensed up even more. I tasted Melanie's lipstick and smelled the bouquet of her makeup. A soft, low moan rose from her throat. To be in Melanie's arms was astonishing. I still suspected that my new connection to her father had made her take notice. Nevertheless, I might be willing to go over a cliff with her. And if someone told Ann about it? Ann, who'd had sex with my brother how many times? Ann, who never had interest in me?

Melanie squeezed me, pushed her body into mine, and slid her hand down my back. To ease the pain of their indifference, I used to tell myself the Cantling sisters' sexual sophistication was off-putting, and it was, but with Melanie's tongue making a wet circuit around mine while her hips ground against me, I couldn't remember why. Why be faithful to an idea that was Ann? What had Ann done for me lately? Who was Ann?

Melanie disentangled tongues and pulled back.

"Benjamin," she said, worried, "have you been eating chocolate?"

"Who cares? Don't we have better things to do?"

"Calm down, Romeo. I tasted chocolate. Don't lie to me! Tell me where you got it."

A glance at her blazing eyes alarmed me. "What's the big deal about a piece of chocolate? I had a truffle on the way from our house."

"I don't believe you."

"Let's not lose the moment," I said. "Is a cake more important than this?"

"In this case, yes. I saw you come out of the kitchen. Are you telling me my cake is intact?"

"I can't vouch for the state of your cake. I only know I've done nothing to it."

"If some of it's gone, it will be obvious it was you."

I chose a bluff. "Go check it out. Waste the moment."

"Okay. I will."

Helpless, I watched her stride through the kitchen door. I tried to decipher her murmured byplay with the catering pair. A sensible person might have fled at top speed, but such is the male libido that I stood there and told myself this could still work. The love-starved seductress of moments ago could return to the stage.

The "Fuck!" that arose from the kitchen seemed to shake the walls. Though I couldn't fathom Melanie's extreme attachment to the cake, I knew enough about female tendencies to accept that the chances for sex with her had weakened. And Ann was certain to hear a full recap with unflattering spin, and I would be further diminished in her eyes.

Melanie stormed into the hallway, gripping the closed box like an outraged rabbi clutching a violated Torah. She glared at me with contempt and, inexplicably, amusement.

"They told me you came in and asked for food. They saw you at the refrigerator."

"That's right. I got a drink of water."

"That's your story?"

"It's not a story. It's fact." I felt my lame defiance slice my age to four. "Even if I'm lying, which I'm not, what's the big deal about a cake?"

"You don't get it. It's a very special cake. A gift, baked for me. Aside from the fact that you've screwed up the rest of your evening, you can't just walk into someone's house, open a present she's bought, and eat it."

"It's food," I protested. "Somebody's going to eat it sooner or later."

"My father's waiting for you, right? You're seeing him before the party?"

"I thought you didn't know about me and your father."

"Horrible me, I lied. You'd better find him right away—because in about an hour, you won't remember how much two and two is. When he sees you totally messed up, he'll never trust you again."

"What's this about?"

"A friend of mine's having a birthday party tonight. She loves weed. Ganja. Marijuana. I had a weed cake baked for her. This cake," she said, pushing the box close to my face. "I hear the baker really loads them up. This one's absolutely filled with dope."

"I thought you were drug-free these days."

"I am, more or less. It's a policy. This is for my friend. Have you had much experience with weed?"

I was no stranger to marijuana, but it was appalling that I might have been drugged without knowing it. But I couldn't complain about that to Melanie.

"Experience with weed?" I said. "I smoked some years ago."

"Well, buckle up, stony. You're in for a wild ride. If you ate on an empty stomach, you'll digest it fast. You have about forty-five minutes till takeoff. For about six hours, you won't know up from down. You'll probably be paranoid and goofy. You'll definitely be starving."

"For six hours?"

"I know how hungry you get. Weed will make it worse."

"You're making this up," I said. "You're mad because you think I spoiled your cake."

"Nice try. Once it kicks in, you might start to hallucinate. This is powerful stuff."

"That's enough!" I said. "You came onto me so I'd tell you what happened with your father. Now, to rattle me, you've made up a story about a cake I didn't eat. Admit it. There's no weed in the cake."

"Okay. Would you like another piece?" She flipped open the top of the box and swung the cake to and fro in front of me. Her smile was taunting.

"I'm not hungry," I said.

"You will be soon." She closed the box.

Melanie had been consistent about the weed, and I had to accept the possibility that she was telling the truth. The Cantling kids had no doubt dissected enough live specimens of poor people at posh private schools to learn the circulatory system, whereas we at Stonefield High had learned vascular anatomy from a line-drawn poster of a naked man with strands of black spaghetti radiating from his chest to the rest of his body. I had nevertheless picked up the general idea. Melanie's piercing stare aroused visions of chocolate-covered cannabinoids fanning out through the pasta to make my mind spin and my heart race.

"While you're stoned," she said, "my father might have one of his episodes and start ranting. I wonder what that will be like."

"Episodes? What episodes?"

"Damn you, Benjamin. I don't want us to start out like this."

"We're starting out?"

"We could be. Except you lied! I don't envy you. You know how Daddy is about drugs. We had to hide them all the time. If he finds out, he'll kill you!"

"I still don't believe you."

"Believe whatever you want. Just go to him. Hurry! And get away from him as quickly as possible!" She glided away. If she'd invented the weed, it was a better performance than I'd believed her capable of.

While I returned to the party, I did some quick thinking. I decided that Byrne's warning about life and death was probably a bluff to keep me at the party. Talking to Charlie could wait a day or two.

In the past I had witnessed Charlie explode about his kids using recreational drugs. He had thrown his daughter Nicole out of the house on suspicion—well founded—of cocaine. The relationship had never recovered. That blowup led directly to Nicole moving to Santa Fe and her refusal to come east until Charlie seemed to be dying. If I got caught and tried to blame Melanie and the cake, it would not help me. No, the prudent course was to go home.

An on-the-spot postponement for gastrointestinal reasons was the most promising alternative. The dodge would be more persuasive if conveyed amid bathroom echoes. For greater credibility, I could even flush. Accordingly, I found my way to a baby-blue "powder room." Located near the front door, it was a small, Waspy outpost scented with odor remover and featuring gossamer hand towels. I locked myself in, lowered the lid of the burgundy-colored toilet, and sat on it. I was about to call the Cantling landline and declare a health emergency when I discovered another message from founder and CEO Al Twenty-Four Seven.

"No duck. Poss life and death. Remember: Rules of Engagement."

It seemed Byrne had anticipated my attempt to escape. If I'd been summoned to the Cantlings' to talk about a house, why was Byrne citing rules from the firm's gumshoe days, e.g., no sex or drugs, no money deals with subjects of an investigation? I was trapped. Whether I fled the house or stayed and seemed druggy, I'd face the contempt of Cantling and the wrath of Byrne and probably lose my job. A defense that I'd accidentally eaten weed would only produce guffaws. And they'd completely dismiss Theo's threats.

Luckily, my stomach-bug fantasy pointed toward a solution. Because my scintilla of know-how about induced barfing was wholly cinema based, I tapped at my cell phone to pick up additional tips from the web. Per instructions, I stood, lifted the burgundy toilet seat, and bent over the water. The rich blue additive complemented the walls and stood out against the gleaming white bowl. It struck me that the three-hued toilet's pristine and festive appearance was no fluke. In Cantlingland, the cleaning for the Early Fourth would have been rigorous and the red, white, and blue no accident.

I slid a finger down my throat and, ad-libbing, imagined eating rats. I gagged. Nothing came up. Summoning grisly images from Google's excerpted films, I tried twice more. Alas, despite my love of the stomach bug excuse, I'd been cursed with digestion that only the worst of flus upended, and I couldn't bring up any cake. Face hanging over the blue water, sweaty with worry and failed effort, I thought about—of all things—my father. I found myself agreeing with him that college courses with real-world applications, like Techniques of Barfing, would have been much more useful than A Short History of Finland and other liberal arts esoterica he'd complained about wasting his money on.

Someone rapped at the door. When it crossed my mind that Theo might confront me again, I elected not to respond. I opened a valve at the sink, splashed cold water onto my face, and dried myself with one of the teeny towels. Normally, advice to stay positive was the last redoubt of befuddled sports coaches, but in my condition I needed any psychic advantage. I reminded myself there was a good chance the cake contained no marijuana, and even if it did, I might be spared humiliation. I calculated: if in forty-five minutes I grew dopey, I was likely to be long gone from Charlie, who couldn't have budgeted much time for lowly me.

My face and hands were still wet, so I added the second to my drying regime. A glimpse of my watch jarred me. If Melanie's cake was full of weed, my minutes of not being stoned had shrunk to forty.

There were several more raps on the door and a futile twist of the knob. I had to get moving.

CHAPTER THREE

BENJAMIN

I found Charlie Cantling in his office, a converted bedroom on the second floor with an expansive view of the sloping lawn and the Sound. Cantling stared into a computer screen atop a modest-looking midcentury desk with splayed legs. Cantling standards suggested that the unassuming desk could claim a chic designer, though Charlie wouldn't know the name.

In black pants visible under the table and a white shirt with rolled-up sleeves, Charlie rapped hard at the keyboard, rippling the water in an adjacent pitcher and causing a flanking silo of plastic cups to tremble. A sporty blue jacket, soon to be donned for the ceremony, stretched over the back of his chair. Behind him a cane leaned against the wall, the face of a wolf carved into the curved chrome handle. Charlie's missing necktie bolstered my decision not to wear one.

Charlie's greeting was a grunt followed by the flick of a hand toward a small, armless wooden chair across from him. A black writing pen thrust out at an angle from his mouth. The need to clamp the pen between bicuspids enhanced his surly demeanor.

It wasn't shocking that Charlie would work the internet pre-party. Thirty years ago, Cantling Market Research had been a modest source of walking-around money for the Cantling family when, following the death of her husband, Charlie's mother drafted her oldest son to run it. He had been an unpromising choice, though superior to the childless brother in Hawaii—now deceased from a drug cocktail. Charlie, who had caroused his way through college and business school to become a high-pressure salesman on Wall Street, proved to possess the savvy to create online versions of the previously recondite reports of Cantling Market Research and form a snappy internet marketing operation to peddle them.

A year earlier, Charlie had sold the marketing group for four hundred million dollars to a big ad agency. I'd been told that after closing the deal, Charlie insisted on standing authorization to use the money to add another business to Cantling Market Research—but because of the accident, the money remained unspent. Charlie had that kind of sway with Cantling Market Research because he had insisted his mother put all the company's shares into a trust that Charlie controlled upon his ascension to power.

The afternoon's probes from his near and dear suggested that the cash held passing interest for the family, whose members would have been the sole recipients of every distribution that hadn't happened.

Charlie pushed the screen aside and fixed on me. "Seen some of the family today? Vivian? Melanie? Theo? Ann? They're the best, right? Brilliant. Captivating. Enough to make an old man's heart swell with pride." Charlie, as usual, seemed acerbic. "Four out of five showing up is not too shabby."

Charlie was looser of tongue than I remembered.

"Your dad created the Independence Day tradition around here," he said, asserting the right of the powerful to change the subject. "We owe him."

"My dad?"

"You know the story. For a time, when folks began moving out from the city or Fairfield County, there were few big private parties on the Fourth. I didn't want to compete with the main event, the town parade, but it was terrible. Some old vets would load up with beer, waddle to the square, and belch. Horrible sausages. A boring speech. Finally, your dad couldn't take it. He got a big flag, flew it over your house, and blasted music in the afternoon. The next year we decided to get into it too. But a bigger house needed a bigger flag. Like your dad, we threw in music. And then fireworks.

"We didn't want it to look like a competition, so we had our party a week early. The way I see it, we joined a parade your father started. Your grandfather was a refugee from Hitler. Your dad was grateful to the US. If he wanted to prove he belonged, it was all good."

Cantling's gloss on the Fourth competition seemed to buoy him. I dwelled on the insult.

"Why wouldn't my father belong?"

"Of course he would. And he wanted to. That was one of the great things about him. Me, I've always liked the Goulds. And that name. They changed it, right? From what?"

"Something Russian. Unpronounceable."

"It doesn't matter. I love the Goulds, but we can't live in the past. Does it make sense for two young guys to hold on to that house? From the look of things, you have trouble maintaining it."

"We manage."

"I'll make it easy for you. Let me buy it, sign it over to my offspring, and my little darlings can sort out what to do with it. They're gonna need more space. Some of them might get married and stay that way. They could have children. Can we talk about this?"

"Talk? Yes. Deal? I don't know."

"It seems clear you don't have the income to keep that place. As for assets, I doubt your father left you twenty cents."

"Charlie, I don't want to get into it."

"Just giving you facts. Here's a plan: We split the cost of an appraiser. I pay you and your brother whatever number he comes up with, plus ten percent. There won't even be a broker's fee. A sweet deal."

It sounded like a genuine offer, but I was skeptical. Why would Al Byrne have texted me about the possible sale of our house?

"Even if I was tempted," I said, "Jody has experience in real estate. We know how it works. The appraiser will tilt things your way to keep the relationship. More important, Jody doesn't want to sell."

"Okay. Let's assume the appraisal will come in on the light side. I'll pay you appraisal plus twenty percent. The way I see it, after taxes, you and your brother will end up with three-quarters of a million each."

My parents had stretched their budget to buy the house decades ago, before the better-heeled had arrived in droves and inflated prices. But close to two million for the house? I had shown up to humor Charlie and Jody and Byrne. Now it seemed the offer was rich. I reminded myself that my connection to Jody partly depended on the house. What would happen to us if we sold?

"I'll talk to Jody." I stood to leave, safely in advance of any possible weed high.

"Let's keep the deal moving," Charlie said, reaching for the cane behind him. "We'll start the inspection right now. Ever been up in a helicopter?"

"No."

"There's a first time for everything."

"I don't want to put you to any trouble." A weed high in a helicopter presented a horrifying prospect.

"No trouble. Do you want the ride or don't you?"

"Don't you have a party to host?"

"We'll be back in a few minutes. The chopper's the best way to look at the house and the properties. And we can keep talking with total privacy."

"Why is that important?"

"These walls are so thin. And we might have other matters to discuss. Al Byrne said I should take you on the ride." Cantling held out a cell phone. "Call him if you don't believe me."

Cantling had me. I'd look pathetic, and insulting, if I made the call. But why would Al Byrne care about the house and the helicopter? It seemed peculiar. "How long's the ride?"

"Five minutes. Ten tops. You'll be down before you know you're up."

I checked my watch. At least thirty minutes to weed time. There was no risk in a short flight.

With the cane's help, Charlie stood and limped toward the door.

"Your leg's strong enough to work the controls?" I said.

"Don't insult me. Do I seem reckless to you? I started flying again weeks ago."

I saw the bulge at his ankle and remembered last night. "Are you still carrying a gun?"

"Damn right I am. I need to get used to it. Does it make you nervous? Okay, I'll leave it here." He slid the pistol from its holster and locked it in a desk drawer.

"Why a gun?" I asked.

"There's a lot of kidnapping these days."

"In Mexico City."

"And then there's friends and family," he said with a grin.

I followed him to the helicopter. Why? First, I wanted to prove to the Cantlings, especially Ann, that I was more than an overcautious grinder out of corporate pabulum—that even under threat of weed, I could venture into the skies. And I confess that as we strode to the beast, swagger cloaked the dread. Also, I wanted to impress my brother.

Soon after our father died, Jody, citing supple women and brotherly bonding and Imodium A-D, had asked me to buy a ticket to Africa and climb Kilimanjaro beside him. Since this struck me as wasteful and hyperbolic, I invented a strained knee that would take months to heal. I also mentioned my well-paying job and the taxes on the house, not foreseeing that Jody would torture me with summit photos and tales of condom resupply, and that jabs about bogus knee pain would be thrown at me forever.

As I strapped into Charlie's passenger seat, I hoped a gutsy whirl over Jody—currently knocking a fluffy ball back and forth with girls—might bring a modicum of relief from his macho slings and arrows. But I knew this was a secondary consideration. Call it an excuse, call it self-pardon, but the reason I agreed to fly with Charlie was simple: I couldn't brush him off. I flew because I had to.

After we donned headsets, Cantling pressed a button overhead and swung a lever forward. The labored rev of the engine made me hope it wouldn't start. I followed Cantling's gaze to the instrument panel where, to my disappointment, indicator lines in gauges flagged growing numbers. The grind and spin of motor and rotor accelerated, and a downdraft flattened the grass below. Cantling gripped what he called "the stick" with both hands. My fear and excitement suggested that weed was asserting itself. Slow down—stave it off, I told myself. I recalled a yoga-loving date who in lieu of love had taught me deep breathing, and after a brief session of ins and outs, I had intimations of calm.

Nose to the sea breeze, the helicopter lifted off. When we were several feet off the ground, Melanie emerged from the house. She seemed to recognize me in the helicopter and, with both arms waving and a grin so broad I could see the whites of her well-straightened teeth, gave the trip a sarcastic blessing. Whether or not dope was coursing through me, she clearly wanted me to believe it was.

We floated over Cantling's house toward the party preppers and saw heads tilted backward to watch us and hands raised to cover ears.

We swung around and hovered over the tennis court, which appeared as a symmetrical blue-and-green patch peeking through the treetops spreading around it. Four figures stood on court and darted about, swinging rackets in succession. Cantling piloted a dive toward the net.

Ann motioned the roaring machine away. Cantling, never one to accommodate, lingered while his prank grew annoying. We watched the players flub a few points before Cantling took us straight up. There he made the helicopter hover again, slowly turning round and round. While I grew numb to the beat of the engine and the interior vibrations, all of Stonefield and its environs spread out beneath me, washed in the angled light of late afternoon.

Much of the area was a thick forest green, but at the eastern edges of woodlots, long shadows of trees extended along the ground. The houses provided blotches of civilization where shards of sunlight bounced off windows and skylights and the metal tops of cars. Further out, I saw rows of shops on Main Street, a mall in an asphalt sea, and lines of late traffic on the roads leading inland from the harbors and beaches. In the Sound, undulating swells glided to shore and broke with a wisp of foam.

Cantling seemed to wince with every push of his injured leg as he worked two pedals at his feet.

"Charlie, are you okay?" I said through the microphone attached to the headset.

"Never better." Cantling rubbed his thigh with his free hand and grunted.

"What's with the leg?" I asked.

"A bit of pain—just to remind me the limb isn't somewhere else. It's bad today. Usually, the painkillers handle it."

"Painkillers?"

"You know how I feel about drugs. I fire people on the spot if they fail a test. But now and then, I need these. The side effects are mild—some drowsiness, a bit of confusion. Nothing to worry about. I keep the dose low." He yawned. "Pinch me if I fall asleep."

I couldn't figure out where truth ended and teasing began. "If the leg's really bothering you, shouldn't we head back?"

"Not yet. We only need a few minutes."

He dipped the nose of the helicopter and headed lower toward my house, which we reached in a matter of seconds. It was a middling example of the old Cape Cod variety—shingled, rectangular, squat, and unimaginative. Nevertheless, to see it so close from the air was wondrous. The empty chaise on the patio brought memories of my mother reclining in that very spot, with a sun like this one illuminating whatever book she happened to be reading. Now and then, she'd drop a hand to pat the fat, lazy dog lying beside her. A triple threat of intellect, Mom taught the resistant undergrads of Stonefield College philosophy, logic, and, like any sensible atheist who could use the income, religion. In her too-short life, she tried without success to correct the excesses of her adopted younger son. I suppose she was easier on me, well behaved and a thinker.

Dad's steady conviction that a better deal was coming and we could blithely run up debt must have brought her constant distress. I doubt she knew at the wedding what risk she was assuming. I never saw her take another such risk, unless you count her telling a music professor at dinner that Haydn was better than Mozart. She must have reminded herself over and over that Dad, whatever his foolishness, was devoted. Her salary was our bulwark against foreclosure, with the result that she left in her wake two adventurers and me, a precocious worrier about financial doom. Luckily, widower Dad, possessed by an angel of caution and renouncing all fliers, found steady income. We kept the house.

With the helicopter descending, Charlie said through the headset, "See? As you know, there's raw land to the northwest—several building lots. Which means somebody could put up a house next to you anytime. That would cut the value. Your property would be my buffer to all that."

If Cantling was faking interest, he was adept at it. "Have you heard something?" I asked. "Is anyone planning to build next to us?"

"There are rumors."

"There's always rumors."

"When are you going to get real?" Cantling said. "Your place is almost a dump. I can't even fly close. I might blow those old shingles right off your roof."

"Do I need a guided tour of our shortcomings?"

"Yes. Your chimney's crooked. You call the lawn a field so you don't have to mow it. Your driveway's an obstacle course. Appraisal plus twenty. It's a great deal."

"We'll give it some thought."

If we took the offer, I calculated, I'd lose living with Jody and my chance Stonefield encounters with Ann. I'd have a paid-off mortgage, a bit of money, and not much else.

Charlie swung the chopper toward the Sound, and soon we were over blue water. With the still-brilliant sun descending behind us to the right, this promised to be a last spin before landing. Below, a hodgepodge of boats converged toward cluttered harbors.

"Beautiful," I said. "I'm glad we did this."

"Funny, isn't it? People rave about Long Island, put up big bucks to live there, but I've always preferred our coastline to their North Shore. What do they have? Stony beaches. No harbors east of Port Jefferson. Dull. On a day like today, you can see it all. Hell, I'll show you."

"What? Shouldn't we get back?"

"I'll have hours of that party. The fireworks don't start till nine. Don't forget, I'm still recovering. All that smiling at neighbors, it strains the ailing body."

"You have commitments," I said. "I don't want to keep you away."

"Ten minutes there, ten minutes back. We'll be on time."

I imagined Connecticut receding behind me and weediness poised to rise. There was no way I could explain and beg to land. If Byrne found out I'd blamed my drug use on a potential client's daughter, I'd be out of a job. "Charlie, I want to go back."

"Relax. It's gonna be a treat. And don't give me any nonsense about your stomach. I promise a smooth, straight flight—nice and low to stay away from airplanes. You'll love it." He grinned and aimed us toward Long Island. My captain began to rub his thigh again. I felt grateful for pain or anything else that might keep him alert. Then I giggled.

Racing away from the sinking sun, we stayed low enough to watch the helicopter's elongated shadow lead us to Long Island, which appeared as a dark-gray mass on the horizon. Details that would prove we were closing in—lighthouses, shoreline, towers, homes—were slow to emerge. It had been a half hour since the forbidden slice of cake. I found it funny that I was worried. This led to my second giggle.

Cantling said, "On your way to see me today, did any Cantlings talk to you?"

"I had some chats. I tried to stay out of the middle."

"Did they try to co-opt you? Did they tell you about getting theirs?"

"If they did," I said, tapdancing a bit, "I didn't pick up on it."

"Did they happen to mention they've decided I'm not fit to run anything anymore?"

"Why would they think that?"

"They say that after the accident I have serious issues. Not just medical, if you know what I mean. My daughters, with their legs, their looks, their degrees from third-rate colleges—have they already turned you? They asked you to spy on me, right?"

"No way."

"I can't tell you how relieved I am," he said, sarcastic. "So, what do they want from you?"

"You might ask them. At your house, you said you wanted to help them."

"That was when I thought they might be listening. Thin walls make weak secrets. Don't get me wrong. I do like to help them, but in proportion. My children are already formidable. The daughters: beautiful, good dancers, a couple of them with brains. And Theo, the honey tycoon? He gave us a jar. It reeked. But he won't give up, and somebody's funneling him money to keep going. All of them, plus my wife, they've been living high off Cantling Market Research. Dividends, special distributions, spousal dipping. Every day a holiday, in designer clothes, with perfect hair.

"So, what happens? The more they get, the more they want. They plow some of it into their so-called careers. Which means it's gone. Then they look around and there's always somebody who has more. Give a kid Buckingham Palace, and he whines about Versailles. They don't care that I have big plans for that four hundred million," he said, oblivious to the possibility that I might miss the reference. "Very big plans. It will take this company to a whole new level. But to make it happen, I need every dollar the company has. Instead the family wants me to divvy it up and dole it out. What would happen? Ann, because she's got sense, might hold on to her share. The rest of them? Forget it.

"You're a smart guy," he said as a line of transmission towers came into view, followed by what looked like a radar station. "You can understand what they don't. If I don't reinvest that four hundred million, don't replace dying properties, the company will go into a deep sleep. But all that means to them is Charlie's in the way. They think: Get rid of him, grab the money. That's where your house comes in, Benjamin. I'll throw them a bone and give it to all of them together. They can all pay for the upkeep, get the roof replaced, keep the toilets running. They'll fight like crazy. Which, when you think about it, would be helpful. Since they can vote me out of the company, do I really want them to develop the habit of cooperation?"

The possibility that Charlie might use our house as a grenade irked me. Reluctant to disturb my pilot, I eked out payback with, "Aren't you concerned I might tell them this?"

"If they believed you, they'd chalk it up to one of my moods."

I giggled again. Charlie heard. "I knew you'd like it up here," he said. "But do you see how boring the North Shore is? They have vineyards. So what? Go to New Jersey, you see all the vineyards you need. But who wants to live there? Let's head southeast to the Hamptons. I promise you some sights."

Now I was terrified. "The Hamptons? How long will it take?"

"Less than ten minutes."

"Round trip?"

"One way."

"And the party?"

"I told you. It can wait."

I told myself: There are thousands of helicopter rides every day. Millions. Almost none of them crash. This one's just longer than planned. Maybe we can go all the way to Portugal on our cushion of air.

What choice did I have? Try to stop him, and he'd laugh and keep on flying. Whoopee!

When he'd entered the helicopter, Charlie had slid his cell phone into a cradle attached to the instrument panel. Now he tapped at the phone and said, "How about some music?" Before I could answer, snappy hip-hop sprang into my headset. Between the static and the thumping and the pronunciation, I couldn't decipher much. "Ann picked the station," Charlie said. "My daughters are up to date."

Curious now, I tried to discern the words, which were something like "There's a man with a plan in a minivan and a bank we can yank for a prank. Oh, let there be bills in the tills, Diane. Let there be bills in the tills."

My taste runs to Mozart, with a dash of Schubert, but Charlie's rhythmic tapping on "the stick" proved he was awake, which was reason enough to endure the hellish noise. It raged on while we crossed the shoreline and whirled past small towns and green flatlands. Ahead spread boat-dotted inlets and bays, and beyond them the endless thread of sand beloved of beach-surveying websites with top-ten lists, and beyond the beaches, the deep blue sea. I was dizzy, thrilled, terrified. The thumping music battered my brain, which I imagined careening about in its cushioning fluid. I had an impulse to dance. I felt I was falling forward but not dropping down.

"Funny thing," Cantling shouted above the music. "The family thinks I lost my mind after the accident."

"You've lost your mind?"

"The doctor gave me a clean bill of health, more or less. No major impairment, or at least none we can see. The family wants to believe something else."

"Do they have evidence?"

"They imagine they do. There's the pistol I've been carrying. I don't know why it bothers them so much. It's me that has to worry. That's why I have the pistol."

"What are you worried about?"

"I'm pretty sure it's nothing. I just want to take precautions. My loved ones tell me I'm delusional. I guess, from their perspective, it adds up."

"You have delusions?"

"Benjamin, you look pale." I turned toward him and saw him studying me. "Have I scared you? What do you think I'm gonna do— blow my brains out?" With thumb and forefinger, he formed a pistol shape and jabbed it into his mouth.

I managed, "I'm glad we left the gun behind."

"No problem. I have a flare gun. You do remember flare guns? Trust me, if I wanted to die, I could have. Many times these past months, it seemed like the sane thing to do. If I crash this bird headfirst into the ground, some people would grieve, some would be happy, most of my kids would grab calculators. Don't worry. I didn't suffer for months, take the pills, do the rehab, just to end everything when I was mostly recovered. Bottom line: I'm too mean to die."

We pressed on toward the southeast while I groped in vain for a noninsulting reply. Approaching the Hamptons, Charlie turned the music off, which, on balance, helped my nerves. As we passed over the last farms north of the coast, he reduced altitude for a close view. This brought us low over a golf course, where a few roused sons of privilege brandished clubs at the sky to protest the noise. Then we flew over an inlet and a line of trees behind the beach. The shingled roofs of Cape Cod houses there looked stolid and reticent beside the white geometry of gigantic modernist mansions built, it seemed, on sand.

"Do you know what it's like to have children who think nothing of your life's work, who feel you're a failure as a father, who might want you dead? No, you're young. Full of yourself. Educated. And that, my friend, is why I contacted Al Byrne about you—and why you're here now."

While my fried brain parsed the affront, we passed over the beach and reached ocean. It seemed that all that remained between us and Portugal was the immense blue water and a handful of boats. I still wondered if I'd been brought along as a kamikaze sidekick. Would he continue southeast and run out of fuel, plummet, float for a minute on the waves, and sink? To die amid such beauty seemed preposterous. But Charlie had promised no suicide.

"Idiot," weed said. "Do you trust him?"

Charlie swung the helicopter around and turned it northwest toward home. My relief gave way to daggers of pain, for squinting into the sun with dilated pupils was excruciating. I closed my eyes and tried deep breathing. In. Out. In. Out. Worthless. A tap on the shoulder opened my eyes to a pair of very dark sunglasses dangling from the hand that had tapped me. I accepted, sliding the temples of the glasses under the headset's frame. My brain teemed with hopes, images, worries, memories, and somewhere a cloud, an unsettled feeling I couldn't account for. I slumped in my seat and fixed my shaded eyes on Long Island below, sure that in glumly facing downward, I cut a very druggy figure.

"I didn't believe the little darlings had the guts," Cantling said, "but they did. It didn't take long. You'd think a hundred thousand every three months would satisfy them. No, within weeks they doubled their payout. Eight hundred thousand a year—to each of the five kids. Four million dollars a year!

"Why did they need more money? They said it was a temporary measure to cope with new expenses because of my accident, like the occasional visit to the hospital in New Haven. And outfits. The worry cost them, too. Botox by the gallon to get rid of frown lines. Why do women in their thirties need Botox? And high-priced shrinks. And outfits. Two acting coaches for Melanie. And first class to Paris to lift their spirits. They even brought up money for their children."

"Children? They don't have any."

"But they do have dreams. There's a clause in the family trust that says the lead trustee can decide to pay an extra half-share to each of their children."

"Would you agree to that?"

"Not now. Maybe not ever. Unfortunately, there's a way for them to vote me out. It's not likely, some loyalties run deep, but it's possible. If it happened, they'd get to dispense their kids' money. Millions more would go down the drain every year."

The thought of the Cantling sibs as parents was jolting.

"Who pushed the most for more money?" Charlie said. "Who was the big force at the trust? Vivian's the oldest and bright and bossy, but do they really listen to someone who walks around in riding clothes? Can't be bothered to work much. Loves horses. Pays thousands. You might think the idea came from Theo, the only guy and oldest after Vivian. They had plans for the company, too. Luckily, the lawyers did what comes natural—spun them in circles and stopped much from happening. Business is very different from what the kids are used to. It's a grind. Every day there's decisions. Get enough of them wrong, there's nothing left. Thank God they had a savvy guy to run things. Phil Weller, my number two. Imagine him having to deal with five little Cantlings. They gave Phil an extra payout, I suppose to buy him off.

"When I found out how much they were taking, I told them, 'With me out of the hospital, your expenses are down. You need less.' I couldn't cut all the way back to the previous status quo. Bad politics. Risky. I told them I had plans for that capital. They weren't interested. They don't care how the money gets made. I left them with a fifty percent increase and gave Phil a bonus. I should have been tougher on them. A hundred and fifty K every three months to each of them is still too much. They didn't argue, but they'd gotten used to more. That's what this is about. More! Always more! They tried to smother me in the hospital. With a pillow."

"A pillow?"

"I can still taste it."

POSS MATTER LIFE AND DEATH: Byrne hadn't made it up, after all. Shocked into coherence, I asked, "Is this real? Who's the 'they'? How many?"

"One of them, maybe two. I think I heard them talking. Were they family? People I work with? How the hell would two of them get together for this and keep it a secret? I remember something like 'Put the bastard out of his misery.' Very sweet. For all I know they might try again. Maybe there's a bomb in the helicopter. Boom! One blast and it's over. How's that grab you?"

"Not well," I said, afraid I might throw up. That I knew my paranoia was weed induced only heightened it. I thought: This can't get back to Byrne. How would it sound? "I stole a piece of cake, Al. It was full of dope." There'd be no more job for me.

"Benjamin, are you saying you're not well? Do you get airsick?"

"Not really."

"Try to relax. Keep still. Breathe slow and easy."

"I'll be all right."

"It shocks you, doesn't it?" Cantling said. "Even if it was an attempt at a mercy killing, it's against the law."

"So you want people prosecuted?"

Cantling gripped the stick and stared fiercely ahead. "I don't know. Everything stays here, right? Since my head cleared, you and Al Byrne are the only people outside the family I've told about the pillow. But I must have babbled it in the hospital. It went up the chain. The doctors came and said it didn't seem likely. 'You were so weak. If someone tried to smother you, they'd have succeeded.' But these doctors did say, 'People can surprise you with their strength when their life is threatened. And maybe you weren't as out of it as we thought.'"

I was shocked. Cantling had alerted the authorities about his own family.

"The hospital people started to cover their asses. It got to the lawyers and then management, who decided they had to report it. It was a 'statutory requirement.' I haven't heard anything since. Is law enforcement looking into it? Not that I know of, but it could happen. The whole situation drives me up a wall."

"If you found out somebody did it, how would you feel?"

"They might be a hero, they might be a villain. One thing's for sure: it's so damn vivid! Who'd have thought anybody in the family had the guts? I wasn't really suffering that much. I was too drugged. Did they see a lot of suffering ahead? Like a lifetime? Is that why they did it?

"There's other possibilities. Phil Weller or somebody else from the business might have done it. But my money's on the family. Which means one or more of them is living with the consequences of failing. But I don't pick up any hints, like weird hugs or embarrassed looks."

Cantling's mental state seemed a jumbled combination of confidence and uncertainty, of clarity and confusion. Like mine. I'd have laughed, but my life was in his hands. I tried to focus. I said, "I assume there was no camera in the room."

"Right."

"Does the hospital keep visitor logs?"

"Yeah, but they tell me a lot of people slip through. For what it's worth, they put together a list for me. Just about everybody's on it, even a guy who used to drive for me. I talked to some of the kids. I started with, 'You must have thought some things while I was on the brink. You must have had ideas about who would get how much and who would take over at the company.' And they all said, 'No, no, we were too shell-shocked.' I told them I'd been in a very bad way, and if somebody tried a mercy killing, I admired them. They just sat there and looked at me like I was a lunatic, like I imagined the whole thing.

"Of course, the family's always afraid I might come down on them, cut off the old cash flow. Nobody wants to raise their heads out of the foxhole, even if I might hand out medals. So I stopped asking. I told the family it must have been a dream. I don't want to give them ammunition, don't want to prove their point that I've lost it. I've tried to figure out who might have done it. Tessa or Ann or Vivian? They'd be in the top tier. Theo? Forget it. Theo's always on my side. Melanie? The queen of indecision? Is she gay, straight, an actress, something else? She'll do whatever her sisters want. She's almost as weak as Theo."

Charlie's scathing assessments of his family were, as far as I knew, not terribly inaccurate. I felt uneasy. I was not a Cantling. I should not have been hearing this.

"The worst of them is Nicole, doing drugs and God knows what else in Santa Fe," Charlie continued. "I asked her to come today, my first Early Fourth since the accident. Can't head east again, she said. Too busy. It was all she could do to visit a couple of times in the hospital. She could only be with me when I was completely out of it. So now you're in the mix. Talk to Nicole, talk to all of them. If they thought it was for a good reason, why not admit it? I need to know who did it and why."

It struck me that Charlie's anger was the best indication that he was recovering. I wished I could point out the irony.

"Benjamin, can you keep another secret? A big one?"

"I guess I have to."

"Good boy. It's about that four hundred million. We may need all of it. We're in advanced talks to buy another company. It's a huge opportunity!"

"You're trying to buy a company now?"

"I am! And if I decide to do it, they can't stop me!"

Yeah, Charlie Cantling might have gone bonkers. Or maybe he always was, and this was just an exaggeration of his old self. In family lore, he had slapped his son Theo at nine years old for running from a fight. Nothing angered Charlie more than weakness. And he himself had been weak, and now he would prove that he was strong again.

"I want to get this smothering behind me," Charlie said. "Your boss and I decided for so many reasons that you're the guy to find the answers."

Canting had mentioned Byrne before, but I was astonished. Wisdom or weed told me this was the worst idea I'd ever heard. I realized that the feeling hanging over me, a feeling I couldn't name, had been dread. The events of the afternoon took on a new color. I'd been maneuvered into the helicopter so that Charlie, in full privacy and control, could make his offer.

"You have a sharp mind," he continued. "I'll put you in touch with my executives. I've got a computer guy who'll give you access to all the emails. With the family, it won't take you weeks and weeks to get up to speed like it would with some other guy."

"Will they talk to me?"

"You know them. They love to talk. Because they're Cantlings, they expect people to listen. Plus, I'll make it clear they'd better talk or the checks could stop."

I tried to deflect with, "If you're so concerned, you should rely on the police."

"Really? We had a glimpse of their brilliance last night. Do you believe they can tell a red light from a green one?"

"If somebody wants you dead, they could try again."

"I'm not a zombie anymore. And I've got the gun."

"I'm a pencil pusher," I said. "Why not hire a real investigator?"

"They won't open up to an outsider."

"I have no training."

"Don't worry. Al Byrne agreed to supervise. He'll walk you through everything."

We were over the Sound, with the sun ahead and a highway of glare on the water leading to it. Sunward was homeward, but Cantling had already shown he was indifferent to the party schedule and had changed destinations twice. My history with Charlie made me suspect that, sensing my discomfort, he might prolong the flight again.

I'd have preferred to closely monitor our progress, but even behind dark glasses, I was forced to close my eyes to the doubled light. Hip-hop resumed, something with the flavor of "You broke my nose with a garden hose. You busted my knee in a spelling bee. You're not what I thought I bought, you bitch. You're not what I thought I bought."

I waited as long as I could, which was at most thirty seconds, and lifted an eyelid to a reassuring stab of sunlight straight ahead. I closed the eye again.

"Here's our story about why I hired you," Cantling was saying. "It seems I had a taste of mortality, so I want to take the pulse of the family. Tell them I'm trying to figure out how much to give them now and in my will. I want their ideas about what should be done with the houses and the real estate. And with Cantling Market Research. It's not the main issue, but if they can be halfway honest, I could use some information about all that. Then, when you can slip it in, find out their views on pulling the plug. My daughters may not tell you the truth, but they can hardly refuse to talk to you. My son will talk if I tell him to. My wife, well, you'll handle her the best you can."

"Will the CMR executives cooperate?"

"They'll do what I say, more or less. As far as anyone else is concerned, especially your brother, this is simple fact-finding, necessary for estate planning."

"The way things are now, who would take over at CMR?" I said.

"That's complicated. My mother set up a trust to control the company. Right now I'm in charge of both. But the Lord giveth and the Lord taketh away. With a unanimous vote, my wife and children can remove me from the trust and the corporation anytime. I'd bet two or three would do it tomorrow. So here I am, a successful businessman, and I'm forced to try on tippy-toes not to offend a bunch of addled postadolescents.

"Okay, I could name my successor. I could look for a solid businessman inside the company or out. But my mother, bless her heart, drank some lawyer's Kool-Aid about empowering the next generation. She set it up so a simple majority can toss out whoever I pick. Get it? If I appoint somebody, the family can turn on a dime and take control. Even Nicole gets to vote from Santa Fe.

"My accident got them started, and they went right for the money. Now they've gone to ground. They hide behind smiles and concern for my health, but they're full of intrigue. Who has the votes and how many? Who wants the power? Who might do what to get it? You, Benjamin, are going to figure it out."

"What if they ask if I'm investigating the business with the pillow?"

"You'll tell them it came up and old Charlie shrugged it off. I decided the drugs got the better of me."

"They might say, 'If he wants to know what we want, why doesn't he just ask?'"

"Easy. My kids are adolescents refusing to age out. You think I get reasonable answers out of them ever? Now and then, they throw some outrageous accusation at me. The rest of the time, they say yes to whatever I ask them and then pile on the bullshit. They're scared. And hostile. Someone said I intimidate them. I wish I did. They might behave better. I'm much better off with a third party who they'll talk to, like you."

We flew on. With eyes shut and blitzed brain reeling, I saw that Charlie had signed me up to spy on his family. And the others wanted me to spy on Charlie for them. How many relationships would this arrangement cost me? How would Theo react? And Ann?

With the Connecticut shore growing closer, I said, "This is a big surprise. I'll have to talk about it with Al Byrne."

"Blame me for the surprise. You and me have an old connection. That's why I went to Byrne in the first place—and why I wanted to talk to you today."

"To check me out?"

"I wasn't sure you had the cojones. Now I'm optimistic. You looked at my situation from several angles. You asked a few sharp questions. If you'd have been spacey, if you'd have been dumb or played it that way, I'd have dropped you right away. I'll confirm with Byrne that the deal's on. I can cancel the contract anytime if I feel you're not making progress, so don't even think about dragging it out. Results, young man, results. We negotiated a retainer for your services and for Byrne and Company backup. And Al Byrne will give you ten thousand a month extra."

"Ten thousand? I guess I don't have a choice."

"Do you want a choice? Are you balking?"

"No," I said. "I'm confused. I'd make enough money to keep the house, at least for a while. And you don't seem to mind. Your offer to buy, was it real?"

"Bright boy."

"So, the house deal was an excuse to draw me in."

"Let's say I was laying the groundwork for a deal and reminding you how much you have to gain by working for me."

I peeked again and confirmed we had nearly reached the shore. "Will you agree to stop flying over the house?" I said.

"Okay. I'll only approach from the Sound side."

"Even when there's wind?"

"In any wind or no wind."

Much too easy, I thought with weedy insight. Won't happen.

"By the way," Charlie said, "your brother's a loose cannon. Keep him out of this. Let him think you're just interviewing people about what they want from me. My daughters will be talking to him. Let's not encourage loose talk about mercy killing."

I shut my eyes again. If liftoff had seemed unnatural, then landing felt impossible. How could a large, screaming, ungainly machine squeeze between trees and houses and power lines and settle safely on a microscopic piece of lawn? The Goulds were good Jews and atheists, but right now I wished to God for a God to pray to.

I felt Charlie turn the helicopter and point it into the wind. I opened my eyes. We were back. Below, a profusion of newly parked cars spread inland from the Cantling house, and guests had fanned out onto the patio and lawn. The tennis court was empty.

"Charlie, this won't be easy. You have more confidence in me than I deserve."

"Don't push humility. It's overrated. You won't try to wiggle out of this with Al Byrne, will you?"

"Not in the cards," I said. "By the way, can I keep the sunglasses?"

"No problem. I've got a dozen more. Now shut up and let me land."

I stayed silent during the landing, steeling myself to the phobic possibility of a snickering welcome committee drummed up by Melanie. I resolved to claim the flight was lovely and lie to Melanie that I'd had no indications of weed, and by the way weed has no effect on me. But when we settled onto the ground, the only greeter was Tessa, motioning forcefully from the doorway to summon her husband to the party.

Charlie seemed to forget me. He hopped out of the helicopter and hurried toward the house. After he passed his wife, she pointed at me and mouthed, "We'll talk."

A weedy insight explained the lack of Melanie. Out to boost the company payout from drug-disapproving Dad, she couldn't risk exposing her own involvement with drugs.

Cantling chaos. Cantling intrigue. I was learning.

Stepping onto terra firma, I let out a whoop of joy that went unheard under the engine's throb and the swish of the blades. I craned my neck to watch as the rotors, with quiet majesty, slowed and grew still. Time was still distorted. Only a few seconds seemed to have passed since we'd landed, but when I looked away from the rotors, the engine had shut off. I heard the murmur of cocktail chatter and the purr of the string quartet. I took a step toward the patriotic tipplers and stopped.

No mere cannabinoid could make me forget I wasn't free of dope and hunger. Wasted and talking too much, I might break Waspy taboos and embarrass myself, lose friends, and expose my drugged-up state. And what good could come of seeing Theo again? Or Melanie?

Reversing course, I found the path to our house and was grateful to escape undetected. Lit now and then by shafts of late sunlight slanting through the trees, I discovered I was famished, just as Melanie had predicted. I longed for something sweet and fresh, or at worst recently expired, in our woefully stocked bachelor's fridge. My best hope was the mainstay of Jody's diet, the only item he reliably resupplied: Big Sugar Frozen Waffles. My pace quickened. My saliva gushed. I yearned for a tower of toasted Big Sugars drowned in cheap goo and piled high with butter.

I passed the empty tennis court. On the sound system I heard the string quartet stop midmovement and the crowd murmur die. After an electronic screech, there arose the reverential silence that only a master pitchman can create.

"Same body. Same voice. Same party," Charlie began. His amplified voice surrounded me. "But I am not the same man I was. I have learned that life is beautiful, life is precious and, above all, finite."

A crow stirred from its afternoon torpor squawked from a hidden perch.

Every year, Charlie turned profound on the Early Fourth, but it was beyond me to determine how much the old pirate believed himself. His recent ordeal and his domineering ways combined with the weed to move me, and as his reverberance accompanied me to the property line, my dilated pupils were wet with tears.

"I intend to use my remaining time," he boomed, "to pass along to others everything I have of value. I don't mean the tangible stuff like wealth and property. These are temporary. The tide rolls in and takes them away. I'm talking about the real stuff: wisdom, understanding, children, love. Ah, don't listen to me. Sermons are a waste of time. It's a beautiful afternoon in June. Happy Independence Day."

CHAPTER FOUR

BENJAMIN

At home I stuffed myself with waffles and stumbled into the living room, where I stretched out on a couch and set my cell phone beside me. For at least a couple of hours, it didn't ring or ding, and I didn't stir. There was no need. Behind my sunglasses, my eyes—sometimes open, mostly shut—were bedazzled. My mind was a kaleidoscope of fractured fantasies and incoherent dreams. Much of the time I didn't know whether I was awake or asleep, insightful or delusional.

Suddenly, a lamp turned on, and I discovered Melanie Cantling standing over me. There was curiosity, and possibly concern, on her fair face. In the window behind her, the evening sky was turning dark. I hadn't heard her enter the house.

"Benjamin, I'm sorry if I startled you." She spoke slowly, as if to an uncomprehending child. "Are we alone? Is your brother around?"

I heard myself say, "I don't think so."

"Are you expecting him?"

I recalled her tongue in my mouth. "He's out for the evening."

"You're sure?"

"Very." I was lying.

"Then it's good I stopped by, for a lot of reasons. I've been thinking: I should not have come onto you like that. I guess it was because I hadn't seen you in a while. But it's the Early Fourth. And you were with my family again. I got overexcited."

"No problem. Stuff happens." I reached a hand toward her. When she ignored it, I let it fall to my stomach.

"I have a new idea," she said. "Something that will bring us closer."

"I'd like that. Now let's have sex."

"Here? Now? You're all drugged up. I will not take advantage."

"Please do. I'm okay. Anyhow, weed doesn't affect me."

She reached for my sunglasses and, when I failed to react, lifted them off. "Your eyes are black holes. You can barely move. You seem half out of your mind. That's your idea of okay?" She replaced my sunglasses on my face. "If you can, pay attention. I know you didn't mean to get high, and you're not used to it. I feel bad about it. I should have stayed to help you get through. That's the main reason I'm here—to help you."

"Thank you."

My cell phone pinged. Melanie picked it up from the floor and studied the message. "It's Jody. He says, 'Party dull. Home soon. Stuff to talk about.'"

She set the phone on the couch. "Benjamin, we don't have much time. There's another reason I came to see you. After what you did to my cake, don't you think you owe me a favor? I've heard about the man who runs your company. He sounds fascinating. I might like to talk to him."

"Al Byrne? You want to meet him?"

"It might be a good idea, it might be a terrible one. I can tell him things I can't tell you—because of our history."

"We have a history?"

"We do now."

"I don't know if he'll agree. He's busy. He wants the Cantlings to talk to me."

"If I can't even talk to him, I won't help. And I may have to tell everybody you were stoned."

"That was because of you!"

"Very nice. Blame it on the client's daughter."

I was developing a bit of respect—or was it fear?—for Melanie. I said, "I'll see what I can do."

"You don't have to do much. Just back me up. I only want to talk to him. If he asks, tell him you think it's a good idea."

When my brother arrived minutes later, I sat up grinning. In a delightful reversal of the old pattern, Jody had happened upon a Cantling girl looming over me.

"So, bro, what everyone's talking about is true. Charlie wants you to work for him."

"How do you know?"

"Because Mel's in our living room. How many times has she chased you over here before? Does 'never' sound right?"

"You're saying I have ulterior motives?" Melanie asked him.

"You're here, aren't you?"

"If Benjamin and I have business, it's none of your concern. To be honest, you're sort of in the way."

My grin grew wider.

"I live here, Mel. Or have you forgotten?" Jody said.

It struck me that they'd been caught off guard, for they were talking in a way I'd never heard before—directly, like old intimates. Melanie's allure began to weaken.

"Listen, Jody," she said, "Benjamin can have whatever relationship he wants, more or less, with my father and with me. It has nothing to do with you. Benjamin, don't forget what we talked about. We might be able to help each other."

"Stop messing with my brother," Jody told her.

"I'm the one who's messing with him?" she said.

"What are you two talking about?" I asked.

"Nothing," she said.

She left soon after, and Jody said, "You're not seriously thinking about doing a project with Charlie Cantling?"

"I might have to. He made a deal with Al Byrne."

"Bad idea. Have you forgotten who Cantling is? The man Dad called a big, hungry python?"

"I can take care of myself."

"Trust me, he'll squeeze you bad. That's what pythons do. Look at you already! Why are you wearing shades? If it's too bright in here, turn the lights off."

"I have a migraine. The shades take the edge off the light."

"Bullshit. Aren't you a little bit suspicious? All of a sudden Cantlings are falling all over you, and you think that's normal? Tell me something: were you stoned when you started flying, or did it happen after?"

"I'm not stoned," I said. "You know how I feel about drugs."

"I could settle this," he said. "I could pin you down, grab the shades, and get a look at your pupils."

"The shades will remain on my face, and you know it." Checkmate. Since the day our mother died, we had never had a physical row.

"I get it. You think you need to stonewall everybody about the dope, me included. This is too much. I leave you alone for an hour, and you get all tangled up. Cantling. Spy games. Drugs. A pack of lies. How can I help when you won't tell the truth?"

I was about to answer when from outside we heard POP! POP! Then came a screechy whistle. Through a window, I saw two narrow, parallel streaks of light zip into the night sky. At their peak the comets burst and spread into two circles, each of which resolved into multiple exclamation points that dripped with fire. The fragments floated down in concert, dimming to embers before they disappeared. The night reverted to darkness. Neighborhood dogs barked. Small waves broke against the shore. Jody, who knew the firework sequence from other years, left me in the kitchen for the patio.

I joined him there, our eyes fixed on the sky. Stonefield loved its Fourth of July fireworks, which started a week early and ended a week late. I imagined rows of craned necks at various houses, and oohs and ahs, and hired pros with missing fingers tending rockets at the water's edge. A dozen small boats had edged close to shore to watch.

"You haven't watched fireworks for years," Jody said.

"But they're amazing."

"You're stoned."

"You won't believe me if I deny it."

"Correct."

Explosions. Bangs. More comets streaked through the sky with brilliant colors ablaze—reds, oranges, yellows. Starbursts. Skyrockets. Pinwheels. The chatter of popping gunpowder. My face was strained from a grin too wide. After ten minutes, another lull and dogs barking again. It was too soon. This couldn't be the end of the show. Sure enough, a colossal mass of munitions rose up and exploded, raining down huge bursts of shattered fire. The entire sky ignited.

Moments later, it was over. In my eyes, shimmering electrons created ghost images of fire. The handful of boats in the Sound honked horns in appreciation and with fading engines stole away.

We sat side by side on the patio, Jody in a lawn chair and I on our mother's chaise, the wood gone gray for lack of oiling. From the party we heard goodbye shouts and doors close. Motors started, cars drove off. Of the fireworks, only a sulfurous haze remained, wafting our way on the faintest of breezes. But for a few extra lights at the Cantling house, the Early Fourth extravaganza seemed forgotten, as if no one had shown and nothing had happened.

A sprinkling of stars unfurled across the sky. The fireflies returned, flashing their lightning lures. In the direction of the path to the Cantlings, we noticed, mingled with the fireflies, three pinpricks of lights growing stronger. They moved horizontally and didn't blink. The lights intensified and stopped, holding steady. Now, from that same direction, a flash and an explosion.

Another flash. Another explosion. Was someone launching extra fireworks? I scanned the sky for fire and saw only blackness and stars. Something flashed. BOOM!

"Unbelievable!" Jody said. "Who's doing that?"

"Probably kids with bangers. Let's just go inside."

"I don't think so. It's too big for bangers. I'm heading down there. We can't have this crap close to our house. They might be on our property!"

"Jody!"

It was too late. He had started down the lawn at a trot, holding his lit cell phone close to the ground to light the way. I called, "I'm coming with you" and jogged after him.

"Don't," Jody said over his shoulder. We kept our voices low. "You're useless even when you're straight."

"I should be there."

"Try not to fall on your face."

The slight downward slope propelled me forward. I may have stumbled a bit but didn't admit it to Jody. BANG! Another explosion, closer now. Cantling voices rose from the woods.

Ann: "Stop it. You're making a fool of yourself."

Another voice, probably Vivian's: "Stop it!"

Jody rushed into the dark grove of trees connecting the properties. The weak glow of his cell phone became intermittent, forcing me to slow down. I hated hearing Jody's hurried footsteps fade, but I couldn't see the ground and had to be careful of obstacles. If I turned an ankle, if I wrenched a knee, what use would I be?

A strange scene came into view. In an open space among trees, two flashlights shined on Theo Cantling, who gripped a shotgun across his thick chest and gazed into the night. Theo had donned protective earmuffs resembling his father's helicopter headphones. Clamped around his angry, bewildered face, they made him look ridiculous, but the shotgun ruled out laughing. Behind the flashlights, two dim figures lurked.

Theo spoke to a shape in the darkness. "If I hadn't dropped my flashlight, this would be different."

"You'd shoot me?" Jody said.

"You shot flares, I've got a shotgun. What's the difference? I don't want to hurt you. Where's your brother?"

"You're drunk," Jody said. He stepped sideways. I assumed it was to keep Theo from facing in my direction. "Go home."

"Good idea," Ann said from the darkness behind the flashlights. "Come with me and Vivian. We'll help you get there."

Theo, I realized, was enacting a parody of last night, but with a shotgun and shells. "I don't need help," Theo said. "Hey, Benjy. If Jody's around, you are too. I've got Cantling cash. That's what it's all about. Jingle-jingle. Come get it."

I couldn't leave Jody by himself. Plus, any motion might attract Theo. I didn't move.

"Hey, chickenshit! Let's have a discussion," Theo said. He extended the shotgun, aimed it into the night, and swung it to and fro. "We'll talk who's productive and who isn't. Some guys sit on their inheritance. Not me. I'm the future Cantling king, the man who fought Varroa mites and won. Every bee in Western Connecticut's gonna work for me!"

Before tonight, apart from trying to push me out of a treehouse twenty years ago, Theo had seemed essentially harmless. But he was drunk, with a gun in his hand, and he had threatened me earlier. Each time the shotgun swung and unwittingly pointed at me, I froze.

Theo said, "I've seen the future, asshole, and it buzzes. You? A party-line Socialist. Kill honest businessmen with taxes and idiot regulations. Fuck you! Who says I can't spray my tomatoes? When I find you, I'll blow your head off. I'll leave your flesh for the raccoons."

From Ann and Vivian, gasps. From me, silence.

"Theo, have you ever made a profit with Theo's Aromatic?" Jody asked by way of distraction.

"Judy, you would say something dumb," Theo replied. "Fuck profit. Theo's Aromatic is growing like crazy. When my bees stop dying, I'll be the fourth biggest beekeeper in Western Connecticut. Who else can say that?"

"If there's no profit," Jody said, "income taxes ain't relevant."

"I'm patient. The honey market is ripe for the taking, and Theo's Aromatic is the top brand. Ask anybody."

I'd have loved to critique Theo's honey then and there. The handful of licks I'd ever dared had smelled of ammonia, but in deference to the shotgun, I kept the ammonia angle to myself. Theo was also dedicated to illegally shooting birds, which explained his drunken ease with the gun.

"People look up to us," Theo said with a growl. "We're the best fucking people in the world—and now we have bees. One car crash doesn't ruin the Cantlings. One lousy truck that couldn't get out of the way. Benjy's gonna make us stronger? Benjy's gonna help? Give a little man some power, and guess what? He'll try to steal everything. This is Benjy's big chance. Dad's backing Benjy and not me. What the fuck? It must be the drugs Dad takes. I'm going to kill him."

"Can we clarify?" Jody said. "Who are you going to kill? Benjamin or Charlie?"

"Keep it up, and I'll kill you too."

"Theo, you are absolutely right," Ann said. I couldn't see her in the darkness. "This is a great family. People look up to us. We stick together. Part of what makes us who we are is we get the right people to work for us. Dad has decided Benjamin can help. We should accept that. Let's go home, sleep on it, and talk it over tomorrow." I knew the Cantlings enough to be certain tomorrow's discussion wouldn't happen. And Ann knew it too. "We'll sort everything out."

"You're in the wrong woods, Pollyanna," Theo said. "The Goulds want us out of the way. It's us or them, baby."

He lifted the shotgun and fired into the air. The noise was excruciating, and in the sudden light of the muzzle flash, I felt dazed and exposed. I ran five steps and dove to the ground. When I looked up, I saw Theo, still lit by flashlights, aiming the shotgun into the darkness and scanning. "Oh, Jody, Benjamin? I still have one in the chamber."

The gun rotated toward Jody. This was, at last, too much.

"Asshole!" I shouted. "I'm here! Fire away!"

One of the flashlights found me. The other went dark. "Fuckhead!" Theo screamed.

"Vivian, turn your light off!" Ann said.

"Shit!" Vivian said.

The flashlight switched off, but it had been enough to divert Theo's attention from Jody to me. I tried to roll away from where Theo had last seen me, but even without light, he could listen and probe the ground and find me and shoot me.

Sober, he might be a harmless oaf, but under the influence, who knew? I heard his slow footsteps nearing me on the soft earth. It was too late to get up and run. It struck me that, yes, he really would get away with it. Cantling lawyers. What a shabby end: my face to the ground, the smell of dirt. "Ann!" I called. "Ann!"

"Why Ann?" Theo said.

Now came quick footsteps, thumps, and a loud exhale from Theo like a flopped-on cushion. "Theo, you goddamn idiot!" my brother shouted. "You think this is all a joke? I should beat the crap out of you." There was the sound of maybe a foot impacting on flesh—and Theo again on the exhale.

"No more," Theo said. "It hurts."

"Good!" Jody said. "Pointing a gun at people. Moron! Benjamin, great diversion. I didn't know you had it in you. Ladies, let's turn on the lights."

In an instant, three flashlights were fixed on Theo, who sat clutching his midsection and rocking. Such was the drunken allure of victimized grandeur that as he whimpered and moaned, he wasn't embarrassed. My brother—cool under fire as always, as if fire were his element of choice—stood tall and calm over Theo and held the shotgun at his side. I rose to my feet, brushed at my clothes, and tried to cope with a cascade of stoned emotion. I felt apoplectic about Theo, relieved beyond measure, grateful to my brother, humiliated that I'd needed him.

"Fuck the Goulds. I should sue," Theo said, catching his breath. "Your Honor, one night they fire flares at us. So I shoot some blanks—can't hurt anything—to try to show them the error of their ways."

"Blanks?" I said. "I don't believe you."

"Yeah, blanks. Your Honor, I was kidding around. Then they assaulted me on my own land."

"Isn't it your father's land?" Jody said.

"Splitting hairs," Theo panted. "I'm going to puke."

Theo pushed forward onto hands and knees and lowered his head. Ann and Vivian knelt beside him and patted his back while boozy vomit gushed onto the ground. I'd have preferred that Vivian rap him with the riding crop tucked under her arm.

Impatient with comforting, Vivian said, "Our father heard the noise. He'll know we went out here. What will we tell him?"

"Raccoons," Theo said.

"Raccoons won't explain what a mess you are," Vivian said.

"Talks like a dog, pukes like a dog," Jody said.

"Kill you some other time," Theo managed between heaves.

"Neighborhood kids with some mischief?" Ann said.

"He aimed a fucking gun at us," Jody said.

"He says he didn't mean to," said Vivian, sarcastic.

Theo spat. "Fuck you."

"She has a crop," Jody said. "Be respectful."

"Some kids in the woods were making big noises with firecrackers," Ann said, showing unexpected invention. "Theo went to shoo them away. He tripped and spilled beer on himself. Charlie might see through it, but we'll back it up. Benjamin? Jody? You don't need more trouble, especially if someone calls the police."

Ann had a point. The cops had seen too much of the Goulds. "Jody?" I said.

"Whatever."

"Here we go again!" Vivian said. "Let's rally round. Let's make excuses for the fucking brother from hell!"

"Vivian!" Ann said.

"I should kick him in the balls," Vivian said. "But we might need his vote."

"For what?" I asked.

"My vote?" Theo said. "Never."

"Why don't we take him to the house?" Ann said. She tried to pull her brother to his feet, but he was too sodden and heavy to budge.

"Let me," Jody said, yanking Theo upward.

"Don't need your fucking help," the sot said, on his feet at last.

I let the three of them lead Theo away. Light from the rising moon filtered through the trees to guide me, and I started toward our house to the fading accompaniment of Theo cursing his helpers.

There were rapid footsteps behind me. I stopped and turned.

"Benjamin, wait," Ann said. I braced for questions. After all, I'd called out to her and her alone when Theo pointed his shotgun at me. She said, "I'm sorry for what happened. You'll see: Theo has good qualities, too."

"I'm waiting."

She leaned close. "It might be fine that Charlie wants to find out what we want. You might help the whole family. But be careful."

"About what?"

"People may have to do things you won't like."

"You included?"

"They're my family," she said. "You're not. If you really knew me—I mean, really did—I wonder if we'd be friends."

Before I could ask what she meant, she kissed my cheek and strode into the darkness. The beam of her flashlight dwindled on the path to her house.

The other sisters might seem more appealing to the rest of the world, but not to me. With all Ann had to offer, why had she just put herself down? Was that new, or had I simply noticed for the first time? She'd always been the sister who didn't seem to flirt, had never favored bait and switch, but she'd kissed me and told me she might grow distant, had warned me about things I knew and things I didn't.

We needed to talk more. But when? How much? Her flashlight disappeared, but my excuses were fully illuminated: friendship, work, terror, brother.

CHAPTER FIVE

BENJAMIN

The next morning, I was groggy, depleted, hungry, and in need of a plan. Wary of a Sunday communiqué from Al Twenty-Four Seven, I avoided my cell—until an impatient peek revealed a one-word Byrne message: "So?"

I assumed he'd prefer something in writing. Which would play, of course, to my strengths. I replied in the Byrne style: "SENDING REPORT MON."

His answer was swift: "SHORT. NO ADJECTIVES. MEET TUES 10."

His swipe about adjectives was apt. A year earlier, he'd assigned me to edit an op-ed he had drafted for *The Times*. I'd had to rewrite the piece entirely. When I sent him the new version, I told him I hoped he liked the smell of varnish because I had deleted a few adjectives but otherwise barely touched it. Whether or not he saw through me, he accepted the draft without complaint—and "There's No Good Time for Cybercrime" was published to broad acclaim.

Though my back-and-forth with Byrne had cost me a part of speech, my promise of Monday had bought me time. On the

Sunday-evening train to New York, words and phrases began to bubble up: "Compelling." "Intriguing." "Good case for somebody else." Al's ban on adjectives forced me toward the essentials, and my draft was ready at midnight and polished in the morning. I had decided to confess everything and cast my encounter with Melanie in the worst possible light. This seemed clever and would at the very least immunize me against Melanie's blackmail. At best, it would get me off the case. On Monday, I massaged and clarified.

Around dinnertime, I emailed my first-ever field report to Byrne.

Al had positioned Byrne and Company to appeal to a flush clientele. "Our mission is twofold," he'd say. "First we protect our clients. If it's a question of physical safety, we control access and lines of sight. We monitor electronically. If it's cybersecurity, we erect our firewalls and, as a test, ask some of our magnificent nerds to breach it. They rarely do. We're the best and everybody knows it.

"And I say: so what? There's another part to our mission. We need to convince our clients that they really are protected. We need to shield them from fear. If this means standing guard against kidnappers while a client rafts in an empty ocean, so be it. If it means closely monitoring the house they never use, with the Picassos inside they never see, so be it. If we fail, if we protect them but they don't feel it, if they don't in their hearts believe they're safe, they'll send us away and hire the competition."

To help persuade the target customer that his was a classy firm, Byrne had leased a floor in an angular, modern tower with floor-to-ceiling glass and an architectural pedigree. As I kept telling outsiders, most of Al's agents worked at screens, eating junk food—but perhaps to impress clients, perhaps in a nod to a time when agents needed muscle tone, Al wanted his people looking fit. He had set aside a room for bizarre contraptions with pedals and pulleys and wheels and brand names that hinted at televised sports. Like the rest of the staff, Al had for the most part remained a stranger to the equipment, but now newly separated from his third wife and trying to shape up for the fifty-something dating scene, he summoned me to the exercise room at ten on Tuesday.

Ghost-white walls and heavy fluorescence above rows of workout machines gave the room the gloom of empty brilliance. Between the machines were padded mats that seemed to sag under the imprints of stolen naps. The contraptions themselves were in mint condition, and I was optimistic that Al's unusual bulk wouldn't harm the cross-trainer I found him slow-pedaling on top of. In his hand was a large cell phone, which he aggressively poked while ignoring two upright levers meant to tone the arms. A small screen facing him at paunch height offered settings and controls. We were alone.

The short, squat, narrow-eyed, and balding Al had long gray sideburns meant to lend distinction but failing. It was a tribute to his prodigious capability and salesmanship that he won deals despite his appearance. Today he had stripped down to sneakers and undershorts and a T-shirt swollen at the waist by globs of flesh. The tastes of three ex-wives warred on in Al's closets and made for morning guessing games about what he'd wear to work. The navy-blue suit, white shirt, and deep-blue tie draped on a nearby apparatus told me this was a third-wife day—conservative. An unlit cigar stub was clenched between his lips.

He saw me and, continuing his slow exertions, dropped the stub into a tray on the apparatus.

"There was some action with the Cantlings yesterday," Byrne began. "Charlie sent over paperwork for you to sign. Routine stuff: a card to gain access to the building, an agreement that we'll keep everything to ourselves. And Melanie Cantling wants to meet me. She says she might have some useful information. It doesn't occur to her

I might be a tiny bit busy. Does she have anything on you? Did you screw her?"

"No. Not even close."

"I googled her. Headshots. Bikini shots. You name it. She is definitely a looker."

"She told me she just wanted to talk to you. She didn't say anything about a meeting."

"Presumptuous, isn't she? Not the way we handled things in Kew Gardens," Byrne said, bragging of his humble beginnings in Queens. He started to pedal harder. "The Cantlings want something, and everybody's supposed to fall in line."

"You won't see her?"

"I didn't say that. Do I look like a guy who turns away knockouts?"

"So we're moving forward with them?"

"We are," he said. "Charlie told me your discussion went well."

"Didn't I make it clear there were impediments? Showstoppers." I was proud of the jargon.

"What showstoppers?"

"For one thing, Cantling might be losing his mind. Do we really need a client like that?"

"You expect me to believe this?" Al said. "A business leader like Charlie Cantling, who fields all kinds of problems every day, has suddenly gone crazy?"

"He flew me over the Sound and rattled on about all sorts of things, like he forgot where he was and who he was talking to. His ordeal may have driven him crazy. Or is 'demented' the better word?"

"I forgot your degree in psychiatry," he said. "Remind me: where'd you go to medical school? This doesn't have anything to do with you wanting off the case?"

"I don't want off. I want what's best for the firm."

"So I'm supposed to turn down good business from what might become an important client because you got a bad vibe."

"This family won't cooperate. Charlie, if he's halfway sane, will never let me in on the real secrets. None of them will. Talking to them is a waste of time."

"If that's right, why did he sign our contract and wire a retainer, no questions asked? Everything looks smooth. If he's crazy, he hides it well. Which would make him a little less crazy, wouldn't it?"

"He signed?"

"Don't get too puffed up. There's at least one real problem with this assignment. It seems there's some sour history between your family and the Cantlings. Because Charlie hates your brother. He doesn't want him anywhere near this."

I saw a fresh opportunity. "Al, if you need to take me off this, I'll be disappointed, but I'm a big boy. I know there's a lot of people here who might handle it better than me. I have no experience. No training. And there's Jody."

This felt deft. Al's great pride was the firm's case-study training, with annual refreshers, where our recruits and agents reviewed real security events and lessons learned. To gain traction at the firm, recruits had to pass muster on tricky "Scenarios" presented by Byrne. I had never faced a Scenario.

He said, "You'll be happy to know I told Cantling your brother is not a major stumbling block. It will be your responsibility to keep your brother out of the loop. Client confidentiality says your brother can't hear a thing."

"I'm not sure that's possible."

"Why?"

"My brother's close to the Cantlings. Except for Theo, it's likely they'll all talk to him."

"I knew it," Byrne said, thumping the screen that controlled the cross-trainer. He sped up his pedaling again. "You could look at this as your big chance—a way to make some real money, advance at Byrne and Company, and be a hero to an important family. When this is done, the Cantling daughters could be all over you. It's not like it's a tough case. It's five to one an old man had a bad dream. Really, I'm not exactly sure why he'd bother. I have my theories. But I'm betting it will all become clear in the end. In the meantime, you ask a few questions, make notes, and go home. Instead you're acting like a goddamn bureaucrat. You claim you're trying to follow rules, but what you really want to do is nothing."

"Not true," I said. "I want to do what's best for the firm."

"Really? You grabbed onto this brother situation like it was a life raft. Well, I hate to disappoint you, but half the world has a brother. Just keep yours away. And this field report you came up with—you go on about attempted sex, drug use, and physical danger like I'd have to ignore the rules against all three to keep you on the case. Tell me: exactly what field were you in? You made a sales call. You should have written a sales report. And salespeople want sales, not imaginary showstoppers."

"Imaginary?"

"Sex. Drugs. Violence. We try to avoid them all. But nobody fucked you, the drug was an accident, and nobody shot you. Your report should have only said what the client wants and what you had to tell him to keep the deal alive."

I tried: "Cantling's son threatened me with a shotgun."

"We get threats every day. We get drunks waving their fists, nerds promising to hack us, heavyweight assholes threatening to ruin us. It's a cost of doing business. If we give in, we're nothing. That's why, when they threaten us, we come at them with everything we've got."

Byrne pedaled harder, beginning to work his arms.

"Frankly, I had doubts about you from the day you first walked into my office. Most of my agents, they're great with bytes and software and electronics, but they write so bad the computers can't correct them. They needed help. Even so, you looked like a bad fit. Yeah, you've got a brain, but it matters too much to you. I've known a lot of arrogant losers with brains.

"In the end, I more or less tossed a coin, and you won. We'd bring you in to do brochures, keep up the website, edit reports, smooth whatever we send out. Now, all of a sudden, there's a big opportunity for you. Are you ready to get up from your desk? Can you stop sucking your goddamn thumb? Because if you fuck this up, everybody here will know, and it will be just about impossible to get you back to where you are."

I noticed that the talk and unwonted exercise seemed to be taking a toll on Byrne. His breathing had quickened, and his face was red. I ventured, "I thought I was doing well here."

"You were, until a few months ago," Byrne said, and I saw my mistake. "Remember when Cybernuggets.com contacted us to do a profile of our company? They said they wanted to show the world what the best looked like. They said they'd be careful, with no trade secrets revealed. I took a chance and went along with it. But I told everybody you can't trust journalists, be careful, and almost everybody was. Most of what Cybernuggets wrote turned out okay. The firm looked good. I looked good."

"It worked out, didn't it?"

"It's possible you remember the sour note," Al said, breathing heavily. His face was redder still. "Cybernuggets.com wrote that somebody at the company had described me as, quote, 'an unwavering and perspicacious vulgarian.' Who talks like that around here? Check any cubicle. 'Perspicacious.' 'Vulgarian.' Is that science fiction? 'I'm from the planet Vulgarr. We're gonna blow up your moon.' I know. You're embarrassed to be here. You'd rather be a brilliant journalist—and starve. To prove yourself, you showed off for an underpaid interviewer from Cybernuggets."

"Look at that noun, Al. 'Vulgarian.' It's not even a proper word. And I detest long adjectives. Somebody did a bad job pretending to be me."

"Those adjectives saved you. If it was just 'vulgarian,' I'd have cut your balls off."

Further denials would have been useless—and untrue. During my call with the reporter, a young woman with a voice that purred, that description of Byrne had sprung to mind. I pictured a long suspension bridge with three polysyllables as stanchions. Unwavering. Perspicacious. Vulgarian. To invent that melodious phrase, to form that image, to make adjectives sing, was brilliant. To suppress it would have been criminal. Byrne pedaled harder than ever. His face was crimson. His eyes bulged.

"Al," I said, worried, "slow down."

"Can't. Gotta get trim."

"You're scaring me. Turn this thing off."

"I'm rich," he wheezed. "That alone spreads the female knees a few inches. If I was rich and fit? Wide open. By the way, the second fuckup's a charm. You're fired."

"What?"

"Insubordinate," he said, puffing. "Trying too hard to get out of the Cantling assignment. You're done."

"Al, I like it here. I like you. I like the assignment."

"I don't believe you." Suddenly, he clutched his chest and let out a roar. I watched in horror as he fell off the machine and crumpled onto the padded mat alongside.

"Al!"

He lay panting on the mat. Saliva dribbled from his mouth.

"Al! Al!"

He mumbled. He moaned. I remembered that cardiovascular events required immediate action. I was about to run for help when he looked up at me and winked. His breathing eased.

"Did you believe it?" he said. "Did you take the heart attack seriously?"

"You were faking?"

He rolled to his feet, grinning. His face had lost some of its red. "This is your training test. Pass it and you'll keep your job and, with it, the Cantling assignment. You do want your job, don't you?"

I nodded.

"It looked like a big heart attack. Did it cross your mind I might never recover consciousness?"

"Yes. Sort of."

"If I did, only we would know I'd fired you, and I'd be dead. Right?"

"Yes."

"So here's your test question: if I'd never woken up, would you have told people you'd been canned?"

I shuddered. I was already confused from the heavy dose of Byrne. If the heart attack had been real, I had no idea what I would have done. I might have revealed all. I might have revealed nothing. The bigger question: what to tell Al right now? I channeled Jody, who would have definitely hidden the firing. But how would Jody handle the living Al?

"Time's up," Byrne said.

All I could offer was an observation. "I don't think it matters, Al. Whatever answer I give, including this one, you'll tell me I passed the test."

"Brilliant!" he said, raising both fists. "Now stop worrying. I would never send you over there untrained if I thought there were real risks. Even if Cantling has it right and somebody tried to kill him, no one would ever be able to prove anything. Would the authorities even bother? I had an aunt in a nursing home. Near the end, they dosed her up with so much morphine they could have sold her body parts on the street. The police wouldn't investigate. They said something like my aunt was left-handed, so the drug test was invalid. What do we have with Cantling? At most, a failed attempt at a mercy killing. And a bunch of kids, according to Cantling, without the balls to do it or live with the consequences. You'll report what you find about the mercy killing and everything else, and that should be the end of it."

"I'm not so sure. One of them might have murder on the brain."

"You mean the son?" Al said. "Be careful of your prejudices. Investigate. Appear to help the client. If you sabotage in any way, if I even suspect sabotage, you'll be out on the street in a heartbeat. Take notes and talk to me—and don't let the Cantlings spin you around."

I could hear my brother call me a wimp, but further resistance seemed pointless.

"I'll be careful," I said. "I do know them pretty well."

"Do you know them when they want something they might not get? The only answer they're used to hearing is yes. Famous people are worse. Their asses get licked clean on a daily basis. And Cantlings are halfway famous. So keep your distance, especially from the daughters. No more drugs. And no sex. If you need a role model for good behavior, look no further. I'm it."

"You?"

"Don't be so surprised," Al said. "In my private life, I make it a matter of principle to never turn down a blowjob. But sound business and a hard-on don't mix. That's why I wrote the company rules the way I did, why I'm a dedicated puritan on the job. When I get offers, I brush them away. When I get my own ideas at the wrong time, I keep them to myself. If I agree to meet with Melanie Cantling, I guarantee there will be no sex. If that makes me horny and I don't sleep so good, I know I'd sleep worse the other way. I run a class operation. Keep it in your pants."

"Will do. But I still think this is a waste of time—or Charlie's making some sort of point."

"Enough. You're backsliding right in front of me. Cantling has confidence in you. Go help him. He says he's got this genius IT guy who'll give you all the passwords to the company server. It will be total access. You'll see every email communication and bank account. His kids use the company server to discuss the family trust and the company. It'll be child's play to trace the flow of funds, and the decisions, and the reasons, and what they all want. Pretty soon, you'll understand all the key questions and a lot of the answers. You'll sound like you know what you're doing. My assistant has the paperwork Cantling sent over. Sign it. Now."

And I did. What choice did I have?

CHAPTER SIX

ANN

As the Cantling who's never late, I walked into the boathouse restaurant in Central Park right on time for drinks and dinner. The restaurant consisted mainly of one very large room with wide frontage mere feet from the boat pond, which was crowded with ungainly rented rowboats now that the workday was ending. At the shoreline, a row of white columns with windows in between propped up the low roof. The interior lights had been turned on despite the abundance of natural light.

I scanned the bar area and couldn't locate my dinner partner. I felt alone and uncertain amid the noisy tourist clamor. At the maître d' station, a short-skirted hostess smiled like a chorus girl and stopped me.

"Reservation in the name of Gould," I said. "Two people, six o'clock."

She bowed her head to a computer screen and grimly shook her head. "Sorry. Nothing here. Did you make the reservation yourself?"

"No, my friend did." I wondered whether Jody had managed to forget dinner. "Do you have a table anyhow?"

"We're fully booked. We can't accommodate walk-ins."

"We're not walk-ins," I said. "Try Cantling—with a C."

"There it is," she replied, brightening. Jody, likely aiming for a better table, had used Cantling instead of Gould.

While an American standard played on a hidden piano and tourists half shouted in multiple tongues, the hostess led me to a table at water's edge. A waiter glided up to ask if I'd like a drink. I didn't want alcohol to numb me, so I said I was content with water. I gazed out at the rowers as they yanked clunky metal boats along the pond and tried to dodge harmless collisions at a mile an hour. I thought: Everyone's a navigator. Especially me, nine-to-five Ann, with courses on psychology.

During a second American standard, I ordered a glass of cabernet to relax. When a large glassful arrived, I called Jody. I left no message on his voicemail. As used to happen too often, I was annoyed with him. After two more songs and another glass of wine, I sent a text message. Fifteen minutes late and counting, I thought. The city intimidates him. He'd brawl with lowlifes in Stonefield, but he wasn't comfortable among sophisticates in town.

He breezed in, apologized, and sat down. He was nice to look at, as always. I'd wanted to dress neutrally, somewhere between inviting and off-putting, so I went with jeans and a shaped pink blouse. Jody's untucked polo shirt over loose slacks showed he understood that for someone so good looking, anything more premeditated made him look like a dandy. Jody's getting away with borderline sloppiness gave me a moment of feeling plain.

"After all these months," he said when he'd ordered his own wine, "why did you want to see me?".

"I like that. Direct and to the point. And that's more or less why I wanted to see you—to cut down on misunderstandings. And secrets.

There are way too many." I sounded preachy, but I meant it. "Secrets from other people. Secrets from each other. It has to stop."

"Not completely, I hope."

"Never," I said. "But as much as possible."

"I'm all for it. So what exactly do you want in the open?"

"First, there's Benjamin."

"Of course."

"I wish I knew more about what's going on between him and my father," I said. "Did Benjamin tell you anything?"

"Just the standard line. He's supposed to find out what all of you want from Charlie. A likely story. Benjamin doesn't understand what's going on, so how could he explain it? My brother, in case you haven't noticed, is pretty much a boob."

"I'm not sure I agree, but we can leave it at that," I said. "There's also stuff between you and me that needs to be made clearer, things we haven't admitted to each other."

"Like what?"

"We had a couple of bad dates when my father was in the hospital. Then things just kind of died away. We were in touch a few times. It was the opposite of before, when we used to talk a lot about breaking up and then we'd get together and find very little changed. Now something really has changed. I shouldn't have avoided talking about it for so long."

"Isn't it a family thing?" he said. "Cantlings don't explain themselves. They just move on. Like there's nothing to talk about."

"You know it's a Cantling thing because . . . ?"

"I just know."

I was happy not to keep probing. I didn't want details, not when Jody's messing around with my sisters was old news. Instead I just assumed that, in those long-gone days, the sneaking away was mutual. I turned toward the pond, where there seemed to be a pair of lovers in every floating rowboat. I was far enough along in ending it with Jody that it almost didn't hurt.

"I've learned some things about breakups," I said. "Talk doesn't matter much. You just have to do it. Really, if you're still talking, you probably haven't broken up."

"But you want us to talk."

"Because we've been through a lot, and we may have a misunderstanding. My father in the hospital, coping with it, that was a huge turning point. I had to get more serious about my life. I couldn't fool around with someone for sex that wasn't leading anywhere."

"I don't know that it was going nowhere," he said, teasing because it was his nature. "But would that be such a bad thing? Wasn't the sex good?"

"Yes, until it wasn't—at the end."

"So that was an end?"

"It seems like it was. When I invited you to tennis, I thought I was making it clear we were broken up and just friends."

"There it is, the Cantling way."

"I'm trying to fix it. During the match, you kept tapping me on the ass. And there was something in your attitude, like you were wondering where this was going, like you saw a chance."

"A guy can dream," he said. "If we're talking about full disclosure, you and Benjamin have been tight. How will you handle him poking his nose into family matters?"

"It's weird. Usually, Charlie explains what he wants and waits for us to agree. Now he sends Benjamin. None of us like it. Theo least of all."

"I noticed."

"Theo's not really a threat. He's just frustrated. After the accident, he expected to inherit millions for his bees. When Daddy recovered, that couldn't happen. I had a feeling, for the first time ever, that my brother might turn against Charlie. But Theo's become his old toady self. He won't discuss the future. Nobody will."

"Why not?"

"Because that sort of talk might look like a power play, and word always gets back to Charlie. To stay on his good side, they pass things along. Theo, of course, is the worst."

"Nobody trusts Theo. I wonder why."

"He has the Cantling name to live up to. Maybe he can't do it and knows it. I mean, look at him. Oh, but I'm talking too much, telling you too many secrets. It must be the wine. Why would you ply a girl with alcohol?"

"You plied yourself."

Yes, I thought, the boy is still handsome. I used to like to hold him, to feel him against me, inside me. What was wrong with that? Plenty. Even while we talked about no more sex, I knew what he was thinking. He couldn't help it. Whoops. Neither could I.

I felt a need to kick up some dust. "Speaking of secrets, who have you been with lately, now that you haven't been with me? Or should I say: how many?"

"Why would you ask that?"

"Why would you dodge the answer?"

"Ann, I thought this was a topic we avoid."

"How noble of you. How discreet. But I'm trying to be more open. Who are they and how many?"

Supposedly seeking honesty, I'd fallen into familiar habits. Now and then, I'd press Jody about work, women, staying east, anything. If I didn't stop, he'd get scarce. It would last a week, a month, several.

"I could ask you the same thing," he said. "Who and how many?"

"And I would answer: nobody. And it would be the truth. Not that there haven't been opportunities." My bragging was an embarrassment. "Jody, I know you too well. I picture you working your contact list, the dating sites, your memory. Once in a while you come up empty-handed, which might lead you back to me. Maybe, out of respect for what we'd been through, you kept your distance. But now that we're here, you sit and figure your chances."

"I didn't ask to see you. You got in touch with me."

"Not for sex," I said.

"So there's really no chance?"

"There is, if you want to go fuck yourself. No, I shouldn't talk like that. When you were in town, you made an effort. I haven't forgotten. And you kept in touch from Colorado. That means something. What I'm trying to say is, with all our history, we're already friends."

"Friends," he said. He seemed irritated that I was shutting the door. "Do you know what always put me off? It was the act like we were just friends, back then when we were more. Okay, some things we didn't want to tell other people. I understand that. But a total secret from everybody? You say you don't want that anymore. Well, it's too late to do me any good. It's like I embarrassed you."

"It wasn't that. It was the questioning I'd get. You can't imagine what it's like in that fishbowl. My father's demands, my mother's meddling, everybody's comments. If I'd been open about us, they wouldn't have said much. But there'd be little remarks that would say it all, like 'What do you think you're doing, and where can this go?' Or 'He's good looking, but is he right?'"

"So, I'm good looking?"

"Don't you see? I'd have been constantly on the defensive. That's why I closed up. That's why all the Cantlings do."

"Secrets again," he said.

I thought: I haven't lied, and I haven't been entirely honest. Why have I kept Jody hidden? For one thing, I refused to be another love-starved Cantling succumbing to his charms. More than that, I hadn't wanted Benjamin to know.

"Some secrets we'll keep forever," I said. "And some we'll get rid of to avoid misunderstanding. So, to put everything on the table, let me answer the big question."

"Which is . . . ?"

"Am I going to sleep with you tonight?"

"That's direct, all right. Aboveboard. And the answer is . . . ?"

"Not tonight. Not ever."

"Wow. You've gone there. Made your point. It's settled. Friends from here on." He reached across the table and shook my hand. "We can handle a breakup. After all, we've had practice."

I eyed him suspiciously.

"Are you taking it well so I'll change my mind?"

"Hell no." He dipped into a pocket for his cell phone. "Let's call Benjamin and tell him the news."

"Can't we leave Benjamin out of this for just a minute?"

"I'm pretty sure he'd be interested."

He set the cell on the table between us. I said, "What are you doing?"

"Don't you want to stop trying to trick him? All the games within the games. What does it do for anybody? When Theo was threatening to shoot him, he called out to you. It sounded like love to me. Is that why you're announcing the breakup?"

"Me and Benjamin? No way. He's so standoffish these days. I don't think he likes me anymore."

"Bullshit. I know my brother. I'll bet he's suspicious again about us."

"Has he said anything?"

"Look at you, dying to know. Tell me how you feel about him, or I swear I'll call him right now and lay it all out—how you and me were off and on for years." He dangled the phone between two fingers and swung it like a pendulum.

"Do you always have to go to the edge?" I said.

"You used to get a kick out of it."

"I don't believe this."

"Watch me." He poked at the phone, pressed it to his ear, and said, "Got a minute, bro? I have a question. Why did you call out to Ann the other night? . . . Is she with me? No way. So, why? . . . Right. You're in love with her. Have been for years. Next time you see her, bro, why not take the plunge and tell her? . . . Me? No, it was good, but she's done with me."

He laid his phone on the table.

Shaking my head, biting a lip, I lifted my phone out of my pocket and tapped at it. "Hi Benjamin, it's Ann. I just heard you're in love with me. I wish I'd known sooner— What? You weren't talking to Jody? There was no phone call? . . . Forget it."

I set the phone down.

"Very clever," Jody said. "We know each other too well, don't we?"

"I guess so."

"But not as well as you think."

"What does that mean?"

"It means you may have secrets from me," he said. "But I keep secrets from you, too. More than you know."

There were questions I was tempted to ask, old confusions I wanted to resolve, but I held back. There'd been enough clarity for one evening, and some burials were best left undisturbed.

For the rest of the dinner, by silent agreement, we retreated to harmless topics. After we split the bill, I wobbled a bit while a last American standard accompanied us to the door. Outside, evening bicyclists rolled down Park Drive, and clusters of tourists strolled on walkways. Bouillabaisse and cabernet conspired with the last sunlight to soften me up even more.

"When I have to break up," I told Jody, "you're the guy. Few apologies. Fewer explanations. Very little unpleasantness. Do you have a place to stay?"

I instantly regretted that it sounded like an invitation.

"I'm on a late train to Stonefield," Jody said, playing it straight. "Can I walk you home? Then I'll head to the station."

I shrugged.

As we strolled to the western edge of the park, I cautioned myself. I couldn't deny that, against all good sense, I was tempted. The subway entrance at Seventy-Second and Central Park West reminded me I could send Jody to his train to Stonefield. I thought: Not yet. Let him walk me home. Don't rush. Think it through.

If I was going to make a mistake, this would be a big one. For anything to develop with Benjamin, I needed to wait until the Jody thing was long over, and it had been half a year. How long was long enough?

We approached the outside stairs to the brownstone where I rented. If I turned him away, I'd be relieved—and alone. Worse, if I turned him away, it would seem like a tease.

When I unlocked the townhouse door, he walked inside behind me. He never broke stride. I detested his confidence.

"You've been waiting me out," I said as we started up the stairway.

"Just seeing what will happen."

"So you're subtle now. You used to just grab." I stopped at the first-floor landing and looked back at him two steps below. "We're not in love," I said. "Not even close. Never have been. Never will be. We've broken up."

"Agreed," he said too easily.

A lock turned at one of the apartments, a door cracked open, and a tiny old woman peered out with furtive eyes, the door chain draped across her ancient chin. I imagined her withering judgment. She closed the door.

At the next landing, I turned again. "If Benjamin asks, you were never here. Whatever's going to happen didn't happen."

"He never asks," Jody said. "As far as Benjamin knows, years ago we fooled around for a while. I won't tell him anything more."

I believed him. As selfish guys go, Jody isn't a bad person. He keeps most of his promises, if only because it serves him. But he's always of the moment, probing for advantage. He's capable that way. He's just not long range. What to do? My mind took me in every direction: yes, no, never, maybe. My career made sense. My love life didn't. My body tightened everywhere it could—and decided it.

"I'm sorry," I said. "Tonight there won't be anything to not tell him. I can't do this, not ever."

"Really? This is it?"

"I shouldn't have let it get this far. I'm clear now. Very clear. Sorry, sorry, go home."

CHAPTER SEVEN

BENJAMIN

A stalwart in a black uniform opened the front door and admitted me to the grand Park Avenue building where, after their children left home, Charlie and Tessa had relocated from their suburban estate in New Jersey. Because I hadn't visited the building in more than a year and wasn't remembered, I had to supply my name to another black-appareled functionary at a lobby security station. He fiddled with an electronic console and then explained to someone in the Cantling apartment that I was on the way.

I trudged through the gargantuan lobby toward a bank of elevators in a distant corner. Low ceilings made the many-sectioned space, with its Turkish rugs and potted plants and facing couches in furnished alcoves, seem even larger than it was. After a couple of turns, I reached an open elevator where, in a display of antediluvian luxury, a waiting attendant with nothing to do pushed a high-numbered button and rode upstairs beside me.

As instructed by Byrne, I'd postponed interviews with family members for a couple of weeks to develop background information.

At Cantling Market Research I'd learned the computer system and read hundreds of family and corporate emails and in-house memos. I also interviewed a few key employees, who made an effort to seem cooperative and explain their responsibilities. If any of them had insight into Cantling intrigues or intentions, they didn't let on.

Stepping off the elevator, I wondered whether my time with Tessa today would be an exercise in luxury and wasted time. I'd emerged onto a narrow landing with facing doors on opposite ends. Two small, sprightly, identically sized floral paintings lent perfect geometry to the immaculate space, which was not air-conditioned and, as a result, overly warm in the Manhattan summer. It was a rare absence of indulgence. When the Cantlings' door opened an inch, I felt the faint caress of cool air.

An unfamiliar young woman in a black skirt and white blouse peeked out. "I'm Mrs. Cantling's assistant," she told me. "Mrs. Cantling is on the phone. She asked me to let you in. You're a friend of Theo's, right?"

"I've known him since I was a boy."

She stepped into the hall, pulled the door shut, and moved closer. She was in her early thirties, lanky, black haired, and pretty. She smiled at me with raised eyebrows, like a child anticipating ice cream. I wondered what she knew of me to inspire such warm attention.

"I'd be grateful," she said, "if you would give him a message from Whitney."

"I'll try."

She leaned back and rocked forward with a grunt, smacking my right shoulder with a fierce punch. I had no chance to avoid the blow. My shoulder stung. The fingers on my right hand tingled.

"What the fuck?" I said.

"Stay calm. Your shoulder should be back to normal in no time. Well now, it seems I could do it."

"Do what?"

"Hit someone. So far all I've hit are heavy bags. Theo said you were an aficionado of karate and would understand. You're not angry, are you?"

"He said that? I wouldn't be angry and I'm a karate aficionado?"

Whitney stood smiling with arms raised and fists clenched as if prepared for more action. I wanted to grab her and present her to Tessa for termination on the spot, but grabbing her seemed unwise.

She said, "Please tell Theo I can land a good blow. And I will—if he gets rough again."

"You took karate lessons because of Theo?"

"I told Mrs. Cantling there are predators in New York. When I said I needed karate lessons, she offered to pay. They love me at the dojo. I've learned kicks. Chops. Punches. Would you like to see more?"

Some feeling had returned to the arm. I could just about lift my hand. "That will be enough," I said.

Whitney's information about Theo wasn't a complete surprise. Charlie Cantling had a raging temper and more than one of the kids had inherited it. And I'd heard a rumor about Theo and sexual assault, but that was in college and more than a decade ago.

"If I pass your message to Theo," I said, "he might try to get you fired."

She laughed. "You don't understand anything, do you?" She reached out and gently rubbed my reviving shoulder. "Just tell him I'm waiting."

She admitted me to the apartment and retreated down a hallway toward the kitchen and servants' wing. I wondered about Theo. If he could get overly rough with Whitney and menace me with a shotgun, might he have stooped to violence against his father?

Ahead of me, a pair of columns between foyer and living room suggested Cantling nostalgia for suburban grandeur. The spacious white living room beyond was decorated in the latest Manhattan style, like a king-size hotel suite awaiting furniture. On each of three white walls was a tiny abstract painting lit from the ceiling by recessed lights, an effect that highlighted the room's vast emptiness. Three vases of tall flowers rose from accent tables to break the white monotony. A small writing table supporting a laptop computer was a new addition.

The room's sole occupant was Tessa, sitting L-shaped with legs extended on an off-white couch, calling to mind a reclining nude but with clothes on. She wore a stylish pantsuit in deep purple and accessorized with silver and jewels. There was a low glass table in front of her and a smattering of lamps and chairs on beige area rugs patterned with black diamonds. Bright windows behind her revealed yellow-brick buildings aglow in the midmorning sun on Park's west side. As I approached her, darts of sunlight reflected from windows across the street and into my eyes.

"Dear boy, pardon the look," she said, playing the grand lady. "We were replacing furniture when Charlie had his accident. My magnificent palace is partway empty. Do you know? They locked up Marie Antoinette in Versailles. Now I understand how the poor girl felt."

It was obvious where her daughters had learned theatrics.

"This doesn't look so terrible to me," I said.

"Oh, the plots that are hatched here! I could tell a tale that would shock your innocent ears. But that's for another time. This situation, this mission of ours, is straightforward. Charlie wants everything to be aboveboard, and so it shall be. We may fight from time to time, but this family rows together in the same direction."

She was openly gaslighting out of resentment at my intrusion, I decided—with enough Waspy deniability to not be called on it. I sat at the foot of the couch in a minimalist plastic chair and said, "I hope you know I didn't ask for this position and don't want it. Your family's business should stay in your family."

"I'd like to believe you. Someone else in your position, someone less pure, might get off on this. He might love lording it over Cantlings. In fact, I wouldn't blame you if deep down, in the middle of the night when there's no one around to see it, you were a little bit proud of yourself. Don't you dream of solving our so-called problems?"

This was more force than I'd expected from her. "You can think what you want about my intentions," I said. "But why not help both of us? Why not tell everybody you don't want me involved and you won't cooperate? It would probably be the end of it."

"Benjamin, it's not a good idea to tell Charlie Cantling to go to hell. After the shouting, he'd say, 'Why are you making this difficult? I'm just trying to learn what you and the children want. Young Mr. Gould's a fine intermediary, a facilitator.' Isn't that what you're doing, Benjamin? You're asking us what we want?"

I nodded.

"Then I'm happy Charlie sent you. I wouldn't have it any other way. Charlie's always been a great father, but—how shall I put it?—he can be a dictator who pretends not to be. This time we'll take him at his word. How can I help?"

Despite the misdirection, I tried to stay on point. "Let's start with the easy stuff. I've been told that when Charlie was recovering, Theo wanted money more than anybody else did. Is it true?"

"Money," she said. "What a terrible word. The first thing on everyone's mind, and the last on ours."

"Last but still present."

"On the back row. In a corner. Overrated. Benjamin, let me ask you: the way Charlie wants to hoard this money, does he have some use for it? One of my daughters heard a rumor he wants to buy a business to fold into Cantling Market Research. Is there any truth to it?"

I recalled Charlie's helicopter revelations about the pending deal. He seemed to have done a decent job of keeping it quiet, until now.

"If I knew something about that," I said, "I couldn't possibly get into it."

"Very deft. But I wonder. I assume you've done your homework. I'm sure you're aware there are dozens and dozens of family emails on the company server. That's where we conduct the trust's business. You've read them?"

"Yes. Charlie gave me access."

"Then you know everything."

"I know what I've read."

"And you don't believe it?"

I hesitated. As a communication specialist, I am all too familiar with the anodyne evasions that pass for corporate speech. The Cantling emails were all harmless and, because the family had lacked handlers, blatantly so. It seemed that to guard against the chance that Charlie might survive, they'd whitewashed as they'd composed: "We need conservative assumptions . . ." "We can't drain resources . . ." "Let's never forget what Charlie would want us to do." If they ever tried to seem spontaneous in email, it didn't show. The exception might have been Theo, who occasionally weighed in with a reverence for his father that was foolish enough to be genuine.

"I'm just here to get answers, and not to believe or disbelieve," I said.

"You're quite the dancer, aren't you? All right, I'll talk plainly. I've had to learn a lot about Cantling Market Research in the last six months to appreciate that the clients need us to target their ads. It's important work. I was reluctant to weaken us in any way by withdrawing funds. But Charlie's accident was devastating for our family. We traveled to see him, we took turns at the hospital, we rarely left him alone. In the end, we did vote for a jump in payout because of those extra demands on our resources. At first, nobody gave a thought to clothes or travel or lifestyle. No one said a word about Botox. Even Nicole, who's barely speaking to Charlie, flew in from Santa Fe. I had to literally beg the children to look after themselves—to resume their lives. Honestly, we were thrilled beyond description when Charlie cut the increase in half. It meant he was feeling better."

"None of the kids want more money permanently?"

"Dear Benjamin, it depends what you mean by 'want.' And 'more.' And 'money.' And who the funds would go to. And for what purpose. Let me tell you some history. When I was growing up, women could still be appendages, meant to wear jewels and shine at events. I suppose that, until recently, I might have been a throwback to all that. My biggest asset had always been understanding the men of my generation. Tall men, short men, rich men, beggars. I knew what they were thinking and where they were trying to go and whether or not they'd get there. That might have been a useful talent in business, but I'd never applied it that way.

"When I was a girl, my talent led me to Charlie Cantling, a young man destined for great things. People might say I should have made my own way and I might be a different person today. Perhaps they're right. The point is, my children are different from me. They have contemporary values. They have interests. They're starting careers. They don't need the whole Cantling apparatus and lifestyle. It's largely irrelevant to who they are. But I say: thank God they've got it. Being a Cantling is not all bad. Some good things come with it, things you don't appreciate until you don't have them, and they've never experienced that deprivation. Am I talking too much? Being too frank?"

"No way," I said truthfully, for I'd yet to witness much frankness.

"The children have been very generous with me." She swung her legs around, sat up, and leaned forward as if to impart the truth in all its seedy glory. "Over the years, Charlie's salary—not distributions from the company—supported me and Charlie. With Charlie sidelined, I, not Theo, was the real reason they voted for the increase in payout. They wanted me to not suffer, to have everything I had before. After all, I was facing widowhood. There would be new pains and new responsibilities. I didn't need extra stress. You'll find out someday: it's wonderful when your children start to look out for you."

Explanation number two for the enhanced payout. Under this theory, it wasn't that there were extra family expenses. Instead, Tessa herself needed money.

I said, "Theo didn't push for more distributions for himself?"

"You and Theo again. You have history, don't you? Some of it good, some of it not so good. If you're so determined to blame things on him, I can't stop you. But it would be wrong of you. Read the emails," she said, pretending they hadn't precensored every word. "The best way to describe what happened is the others wanted to help me and to help Theo, too."

"So Theo did need help?"

"Not really. I'm sure he could have managed with his own resources. But it was winter, and his father was dying, and so were his bees. His refusal to give up was inspiring. Direction. Determination. It's precisely what we were looking for from him. As a boy he was wonderfully promising. He drank his way through college and still graduated with honors. That's the kind of brain he has. And you know how handsome he was before the current waistline. For a time, before he found his bearings, he seemed to be lost. I was so glad he launched himself into this bee operation. I still am, despite some of the difficulties I've had with it.

"Look, at times I've had to hold my tongue. When he invites me to the farm, I make excuses. Swarms of insects buzzing around my head? Stingers? They tell me even a dead bee can sting if you touch it. Well, Theo had piles and piles of dead bees. Because of mites, he said. What would I know about that? He sent me pictures—like that would help. This bee business, isn't it wonderful he turned it around?"

"So you didn't help him?"

"I have savings. I could have invested in the bee venture and made extra distributions to Theo unnecessary. But I didn't want more nonsense from the others about me always favoring Theo. The way we ended up doing it, where everybody got the same amount of extra help from the company, no one would complain. Except possibly Charlie, and we all thought he was out of the picture forever."

This was explanation number three: they'd raised the payout to help Theo. It was dizzying. "You said you didn't have enough money, and that's why the children wanted to raise the distribution. Now you mention that you had savings."

"My, you're suspicious. And so direct. I like that. Yes, I had savings, but the children didn't want me to use them up," she said with a glow, as if enjoying her deftness. "The extra distribution helped Theo at a difficult time. It let him pay his workers, buy new hives and equipment, and cope with unexpected bills. He seemed to be thriving again. Then his father reemerged. After two or three months, Charlie was more or less his old self. He asked a lot of questions, zeroed in on things like he used to do. When he found out Theo had put more resources into bees, it got touchy. With Charlie, it's usually 'my way or the highway.' I was afraid he'd cut all the distributions way back and start a war within the family. Don't misunderstand: the children didn't need the extra support, but they'd have been insulted."

"I've done some research," I told her. "Winter is crunch time. Will the bees get through the next one?"

"Theo is confident. Yes, he may lose some bees, that's normal, but he says he's learned special techniques. He says bees have wisdom that people could use. He plans to buy more and more hives. Don't you like the brand name: Theo's Aromatic Pure Honey? There's a little tagline: 'From the hives of Theo Cantling.' Brilliant. I tell you, Benjamin, beekeeping in Connecticut may never be the same."

Noticing the lack of sample honey, I wondered whether Tessa had smelled ammonia, as I had. My hostess had lied to me repeatedly, had shown no shame at contradicting previous lies, but I may have made progress. I'd learned that Theo had been showering his bees with money. I'd confirmed that Tessa had wanted Charlie to fund Theo more. Had Tessa's devotion to her son led her to try to smother Charlie? Could the solution to the puzzle be as simple as Tessa and

Theo to get money? I told myself, usefully, that preferring Theo to be the perp didn't mean he wasn't.

"Come now, Benjamin," she said, tapping her watch. "How much longer do we keep this up? You're not here to talk about honey. Charlie Cantling gets paranoid, then goes quiet, and you show up asking questions?"

"I'm here because I do what I'm told. Why do you think Charlie went quiet?"

"Damned if I know. He's been looking at me funny. Like I was hiding things from him, personal things. That's not how we used to conduct ourselves. I think he checked my cell phone once or twice when I left it around."

"Mrs. Cantling, your private life is none of my business."

"Is that right? How can you identify what people want unless you know where things stand with them? I need you to imagine something—a situation between two people that's developed over decades. A stable instability, you might call it. An understanding. The husband sleeps with more or less whoever he can, and the wife is understanding. Even when the wife is in the room, the husband works his way around to the best-looking woman there. The wife accepts it because the husband can't help himself, it's his nature, and in his mind it has nothing to do with her. When she confronts him, she accepts his fury and ultimately his shame—because he really does feel ashamed, though it doesn't stop him next time. Nothing can. Nothing will.

"Let's assume the wife wants to keep the family together and finds the husband's business interesting enough to listen to. She enjoys the lifestyle, though maybe not the life. She has to swallow some pride now and then, maybe a couple of times she's packed up to leave, but she puts up with it. This situation marches on, year after year. But then the husband, out of commission for a while and with too much time to brood, starts to suspect his wife has her own agenda about certain matters. Naturally, he can't ask. Because there are questions that are really accusations. So what does this husband do? He hires a young man who acts like he's asking about something else entirely."

"Not my business, Mrs. Cantling."

"But it is, young man. And let's not pretend my story would be a secret. It would be well understood in the circles the family moves in. So now, if the husband is asking about his wife's activities, the best answer might be that she hasn't had as many affairs as he has."

She seemed to be trying to keep me off-kilter, and she was succeeding. I was in the helicopter again with Charlie, being knocked around from here to there. Cantling chaos. She studied me with steely poise. I wondered: Is there much truth in what she told me? Is it misdirection? Or both?

Her manner was just arch enough, and removed enough, to make me doubt her.

"You have to give him this," she said. "When it came to race or religion, the imaginary husband didn't discriminate. I might have seen him eye your mother."

"My mother?"

"Have I shocked you? I didn't mean to. Your mother was attractive, clever, and fairly well turned out for a schoolteacher. But don't go all Gothic on me. She didn't like the theoretical husband. I think she found him rather nasty and full of himself. There was no affair. You're nobody's half brother."

Forced to imagine the unimaginable, I remembered my mother rolling her eyes whenever Charlie's name came up. I filled in blanks and pictured a drunken approach, possibly a lunge, and Mom rushing away. The memory cast the patriarchs' Fourth of July rivalry in a different light.

"Don't worry," Tessa said. "I doubt much of the theoretical couple's marital arrangement matters right now. Your mission may not be about divorce. The theoretical husband likes power over women much more than he likes women. Let's be realistic. To a man like that, women are like buses. He gets off one, another comes along."

"Mrs. Cantling, I don't need to hear this."

"Yes, you do. Because I have another theory, a very good one. Yes, Charlie wants to see how little he has to pay out to his family. But there's something else. He told me someone tried to put him out of his misery. I waved the idea off, blamed it on the drugs they were giving him. But Charlie kept at it. He's not the sort to let go of anything. Naturally, it got dismissed everywhere. So he shut up. No one, especially not Charlie Cantling, likes to hear he's lost his mind. But I can't believe he forgot. And that's the real reason you're here."

"I'm here for the stated reason."

She chuckled. "If you believe that, the joke's on you. Benjamin, you spent the summers next to us, you played in our treehouse, you've known us forever. Hasn't it occurred to you that Charlie will use you in the end, and he won't give a damn about how much he screws you over?"

"How do you know all this?"

"Because it's what he does to everybody. You won't see the fatal blow coming, but it will happen. If you weren't so smart, I'd say you were Charlie's useful fool. And that is not a good thing to be." The tone was still arch, but the eyes shimmered.

"How exactly would Charlie screw me?"

"Let's leave that to Charlie. He's very good at it. Just tell me precisely what your mission is, and maybe, just maybe, I can help you."

I was irritated. After all the folderol, she'd launched a frontal attack. Was I truly Charlie's fool? Why are people with lofty minds so often undermined by the worldly likes of Tessa? I wanted to tell her: I'm not an idiot. Everybody knows your husband can be ruthless.

From another room, a buzzer sounded.

"Oh my, he's early," Tessa said. "There's the walk to the elevator, the ride upstairs. Plenty of time."

"Time for what? Who's coming?"

"Theo, of course. I assumed you'd like to hear from two of us in one stroke." While I tried to guess her reasons for watching over Theo, she stood and told me, "I forgot something in the kitchen. Wait here. Whitney will let Theo in."

I disliked Theo more than ever, but on general principle, I did not want him pummeled by Whitney, if that was her plan. Defying orders, I followed Tessa out of the living room. She hurried down the hallway and vanished into the kitchen. Seconds later, Whitney strode from the servants' wing and met me at the front door.

"Theo's coming," I whispered to her.

"Theo! I wasn't expecting him."

"He wouldn't try anything with his mother here."

"Wrong. He loves a little risk."

"Let me handle it," I told her. "I'll tell him to leave you alone."

"You still don't understand." She appeared to be measuring me for another punch. "Try this," she said. "Tell him, if he comes near me, he's a dead man."

She spun around and returned down the hallway. Moments later, Tessa emerged from the kitchen holding an empty jar labeled THEO'S AROMATIC PURE HONEY. It struck me that the tagline—FROM THE HIVES OF THEO CANTLING—suggested discharge from a rash.

"Charlie and I ate the whole thing," she said, brandishing the empty jar. "We loved it. Theo will be pleased."

Recalling that Charlie had told me he dumped the honey, I watched Tessa march between the columns, head toward the living room couch, and place the empty jar on the table.

The elevator arrived. I opened the apartment door to find Theo in khakis, a boxy madras shirt, and a sweat-stained baseball cap. In one hand he held a small white plastic bag with something inside. In the other was a collapsible walking stick, which he thrust triumphantly into the air while he configured lips and teeth into a broad grin. Beside him, a plump chocolate Labrador retriever on a leash lifted his eyes to me and glared. Theo poked at the door latch so that it wouldn't lock. Then he motioned for me to come out into the hall. The door shut behind me.

"Great to see you, Benjamin!" He raised his arms, ready to hug me like a long-lost cousin. Visions of the Early Fourth shotgun held me back. The Lab, who seemed not to know that Theo's bonhomie was fake, lowered his gaze to the floor in a display of the morose contempt his master usually showed me.

It seemed impossible for the mood divergence to last, and I wondered which of the pair would crack. I put my money on the fat dog. Sure enough, when Theo clamped his stick under the arm that held the leash and with his freed hand vigorously shook mine, the hefty Lab bared his teeth and barked at me in ostentatious fury. The racket threatened eardrums in the once-serene landing. Under the best of circumstances, the charms of dogs—their loyalties, affections, obsequies—are lost on me. My mother loved her dogs, but I didn't. I thought: Will Theo hold me while the beast attacks?

Theo yanked the leash. "Shut up, Rembrandt."

The dog kept barking.

"Rembrandt, shut the fuck up!" Theo released my hand and waved his stick at the dog. Rembrandt, humiliated, grew quiet and slumped near the shut door.

"Now you know the reason for the stick," Theo said. "He needs to understand who's boss." He bent to the dog and said, "Don't you, you little rat?"

Rembrandt, lethargic, didn't respond. Theo beamed at me. "Benjamin, old bud, I hope you don't hold anything against me."

"About what?"

"Do I need to say? That joke the other night about killing you. That business with the shotgun. You understand I was just kidding around. Okay, maybe in the heat of the moment I overstated things. I can see how you might have overreacted. It got sticky—but all in fun."

I, on good behavior, said, "No harm, no foul."

"Glad you see it that way. Honestly, if Jody hadn't shown up looking for a fight, all I'd have done was fire into the air like Jody did the night before. What came over him? Why did he attack me?"

"The shotgun might have been a factor."

"We could discuss it all day. Why bother? Forgive. Forget. Move on." He lowered his voice. "Benjamin, have you been here a while? Have you seen that spectacular West Coast piece of ass?"

"Whitney? Yes, I met her."

"My damn mother broke rule number one of the personal assistant business." His tone was confiding and conspiratorial, as if he and I were in this together.

"What's rule number one?"

"Hire ugly assistants. This one's very clever. You think I'm kidding? All that sucking up to me, that tending to my needs. It fucked with my head. The big smile, the perky boobs, the way of getting under my skin. And the incredible games! Or maybe they're not games. How did she figure me out? It's like I don't have a choice. I love it, I hate it, gotta get away from her, gotta have it. I mean, I'm used to country living. When you've seen horses go at it, and pigs—all kinds of animals—it makes you want it with no bother. Manners? Courtship? It's all bullshit. Right, buddy?"

Conscience forced a warning. "Are you sure you and Whitney are a good idea?"

"You've got to be kidding. We're a terrible idea! But she's got the West Coast thing, like everything's okay and always will be, so come on into the hot tub. If you ask me, she has plans for herself. Me, she toys with. She wants it and she doesn't want it. She's ready and she's not and never will be. But when she goes at it, boy does she go."

"You and Whitney, doesn't it create complications?"

"Like what?"

"She has a job," I said. "A fraught relationship with her employer's son could lead to trouble."

"Not a problem. My mother likes her, and if worse comes to worse, there are other jobs. One thing I know about Whitney, she's not just about a job."

"She's been taking karate. She tells me she can hurt you."

"So, she followed through with the lessons? Good. Let her whack me," he said, waving his stick. "It introduces a new flavor. Like the song says, 'A bit of pain makes the dick grow harder.'"

I saw Theo's problem: a four-year-old male had been given the sex drive of a young adult and was trying to cope. Nevertheless, I kept trying. "Why mess with someone you might keep running into if it doesn't work out?"

"You, Benjamin Gould, would lecture me about that? Have you been asleep these past few years?"

"Meaning what?"

"My sisters are fine-looking women—and usually ready. Who wouldn't want a piece of that? We know one guy who got in early and often: your brother. He plowed through and kept turning up at the house like nothing happened. Don't tell me you're shocked. Can you claim for one minute that you weren't aware?"

The onslaught of probably exaggerated tales left me woozy. I couldn't let Theo see that.

"Not my problem," I said.

"Right. Keep thy head in the sand. I wonder how many he screwed. Two seems like a slam dunk, though I won't name names. Three maybe. Possibly all four. Wouldn't that be something? We'll never get a straight answer out of my sisters. Have you ever asked Jody how many and how often?"

"We don't go there."

"Once more in the sand, right?"

How much could I trust what Theo seemed to be implying? Yes, he knew a bunch of Cantling secrets, and my brother had told me about his trysts with Cantling girls. Had Jody admitted a little to hide a lot? It wasn't impossible. He could have been handed from sister to sister like a dessert tray, to be sampled and passed along, before he'd landed his longer run with Ann. I don't think he'd have minded. Theo was right about one thing: I didn't want to know.

"If you ask me, he's banging at least one of them right now," Theo said. "Who could that be? Well, I don't check sheets. Here's the point: if your brother can do what he does and nobody holds it against him, why can't I mess with a personal assistant?" In a disturbing show of instinct, he poked my compromised shoulder. I winced. Rembrandt barked.

"Cantlings and Goulds," Theo said. "Friends through it all. We've known each other so long. Everybody's a pal. It's an unlikely connection, but it's there. I don't see my sisters as victims. They just get close now and then with a friend." Theo sneered faintly. "Anyhow, if their choice isn't good for them, if they spend too much time on their backs in a losing cause, what the hell can I do?"

"Jody's not a losing cause."

"Yeah, there's other ways to look at it. You could say they got what they wanted from him. Now, you and me, because we're not players like Jody, we have an extra bond. We're on the outside together."

He seemed ready to rap my shoulder again, but I raised a hand to stave off the blow.

"People trust you," he said. "They say you're a nice guy. Picky, but wouldn't hurt a living thing. That's why I don't mind asking a favor. Please don't mention this Whitney business to my mother. She might not understand. And tell Whitney you've known me forever, I'm a fine fellow, I don't bite too hard, etcetera. It could make a difference."

Finally, I was angry. There were limits to how far the Cantling alternate universe could expand. Theo and I were not best friends. I was not his advocate. I said, "I'll see what I can do."

"My man!"

We walked with the dog into the apartment and through to the living room, where Tessa waited on her couch. Theo and I sat in the chairs at opposite ends while Rembrandt slumped on the floor, emitting a low growl. Theo laid the stick across his thighs and set the white plastic bag he'd been carrying on the table.

"What were you two gabbing about?" Tessa asked.

"Honey," Theo replied, pointing at the empty jar on the table. "I see you've been eating yours."

"I can't stop," Tessa said. "It's the devil's fault."

"How's that?" I said.

"What's the cruelest invention of all time? The most infernal device? The bathroom scale. Don't laugh. Mine is vicious. It lies in wait all day. Then it sees me and stares up and yells, 'Hop on, fatty!'"

I noticed that in recent months, Tessa had added a few pounds. "But you're so thin," I said truthfully.

"Not anymore. The devil won't allow it. He disguised himself as Theo and gave me this honey. To bulk up my calves. To give me a belly and bye-bye arms. Revolting. Theo, what's your secret? Why is your honey so good?"

"Lots of reasons," Theo said. "First, we know tricks. The guy who helps me is so good, I don't even need to be there. That's what management's about: picking the right people. And that's my specialty. There's more. Honey takes on the flavor of the pollen and nectar the bees gather. We have a special mix of flowers in the woods—maple, honeysuckle, you name it. It's a resource you won't see on a balance sheet."

"You're getting a lot of orders?" I asked.

"Better than that. My customers aren't like my mother, who gobbles the stuff in a nanosecond. Some of them tell me they want to savor it, they don't want to eat it quick. Are they bullshitting me? Do they think it's overpriced? I doubt it. That's not the New England way. It's lucky they're holding back, because with so many bees dying last winter, we didn't produce as much as we'd like. So my customers, they're like pent-up demand. Honey in the bank—that's what it is, and it's why I'm here. Benjamin, Mom asked me to tell you, but I'm not ashamed. I want you to know where I'm coming from. I need more capital for the business because it's a real winner."

"Of course it is," Tessa said with a thin smile.

"So why be quiet about it?" Theo said. "Mom, you thought it would look like I wanted help from Dad and Cantling Market Research. But the way I do business, I don't hide stuff, even when things go wrong—like that crap with the spraying."

"Benjamin's got a lot to do," Tessa said. "Do we need to bother him with every detail?"

"He'll find out anyhow. One of the sisters will tell him."

"What were you spraying?" I said.

"Some blueberry bushes near the hives. And hay. I wanted to protect them, and they add great flavor to honey. Well, these honey bureaucrats, socialist wannabes, came and ran tests. They found pesticide residue in those blueberries. Big deal. Everybody uses pesticides. The bees don't mind. Their collective knowledge, the wisdom of the hive, tells them a little pesticide doesn't matter. The honey bureaucrats don't care. They fined me anyhow."

"They tested the honey?" I said, remembering ammonia.

"And guess what? No residue. All that trouble over some irrelevant blueberries. I could have used that money—I have plans for a brand extension. Like I said, there's hundreds of sugar maples on my property. Tap the sap, boil it up, what do you have? Theo's Aromatic Syrup. It's a no-brainer."

"From the trunks of Theo Cantling," I said.

"Has a ring, doesn't it? I need some support to ramp up. The way things are going, I can pay it all back with interest in two years, three at the outside. Anyhow, it's boring to just talk about honey. Let's take it to the next level."

He reached into his plastic bag, pulled out a full jar of Theo's Aromatic, and held it above the table for all to admire. "Mom, you kept telling me the honey was wonderful," Theo said, "so I figured you might have eaten it all."

"I don't think Benjamin's here to taste honey," Tessa said.

"The hell he isn't," Theo said. "He needs to see the brand potential—if people have the courage to back it." He twisted the lid off and sniffed the jar. "Sweet as ever. Check this out," he said, pushing the open jar toward my nostrils.

I tried to make my shallow inhale seem deep. I smelled ammonia. "Excellent," I said.

In his corner, the dog thrust himself up and barked.

"Rembrandt! Quiet!" Theo shouted.

The barking ratcheted up.

"Do you see?" Theo said. "Rembrandt wants honey. I try to keep him away from it, but he loves hanging out with the bees. This should shut him up." Theo pulled a plastic knife from the bag, dipped it in honey, and walked it toward Rembrandt. The dog, barking, trotted to the opposite corner.

"I love this dog," Theo announced as he returned to the couch. "He's saving the honey for me. Is that loyalty, or what?"

"Is there something wrong with Whitney's ears?" Tessa asked, half shouting above the din. "Don't misunderstand. I love the dog. But I told Whitney: anytime he comes and acts up, which is every time, get him away from me. Maybe she can't hear him in her office. Where is she?"

Theo brightened up. "I brought Rembrandt. I'll take him to her." He set the coated knife down and approached the dog, who stopped barking.

"Please don't bother Whitney," Tessa said.

"It's no bother." He grabbed Rembrandt's leash and started to lead him out.

"Really, Theo? My personal assistant?"

"Mother, I'm helping out. Don't make something out of nothing."

Theo and the dog disappeared toward the servants' wing.

"Honestly," Tessa said. "The drama in this family. Right in his mother's face, he drools over an employee. You'd think, at the very least, he'd have manners. Not to mention self-respect. He could have any woman he wanted, especially if he lost a couple pounds. Of course, he never could dress. If I see him one more time in madras, I'll kill him."

There were far more troubling aspects to the situation. But if Tessa couldn't stop Theo, how could I? I braced myself for raised voices from the servants' wing and a noisy squabble, possibly with bruises.

"Poor Theo," Tessa said. "He set his own trap today, didn't he?"

"How's that?"

"He doesn't see the risk he takes when he admits he wants more support. He has such strong feelings for his father he can't allow for the possibility that you're here because Charlie suspects he's burning money."

"Mrs. Cantling—"

"I don't want to hear from you, Benjamin. I don't trust you. Because there's a very different way to look at all this. Maybe Charlie isn't making you take this on against your will. Maybe you're the one who's come and outmaneuvered him. Two weeks ago, this family was doing rather well. Two weeks ago, Charlie was alive and back and no one conspired against anybody. Then you show up, and all of a sudden everybody's whispering. 'Will Benjamin find this? Will Benjamin want to know that?' There's suspicion. Intrigue. Everyone wants to get their point across to you."

I nodded, half listening. I wondered: Does karate work against a dog?

"My husband," Tessa continued, "may not be the man he was. He has weird notions. He carries a pistol. He might be vulnerable to manipulation. What did you talk him into in that helicopter? Why are you his eyes and ears and go-to boy? What's your plan? Turn us against each other? Pin this supposed attempted murder on Theo? Don't tell me it hasn't crossed your mind. Not in a million years would Theo hurt his father. Nor would any of my children. Benjamin, I want you gone from our lives. So I'm going to make your job very easy. I'm going to tell you exactly what happened."

Rembrandt abruptly scampered through the foyer and into the living room and slumped onto the floor beside me with a glum expression. "I want to hear this. I really do," I said earnestly, though in light of her obfuscations thus far, I doubted there'd be full disclosure. "But don't you think we should find out what's going on with Theo and Whitney?"

"Whatever it is, it's likely to be ghastly—and none of our business. Sit down."

I followed instructions. I couldn't go stomping through her house against her will. The Lab lifted his head and yelped as if he'd heard something. He began to bark.

"Come here, you beast," Tessa called to Rembrandt, who quieted down and, with a baleful glare at the honey jar, slouched to her. She scratched the dog's ears. "Master Theo, ruff ruff, I love you very much," she cooed. "But, Master Theo, ruff ruff, you do strange things with assistants. And your honey is awful."

The word "honey" seemed to alarm Rembrandt. He broke from Tessa and began to trot around the perimeter of the room, dragging his considerable bulk. He barked outrageously. He veered through the entrance columns and, still barking, disappeared. The racket continued from the servants' wing.

Tessa remained on the couch and sighed. "I suppose you'll have to go sort this out," she said to me. "All this preposterous noise!"

I hurried after Rembrandt and found him barking at a shut door in the servants' wing. He raised his front paws and scratched the white wood. From inside, Theo shouted, "Rembrandt! Go away!"

The dog grew quiet and dropped to all fours. I listened. There were guttural sounds, male in origin, from behind the door. I thought I heard Whitney moan. "What's going on?" I called. "Whitney, are you all right?"

There was no answer.

The Lab stood on his hind legs and scraped at the doorknob. The dog's weight made the door swing open, and he scampered in. A tiny spartan room, probably seldom used, came into view. In a single bed arranged sideways to the door, Whitney lay naked with Theo on top of her. His pants were at his ankles, and the madras shirt looked sweaty. They turned to me, Whitney irritated, Theo glaring.

"Whitney, is everything all right?" I said.

She didn't answer.

"Gould," Theo grunted breathlessly, "get the fuck out."

"Leave us alone," Whitney said.

I returned to the living room, embarrassed. The Lab remained in the servants' wing.

"What's going on back there?" Tessa said.

"There's no problem. They're in discussions."

"Is that what they call it these days? You and I talk of life, death, and the fate of the Cantlings, and Theo does what? I can't blame other women for finding Cantling men irresistible—not when, God help me, I married one and adore the other. Don't misunderstand. I like Whitney. But Theo doesn't need a random girl from California with a hold on him. We don't really know who she is and what she's like. I'd ask her to leave, but she's good at her job, flexible, on top of things, and Theo would be furious. I know his priorities."

I tried a reset. "Mrs. Cantling, weren't you about to tell me something?"

"I thought you weren't interested in our private lives?"

"Talk about whatever you like. Maybe it will shed some light."

"Clumsy," she said. "But here goes. Have you considered what horrors I've been through? I couldn't stand to watch Charlie suffer when there was no hope he'd be anything like what he used to be.

I never would have believed I would help end his suffering, but the more I thought about it, the more I had to take action."

"You?"

"I knew the hospital well. When I visited, there was always bustle in the corridor. Anybody might pass by or walk in. But when to do it? I could have tried at midnight, but on an empty floor, people might have noticed."

"Are you saying what I think you're saying?"

"I settled on late afternoon, when there was a change of shifts and a lull on the floor. I sat in his room and tried to act calm. I read a magazine, I played with my phone. My heart was pounding. I could scarcely breathe—but I held together. When things seemed quiet, I stood up and shut the door. I had to move as quickly as possible.

"I bent over and said goodbye. I was crying like a baby. I took a pillow from behind his head, pushed it as hard as I could against his face, and held it there. He struggled. 'Please don't make this difficult,' I whispered to him. 'It's for us.' He writhed, he grabbed at my wrists. He shocked me with his strength. They tell me the body, facing death, calls on reserves. He kept fighting and finding air. How long could I keep this up? Suppose a nurse came in, an orderly. I could go to prison. I had to accept the fact that I'd failed. I put the pillow back under his head, sat down, and opened my magazine.

"When a nurse came in and examined him, I prayed I hadn't damaged him. She read the monitors and found no sign of deterioration. In fact, from that day, there's been nothing but improvement, straight up to where he is now. It makes me sick to think if I had succeeded, I never would have known this recovery was possible. We never would have gotten Charlie back. You can't believe how happy I am that I failed. But the law doesn't care. I'm a criminal, attempted murder, and good intentions don't count. There. You and your digging—you got it out of me. What are you going to do with it?"

"Charlie says the attempt on his life didn't happen," I said, sticking to the party line. "Why would you confess to it?"

"I know my husband. No matter what he says now, Charlie believes it happened. Charlie believes only Charlie. I don't know why it bothers him so much. Whoever did it might be a hero. But it seems like Charlie will keep pressing until he finds somebody to take the blame. That could be any of us, even you."

"How could he blame me?"

"It's Charlie. He's got imagination. So I'm doing you a favor. Because now he can blame me."

"You tried to smother him alone?" I said. "Nobody helped? Nobody watched the door?"

"I know Charlie said he heard two people talking. He believes it would take at least two people to kill him. Well, it was just little old me telling Charlie to cooperate and pass on. So, are you going to call the police, or should I?"

"The police? You don't want to think it over?"

"What's to think over? You cracked the case."

"I'm not here to crack any cases," I said, though the disclaimer felt weaker and weaker. "And if I was, I haven't done it. First you told me the family raised the payout for you. Then they didn't, they raised it for Theo. Then everybody was happy when Charlie cut the raise in half. Except, you tell me, there would have been a battle if he'd cut it all the way. Now you say you tried to smother him. Alone. This may not be any of my business, but I think you're afraid one of your children, probably Theo, tried to kill Charlie to get extra money and somebody might find out who it was."

"So, this is the new Benjamin Gould." Her smile was bitter. "You really do like your new assignment. You like the bonus they must be paying you. And the power. Call the police."

"You've got a phone. Do it yourself."

"Don't be smug. I'll call them in a couple of days, after I talk to a lawyer. It's a promise."

"How long did it take you to craft this confession?"

"I didn't craft anything."

"I have some expertise about this sort of thing," I told her. "It was too polished. Too perfect. You should have messed it up to make it seem authentic. You should have been upset and possibly relieved to be unburdening yourself. You were toying with me."

"Toying with you? The others maybe. But not me. If you stay in this, they'll all take a run at you. You're not like your brother. You're sensitive. He's impervious. That's why they're drawn to him. They can't hurt him, but they'd like to. But you're the target they have. What an opportunity. The ones you think might be on your side, they'll be the most dangerous. Trust me, their needs will come first, and they have a lot of them. They'll beguile you and dazzle you, and when they're finished, they'll spit you out. So save yourself. Accept my confession. Move on."

"I might," I said, "if I believed you'd call the police and confess."

"I promise you I will!"

A wild thought occurred to me: Did she pretend to make a false confession when she did, in fact, try to kill her husband? Two weeks ago, I wouldn't have believed her capable of anything like this. And I never would have imagined I'd be caught in the middle.

CHAPTER EIGHT

TESSA

Benjamin Gould, the little darling, had been right. I'd been working up the courage for a while. Over and over I'd imagined the smothering and the confession, wondering if I had the nerve to carry out my plan. When it happened, it was—dare I say it?—a triumph. I had declared: Do you see, Charlie Cantling? I wasn't born just to marry power. I can fight for it on my own. I can take command of the story.

Why did I do it? Because I was afraid. Who was this suddenly solicitous husband who sought the wishes of others, who claimed he would carry them out? How could I not notice that, whether Benjamin knew it or not, Charlie was asking the fundamental questions of divorce: who wants what and how much? Charlie could have been trying to find out how little he needed to give me. So soon, husband? After I saw you through your ordeal?

An hour after Benjamin and Theo left, Charlie's name popped up on my cell phone. He started out nonchalant. "What's the plan for dinner?"

"Lobster in the shell," I said. "With sausage and vegetables."

"One of my favorites. Worth coming back from the dead for. Send the cook home early. We'll serve ourselves."

"You're clearing the decks. Why?"

"Can't a man be alone with his wife?"

"Is this a date?" I asked. "It's been a while."

"We have things to talk about. And things to do."

In my heart, I felt a flutter. In my head, I heard an alarm. Was this the Charlie of old, who'd smile and smile and set you up for a knockout punch from nowhere? But Charlie of old wouldn't have shown his hand and sent in a spy. He'd have worked around to it by himself—blunt on the surface, devious at heart. That was my Charlie. They say physical trauma can cause dementia. Well, now this new version of Charlie was suggesting, if I understood him right, sex. Why bring up something he scarcely ever mentioned or practiced, at least with me? Was it a trick, from a master, on the road to separation? Or was he losing it? He said, "How was your time with Benjamin?"

"He hasn't reported to you?"

"Not yet. What did you tell him you wanted from my estate?"

"I said as far as I was concerned, my husband was going to live forever and keep us all happy. But you said you wanted me to talk to him. Some stuff came out. There was a range of possibilities about how we got here and where we're going." I thought: Tessa Cantling, listen to yourself.

"When I was half-dead, you may have spent too much time in meetings," Charlie said.

"Theo stopped by. I invited him."

"So you wanted Theo on a leash," Charlie said. "You'd hear what he told Benjamin—and coach him."

"Why would that be necessary? Theo's brilliant. I just wanted to move things along. This way Benjamin could talk to two of us at the same time."

It seemed like Charlie hadn't heard that I'd confessed. Had Benjamin's bosses felt it was too soon to pass along my declaration? Didn't I convince somebody?

Charlie said, "Did anything come up about business?"

"You know how trusts and stock and voting power bore me. I stayed away from all that. I told Benjamin that I and the children had always been treated generously and I expected that would continue."

"Clarity. Generosity. Continuity. You should run for office."

He ended the call. How like Charlie to leave me in limbo, to delay the confrontation. The powerful need a sense of timing, and Charlie could move fast or slow or not at all, ruthlessly or with care. I felt very small, a plaything, a follower ready for his next change of direction. I wondered what the theme of the night would be.

I ate lunch at home, drank a glass of wine, and decided a trip to Madison Avenue was called for. Leaving the building, I headed west in summer clothes and sneakers and wide sunglasses. Madison used to be where I ruled, not Charlie—where I'd mastered the art of shopping and buying and knew most of the salespeople by name. They'd send me notices of new collections and, not so often, next week's discounts. The posh storefronts, the stylish shoppers who plied the sidewalks with their heads tilted into cell phones, the running into gossipy girlfriends, the cars and taxis that scuttled up the street—I had loved all of it too well.

In recent months, I'd scarcely shown up, so the ladies in Boutique Charmaine welcomed me back like the prodigal daughter. I had decisions to make. Coping with Charlie's ordeal had slimmed me down, but I had gained the weight back and added more. What to do? When I was in bra and panties only, a mirror confirmed my loathsome love handles, though the salespeople denied it. I decided to shop as if I hadn't gained anything. It would be an incentive to slim back down. I briefly had a fright that Charlie might have canceled my credit card on a rampage, but it paid for a blouse that didn't quite fit and a dress I couldn't wear.

I tucked the boxes under my arm, strode east toward home, and started to fight tears behind my sunglasses. I saw how people looked at me. I thought: At my age, to be too thin and own too many dresses can make you look like a loser, a woman who won't grow up, a creature of the plastic surgeon's knife.

But let them believe it. They'd be wrong! I've taken a stand. I've scrambled Charlie's plan. What to do now? I won't retreat. I will not be ditzy. I will not be irrelevant.

I needed to talk to Phil Weller. For the longest time, he'd been Charlie's enforcer and second in command, a smart, bulky, unimaginative man who could dominate every room Charlie wasn't in. Charlie did have a weakness for toadies and kept a few around, but he could also appreciate strength and competence. After the accident, I'd been reluctant to sign up one powerful man to help with the loss of another. But there'd been so much to handle: doctors, family, rehab, business. What to do, indeed!

Phil and I had started out tentative, not sure the other could be relied on. Then we talked more and more—sometimes scheduled, sometimes spur of the moment. We traded impressions and plans and, eventually, secrets. He managed to get the sibs on his side, which wasn't easy to do. How? He agreed the company could send them more of what they wanted. He understood an outsider couldn't hold back like a father. I thought: Smart man, that Phil. Knows how far to go.

Lately, I had reasons to hate Phil. But I didn't.

A half hour later, Phil called. Except at business meetings, we hadn't spoken in two months. "I couldn't get back to you sooner," he said, sounding distant. "It's good to hear from you."

"Is it?"

"I was meeting with Charlie and the executive committee," he said, taking the hint. "You know how he is. He keeps us busy. Even at three-quarters strength, he's a barrage. Texts. Memos. Emails. He's got all sorts of ideas—maybe buy a business, or try a joint venture, or put a lot of selling behind some new service."

"He's got four hundred million to play with," I said. "It must be tempting."

"Right. He gets twelve ideas, half of them crazy, for every one that might go somewhere. We follow up on most of it or he gets pissed. Usually, they go nowhere. But every now and then, something happens. From the way Charlie's acting, this may be the time."

"You sound nervous," I said. "That's not like you."

"I don't know if I'd call it nervous," Phil said, always reluctant to show weakness. "But you and me, we haven't spoken for a while."

"It's more than that. You're giving me too much detail, like you're actually telling me something when you aren't. Talking around things—you're good at that."

The old antennae were buzzing.

"Charlie wants to talk to me tonight," I said. "It sounds serious. If he has a big plan for the business, crazy or not, you need to tell me so I won't be blindsided."

"I don't want to be in the middle of this," Phil said.

"Are you serious? Like you're not already there? Charlie is telling the family he needs the cash that's sitting around. Why would he say that?"

"Because for a couple of weeks, we've been in talks to buy a software company."

"Buy a software company? Shouldn't the family have a say in that? Why didn't he tell us sooner?"

"You know Charlie. Always watchful. The sellers weren't shopping the bid, but he was afraid if word got out, someone would step in and offer more."

"How much has he agreed to pay?"

"A lot. That's all I can say."

"How far along is the deal?"

"Let Charlie tell you."

"Do you think he's sound enough to be making decisions like this?" I asked.

"I'm not going to make that judgment."

"I'm worried, Phil. This sounds like too much for him to take on while other stuff is happening. Have you heard he's got one of our young neighbors nosing around?"

"Yeah, the guy's been to the office."

"Charlie's never done something like this," I said. "I mean, an investigations agency? Does he suspect what happened with us?"

"We were very careful."

"Was it enough? The children say when there were discussions, I took your side too often."

"So what?"

"Somebody at work might have figured it out," I said. "People see your schedule."

"There was nothing on it. Stay calm."

For many weeks after the accident, I had tried to be businesslike with Phil—straightforward affect, firm posture, less makeup, business lingo—but there was this one afternoon when we were alone in his office with no more business to do, and I didn't feel like leaving. Phil's windows faced west, and sunlight outlined his broad body and nuzzled his unruly brown hair. I thought to myself: Well now, look who might be my best bet.

Because I am who I am and need to make a bet.

I began to flirt just a little. Not so much that I couldn't pull it back and deny everything. Just a turn of phrase, a flutter of eyelids, but he had noticed. For a week, he didn't say anything about it. He played it straighter than ever. But in a car a week later, after a dull meeting, he reached an arm around my shoulders and laid the opposite hand on my knee. He said, "Do we stay what we are? Or become something else?"

The voice that tells me what men will do had whispered this was coming. I looked at him calmly, with one raised eyebrow, like I'd learned long ago. The ball was in Tessa's court, in a game that Tessa knew. I sighed and said, "Something else, I suppose."

A match made in a hospital. It might have been too soon, but it was more convenient than my past flings, and I'd wanted to be with a man, any man. I wanted to feel the heat of a man's desire that wasn't mixed with rage, for I had long ago gone cold with sleep-around Charlie. If I was to feel truly alive again, I had a lot of ground to make up.

At the start, there was nothing to be ashamed of. Phil and I had become friends by working together, and he and his wife were separated. I didn't know what he'd been like in his marriage, but with us, there wasn't much passion at first. To be crude: we talked business, fucked, and talked business again. It wasn't exhilarating. It wasn't desperate. Was it wrong? What loyalty did I owe my charming philanderer husband, now that he was just about dead?

The first signs of Charlie's revival were confusing. They told me it might be temporary or he might only come partway back. No one mentioned a full recovery. I decided Phil and I could end it if and when we needed to. We told each other there was nothing sordid about what we were doing, but that wasn't how we acted, especially with Charlie on the mend. We slunk away and stole time in hidden rooms. Treating the matter like sin and betrayal seemed to make it so.

As usual, Charlie took charge, this time by getting healthier. When I told Phil we had to stop, I had to go back to being a wife, he didn't argue. It took me time to realize I hadn't meant what I said. It was like I'd been tricked into saying what Phil wanted. Even as the man I used to believe was the love of my life recovered, I ached for Phil with all my wakened heart. I found the courage to tell him. But he was firm: we couldn't start again. The little voice inside told me he was not about to budge. There was nothing to do but accept it—or pretend to.

We stole no more time. When we met, there were others around. We were always reserved. We never stared, never spoke too frankly. It was unbearable.

"Do you wish I hadn't gotten in touch today?" I asked Phil.

"It's difficult."

"So we never mention 'us' again? We forget it happened?"

"I don't want to forget it. Not ever. I do want it to go away," he said, wounding me.

"Is it necessary to avoid me?"

"I'm not doing that."

"You send email reminders about meetings. You nod when you run into me. It amounts to nothing. Okay, Charlie and I have history. Children. Common interests. I can't abandon him now, not when he's still not a hundred percent, not when he may be losing it," I said, reciting the tired sermon of my obligations. "But I miss you."

"I never asked you to abandon Charlie."

"You should have! What a hand I was dealt! He'd been rotten with me for so long, and then when he was basically dead, I had to act the wife. And I did! Trooper Tessa saw him every day. I sat with him when he didn't know I was there. I held his hand, I talked to him, because the doctors said it would help. And then he was back, and with a flip of a page, you and I moved to the next item on the agenda. I wonder: if Charlie had died and I ended up with you, would I have traded one cold-blooded bastard for another?"

"Tessa!"

"Clever man, you relied on me knowing what you were thinking. What was the moment you realized I'd gotten your message and it was over? Was it in Charlie's room, when a doctor told both of us that Charlie showed more signs of improvement? Was that when you sensed I understood? Because I felt it. I was dizzy! I was nauseous! What timing! When my flesh, for the first time in the longest time, wasn't mostly dead, when at last a decent man could do that to me, Charlie rallies and threatens to dominate me in the shape of a semivegetable. Without the man I loved, without the perks of widowhood, I'd watch over a living corpse. What percent of me was grateful he might survive and what percent appalled?"

"Tessa, I am sorry about you and me."

"Tell me: have you convinced yourself that for you, it was just a few pre-divorce fucks?"

"You know better than that."

"But it was easy enough for you to go away. Except, damn you, you're still here."

"Tessa, you need to accept what is. Too much depends on it."

"Yes. I know. Your job."

"And your marriage."

"I hate your job," I said. "I hate my marriage."

A deep breath from Phil seemed to fan the phone. "I get it. You're throwing a useless fit. It's a bit of the old you. But you're not like that anymore. You're changing."

"How's that?"

"You used to be Mrs. Charlie Cantling, invited onto charity boards to open up your checkbook but not counted on for much else. But there were problems at one of the nonprofits, and you stepped up. It was three years ago. I saw it. You fixed relationships, kept things going, found some strength. You changed. That's why you and me could work together. That's why you can handle what happened."

It was hurtful that while speaking of me, he was so concerned about himself. I recognized he was in a very uncomfortable position. When I was younger, I hadn't sought out power, only powerful men, but here was Phil, who had never been anything but a gentleman with me, who'd operated Cantling Market Research with integrity and a firm hand, who'd kept the children at bay—and his career and livelihood were in my hands.

If I confessed about Phil to Charlie, it would be difficult between Charlie and me, but we'd gotten over worse. Under the circumstances, Charlie could hardly call it infidelity. After a while he might accept it. But he wouldn't abide the presence of my ex-lover, who'd be out of a job in an instant. To be fair to Phil—and, yes, to have any chance with him—I would keep the secret.

I was too angry to tell Phil he was safe. "You want me close but not too close," I said. "You want to eliminate the danger I might become. Do you care about how I feel, except when it might hurt you with Charlie? Is that why you came onto me? To shore up your position when Charlie died?"

"Didn't you want to keep me close, too?" he said. "Wasn't that part of it? We had a lot on our minds. We tried not to hurt each other. Until now."

I recoiled. I didn't want to be cruel to Phil. And it was true that I had needed him from the start. After the accident, I remembered what Charlie had told me: without Phil watching over the business, other executives might carve out territories and spend like crazy, the family be damned. But I knew men and their protections. I'd thought: What can I do to protect myself from Phil, my protector?

So I decided to watch him. And be tight with him. And learn from him. That it had turned into sex, well, I didn't plan it.

"I want to warn you about something," I said. "Charlie feels somebody tried to smother him in the hospital. I told Charlie's spy it was me, all by myself."

"Why would you admit that? To Charlie's spy, no less."

"I was upset about this spy thing."

"He won't believe you'd act alone," Phil said, careful not to ask too many questions. As usual, he was quick to assess. "He'll assume, if you had a partner, it was Theo or me. This is Charlie—hard to fathom, harder to predict. He might already know what happened at the hospital. Or he might know it didn't happen. The so-called smothering is full of possibilities, all bad. The authorities might get involved. Your confession, is it a way to score points, to make a case against Charlie?"

"What does that mean?"

"You stood up to him. You called his bluff, if that's what it is. You know the guy. He sees anybody standing up as a power play. Will he be sane about it? How far will he go? It looks like the opening skirmish of a battle between you and him. Somebody's going to come out on top, and somebody isn't."

"If it's a battle, I need allies. Where do you stand?"

"You mean a lot to me, Tessa. You don't know how much I want to be on your side. But to be honest, it all depends."

"On what?"

"On how you and Charlie play it and whether you stay the course—and most of all, on who has the votes in the end."

Charlie arrived at six thirty, earlier than he used to because he still couldn't manage long evenings of work. Even with pins in his leg and other problems, he still resembled the fine specimen I married—he'd been a strong swimmer, tight end, sometime rower. His mood seemed positive, but Charlie Cantling could attack from anywhere. If he found out about Phil and wanted a divorce, he wouldn't jump right for it. He'd line up his ducks at the company. He'd have women. Whose bed would he climb into? A family friend? An acquaintance? Several?

As usual he was dressed old school, in a well-fitted gray suit, though he'd loosened the top button of his shirt and stuffed the tie in his pocket. He started out genial and unthreatening. We leaned across our oval dining table to clink goblets in a silent toast to, I assumed, surviving in our Park Avenue luxury. We'd already sat for a magazine photo shoot. I set my glass down and told myself not to let it matter too much. Love of the lifestyle had weakened me too many times.

During the salad, which Charlie liked as a first course, there was no mention of my confession. When I cleared the salad plates and brought out the main course, I was still in doubt about his mood and intentions. We had developed a love of lobster stew after buying the second house in Connecticut, and we attacked our cook's thick creation with passion. At the center of the table, a bowl of glass we'd bought in Venice accepted the cleaned-out shells. One thick claw on Charlie's plate demanded a trip to the kitchen and a hammer. I heard him smashing away until the shell cracked on the fourth or fifth blow. When he returned, he brandished a bloody finger and grinned like the crazy predator he might be.

He was a hard man to feel sorry for, but he was bleeding. I used my napkin to soak up the blood, found a Band-Aid in the kitchen, and taped it on. We ate and briefly could have passed for a normal couple. He entertained me with office tidbits, mostly notes about the foibles of underlings, subjects on which he was usually sharp and cutting.

He scraped a final morsel from a tail, chewed, and swallowed. "Tessa, did I ever tell you? Lobsters are cannibals."

With a flash of Band-Aid, he tossed the hollowed-out tail into the Venetian bowl.

"You may have mentioned it once or twice."

"In a tank, they'll eat each other. That's why they put rubber bands on the claws. The strong devour the weak. Sounds about right, doesn't it?"

"For lobsters, darling. Not for people. We've had this discussion too many times."

"It's worth repeating. Like it or not, we all live in a big lobster tank. It's a constant vigil, a struggle to stay alive. I hate it. But there's no choice."

He dropped his silverware and pushed his plate away. Perhaps he was having one of his bouts of conscience, which could be genuine, even if they never lasted. Leaning forward, he pushed both hands against the glass tabletop and braced himself.

"Did you think we could pass a whole evening without discussing it?"

He didn't seem to notice the blood oozing from his bandage. It struck me that he was a bloody, demented caricature of himself. "Without discussing what?" I said.

"Come on. I'm not that dumb. I haven't lost my marbles."

"Has anyone said you did?"

"I see looks on faces," he said, grimacing. "I hear people patronizing me, like I'm some confused old relic back from the dead. I'm not perfect. But I'm here, Charlie in the flesh, and I don't appreciate being toyed with."

"Who's doing that?"

"Tessa, I have a very good picture of what happened today between you and Benjamin Gould."

"What picture is that?"

"The way I see it, you brought Theo to persuade Benjamin that the bee venture is going well. A tough sell, wouldn't you say? You were trying to make Theo look like a winner who wouldn't lobby the family for extra payouts from the company. I'm onto you. You've been bankrolling Theo, and you're trying to hide it."

"Where on earth did you get that idea?"

"From the bank records."

"You haven't seen any records. I have my own account, in my own name. That's been the arrangement for years. You don't have the password to check it online. And there's no paper lying around. I stopped getting paper statements last year."

"So you think you have dark money? Tessa pulling strings. Tessa, mistress of the web. How fucking convenient!" He aimed his bandaged finger at me, and I steeled myself. Would Charlie expose our understanding: my slush fund in exchange for letting him roam? Too much honesty could lead straight to divorce. I reminded myself: That might be what he wants. Do I want it, too?

"I don't know what you're talking about, Charlie, and neither do you. You've got no information."

"Now that you're such a woman of the world, chairman of charities and whatnot, maybe you can tell me: Who fills up this family's accounts? Who brings the bank the big deposits and fees? When they're going after new clients, whose name do they drop? Yours? Dream on. The magic word in banking is Charlie fucking Cantling. Do you really believe they'd stonewall me about Cantling family accounts?"

"If they gave you my information, it's illegal."

"You're right! Take the bastards to court! You against the bank. Tessa versus Goliath. Seven clerks will swear they never break the rules. They'll swear you told them to release the information. Welcome to the world, Mrs. Cantling. It took me all of one phone call. What did I find? Hundreds of thousands of dollars from a US account into a Cayman Islands account with no name, only a number. Very creative. Way beyond what I'd have expected. But why? What secrets lurk in the heart of Tessa? It's obvious, isn't it, loyal mother that you are? Unless you're paying off a lover, which is not you—too humiliating—you're sending cash to one of your children. It doesn't take a genius to figure out who. Is that buzzing I hear? Buzzing and bad honey."

I had a backup story for the account, but instinct told me to let Charlie use up some temper. "If I helped Theo—and I didn't—at least I was doing something for him. Not like you. You're so hard on him. You savaged him most of his life."

"Savaged? I try to teach him to not be a fool."

"Is that what it is? 'Theo, you're not clever. Theo, learn something about people. Theo, you're an airhead.'"

"He's not twelve anymore! He needs to learn!"

I shrank from Charlie's anger, but I was furious. Another grievance night at the Cantlings'. I was tempted to tell him about Phil: Chew on that, Charlie. There was more and better sex than I had with you in years. How does the lobster taste now?

But if I told him, I would lose Phil in every way.

"Can't you cut Theo a little slack?" I said. "It isn't easy for him. You're his father. He has a lot to live up to."

"So I should prop him up?"

"Supporting your children isn't propping them up."

"You admit you sent him that money?"

"I admit nothing. I'm talking about emotional support."

"What does that get you without cash?" he said.

"You'd love it if I sent money to Theo! It would give you something else to hammer him with. Do you hate the kids because they have power in the trust? They could get together with me and vote you out. Is that why you pummel them about their weaknesses?"

"Bravo!" he said. "Brilliant misdirection! Who'd have thought you had the ingenuity for all this—and the guts?"

Despite my anger, the dribble of blood from his finger was too much to look at. He tried to wave me off, but I returned to the kitchen, found a second Band-Aid, and replaced the first on his finger.

I said, "I don't need to justify my spending to someone who broke into my records, planted a mole in our family, and is full of crazy notions, but you're wrong about what I was paying for."

"I'm wrong?"

"You know my weaknesses. Well, while you were in the hospital, they got worse. Those little shiny things? Diamonds. Rubies. Pearls. I wanted them. If anybody ever needed pampering, it was me when you were dying."

"I thought you were done with baubles. That you'd become a serious woman."

"I relapsed. The withdrawals I made, the withdrawals you resent so much, they paid for little shiny things. Nothing else. I kept the payments hidden because if you survived, I didn't want to face the sort of tantrum you're having now."

"What jewels? Where are they?"

"I could show you jewels—whole drawers full. Would it help? Could you tell where I bought them and when?"

"What about receipts?"

"Receipts? Me?"

"Tell me the name of the jeweler."

"I'm sworn to secrecy. He's European. He has an issue about paying taxes."

"Very clever, but you forgot something," Charlie said. "A couple of years ago, we found this genius IT guy. He had hacked some things he shouldn't have, and he had a criminal record. But he was so good, we gave him a chance. Now he's a company man through and through. He'll do anything for us. He went online, got into that Cayman account, and found the supporting documents. You're familiar with the name on the account. You picked it when Theo was born. You should be honest with me. It would save time."

"Shouldn't honesty work in both directions?" I said. "Why did you send us Benjamin Gould? A boy you always looked down on. The girls and me, we used to feel sorry for him. We tried to get him to dress right and find him dates. Okay, he's grown up a bit. But a pigeon doesn't turn into a swan. He becomes a slightly more appealing pigeon. Your Benjamin's going to sort out our problems?"

"I have my reasons. Trust me."

"There's an idea. What are you going to do to that poor boy? It's enough to make me feel sorry for him."

"Damn you, Tessa! Cooperate! And stop trying to distract me from what you've been doing with Theo. How is it support to help him go through cash? If the kid can't stand on his own feet, if he has to come crawling for handouts, you're making him feel like a bigger loser. We need to let him fail on his own."

"You'd feel different if it was one of the girls," I said. "You toss money at them like confetti at a wedding, as long as they obey and adore."

"No, Tessa, this time it may not be Theo versus the girls. I see your strategy. You bought everybody off with more money from the company, to get them all on the same side. And now you've kicked up dust to hide it."

"What dust?"

"To muddy everything with Benjamin, you made up a tale about how you tried to send me to the Great Beyond. It's crazy! You with your shopping and your dainty feet! All of a sudden you're trying to kill your husband to save him from being a vegetable? Where would you get the guts? You think you're protecting somebody, but trust me, you're making it worse."

"You're sure I didn't do anything in the hospital? You think I could stand to see what you'd become?"

"I don't believe it. And you'd better hope nobody else does. Did Benjamin believe it?"

"I don't think so."

"So he was sharp enough to see through you? Just pray word doesn't get to some local district attorney who wants his name in the papers because you've painted a target on yourself. You'll find a bull's-eye clashes with Versace."

"This isn't about the law and district attorneys," I said. "It's about you wanting power."

"How do you know that?"

"Because that's what you always want."

"What I want is no more yapping about mercy killing. Then I want to arrange for everybody to get sensible amounts of money. That's why I sent Benjamin in."

"And you say I'm the one making things up. Let's have real honesty for a change! Have I been giving money to Theo for his bees? Yes. Did

I approve of doubling the payout to the children? Did I try to smother you in the hospital? Yes, I did."

"There's no way you'd have done it alone. Who would you be protecting? Theo? I doubt he'd go along. Phil Weller? You and Phil. It's all I hear about: how you two saw eye to eye, how you ran things when I wasn't around. I know what Phil's capable of. To co-opt the kids, to get them off his back, he might agree to distribute some extra cash. But try to smother me? Take a chance like that with the law? It didn't happen—at least, not with Phil. And not with you, either."

I needed us off this topic. "Charlie, I've never seen you so focused on money, and that's saying something. What's going on?"

"That's shrewd, Tessa. I've gotta give you credit. I've got a deal in the works to buy a company called Celestial Intelligence. They've got very good software for evaluating internet ads."

"How sure is this deal?"

"We have a contract, but there are issues. That's all I can say."

Phil hadn't mentioned a contract. "Damn you, Charlie! This gives you the perfect excuse to cut back the payouts and hold on to cash. How big is the deal?"

"Four hundred and fifty million dollars."

"What? Are you crazy? We don't have that kind of money."

"We can borrow the extra fifty million."

"Borrow? How could you put us in this position?"

"The position where this family is rich as hell? Where they can run to Paris or the Seychelles on a moment's notice? Do you really want to keep paying them a fortune?"

"That's unreasonable. They have expectations."

"What they have are votes. I have to give them enough money so they don't launch a full-scale rebellion—or worse."

"What's worse?" I said.

"A pillow in the face, with weight behind it. You and Theo and the Caymans, it's the last straw. Why do we have limits and rules if people just break them? Starting now, I have someone watching your accounts. If any cash goes out to Theo, I'll close your accounts immediately. Really, I shouldn't let him or any of them get another dime, but I'm not cutting them out completely. I'm putting the payout back to where it was before the accident. A hundred thousand every three months. Not a hundred and fifty like now. Not two hundred like it was."

"You're cutting them back, you'd like to do it completely, and you're spending their money on another company, but you're asking Benjamin to find out what they want from you. Why would they give you an honest answer? Don't you realize they might fight back?"

"They don't have the balls. And they'd need your vote."

"Right. So don't push me."

"You'd back a bunch of babies against me? If they push me out, it would be a mortal wound for the company. If that's your desire, round up the votes."

And there we left it. Grievance night had lived up to expectations. While I served us a pie that didn't taste sweet, I thought: He looks like Charlie, he sounds like Charlie, but who is he?

The old Charlie had tantrums, but he'd change course and talk to people and find a way through. The old Charlie was filled with contradictions, but not like this! Was he angry because somebody tried to smother him or proud because somebody had the courage? Did he want to buy this new company? Or did he want to prove that he could?

He was right about one thing. I did want power—to make compromises, to prevent lasting damage, to keep this family together. I asked myself: Do I have the courage? Who stands up to Charlie, even if he's diminished, and comes out whole?

CHAPTER NINE

ANN

When I started my job as a paralegal, my father told me he could calculate the hourly rates of a New York law firm from the quality of its conference rooms: windowless boxes with dark tables and clunky chairs meant low fees and degrees from so-so colleges, while sleek, modern chairs and polished tables and glittering panoramas promised high rates and the Ivy League.

Glimpses in our top-floor conference-room windows of rain clouds heading east across the Hudson seemed to confirm Daddy's formula—I worked here and knew the rates were high. Luckily, the partners were always looking for new clients, and to create goodwill among the Cantlings, they'd given us the room at 10 a.m. for free. There was little demand for the space in early August.

A pot of coffee and cups, cream, and sugar sat in the middle of the table, facing me and two of my sisters at one end. Nicole's small, sharp features appeared softened on a computer screen near the coffee pot. I liked when the four of us joined up to talk. Because of Nicole's volatile relationship with everyone in the family except me, it couldn't have been easy to set up the meeting. It was odd that I hadn't been part of the discussions.

"I'm on my patio, looking down the canyon," said Nicole from the computer screen. Three cell phones lay flat on the meeting room table. "Beautiful. I used to wonder: how do they keep it that way? How do they make the city a mix of new and old, Mexican and American? Well, they got together and made rules. For construction. Zoning. Parking. They cooperated. And they enforced their rules. If two different cultures can do that, four sisters can. This is our chance to finally have an impact in this family. But we need rules. Cooperation."

Nicole's speech sounded prepared. The strangeness of her asking for rules when her principal drive had always been to break them didn't seem to register with the others. What was going on with my sisters? "What rules do you have in mind?" I said.

"Let's agree right now, with no backing out allowed. It will be like we're taking an oath." Nicole was alert and rapid fire at 8 a.m. Santa Fe time. I wondered if she'd taken pills.

"What are we agreeing about?" I said.

"This: if any of us tells Charlie what we discuss today, the other three will say the snitch instigated the whole thing. Bottom line, we four are in it together."

"I like it," Vivian said. My oldest sister was attractive in the slim Cantling way. Spurning jodhpurs for the meeting, she'd opted for a tight, dark business suit. Whatever picture of control she presented, an outburst was always possible. "If someone runs to Charlie," she said, "it will be one against three."

"Sisters first and death to traitors," Melanie said with a smile. In dark jeans and a light-blue blouse, long sleeved in summer yet stylish, my youngest sister was beautiful in sloppy clothes.

"What about Theo?" I said.

"We can't include him," Vivian said. "He'd go right to Charlie with anything he hears."

"What if the four of us don't agree about something?" I said.

"We vote, and the majority rules," Nicole said. "We stick together."

I thought: Nicole? Promoting family unity?

Growing up, she'd been Charlie's favorite. When at twenty-two she turned against him with a string of attacks leading to the move out West, it was a terrible blow to him. They'd been locked in battle ever since. Now and then they'd show affection, which made the inevitable blowups worse.

"Here's a chance for more bonding," Vivian said. "In September there's a benefit dinner for United Vegetarians. Before Charlie cut us back, I paid for a table. They made me one of the honorees. We should all be there. Solidarity!"

After Melanie and I agreed to show up, Nicole said, "I'll be there, too. I'll come east. Sisters forever."

"Will you donate?" Vivian asked her.

"That's the problem," Nicole said. "I can't. I gave up a lot for Charlie. I came east twice. I sat and held his hand. And whispered to him. And saw him through it."

"We were there too," I said.

"Of course you were," Nicole said. "So what does he do in return? He hoards hundreds of millions of dollars. Oh, he'll send us something now and then if we smile and kowtow. Meanwhile, he's furious about this so-called smothering. He has Mom so scared that she decided to confess. Does anybody believe her? Me, if I tried to smother him, I'd be proud. I don't care what the law says. It would have been the right thing to do. Not to mention he deserves it."

"Nicole, you don't mean it!" I said.

"Maybe I do," Nicole said. "Because until he has answers, he'll keep squeezing us. I asked him what he was trying to accomplish with Benjamin. His answer? 'Trust me. All of you. I'm getting new information. When it comes to light, it could change everything.' What information? And where is he getting it? From Benjamin? Are we supposed to roll over and let Charlie's spy grill us about our plans, our lifestyles, everything? Charlie Cantling wants to know what we want? And I came to Earth from Mars!"

"Maybe he's acting weird because of the drugs he's taking," Vivian said.

"Or maybe he's just crazy," Nicole said. "A certain amount of craziness is fine with people, as long as you're famous or successful. That's our father. Whoops! Can you hear the noise?"

"I don't hear a thing," Vivian said.

"The dogs are up. They're barking. I need to put them in the yard. Schnauzers are impossible! Why do I have three?" She vanished from the computer screen.

This gave me a chance to tap at my cell phone, where a message from Benjamin had just appeared. Instinct told me not to mention it to my sisters. Since Benjamin rarely texted me, I was eager to read it. I bent to my phone.

> *Good morning, Ann. Being in this new position with your family has made me think even more about you, and I want to tell you some of it. I decided to write because I want to be very clear. Of course, since you often know what's on my mind, you probably suspect a lot of it. Ann, if you feel I'm being paid to spy on you, I understand. You're supposed to answer my questions about your family, but I can't answer any of yours. What I want to know about, what I learn, what I tell Al Byrne—I can't discuss it with you. Well, I don't like being a pawn, I don't like these rules and prohibitions. I don't want events controlling me. It's time I turned that around and worked hard for the things I want. So I'm going to tell you some of my secrets, if only to even things out. I'm going to open my heart.*

I stopped reading. I didn't want my sisters to see me distracted. I thought: It's just like Benjamin. Sweet but with terrible timing.

I didn't want him to get in trouble at work by telling me too much. On the other hand, I wanted him to tell me everything. I stood, clutching the phone to my chest. "There's a computer foul-up in the office," I announced. "They need me."

"We need you too," Vivian said.

"I'll be back in three minutes. Please don't make any decisions without me."

Outside the room, I hurried to the fire stairs, stepped inside, and shut the metal door behind me. I was very nervous. Above, a red bulb glowed in its metal cage, spreading warm light across the cold metal of the landing.

Benjamin's message continued: "WITH SOMEONE ELSE, IT COULD BE RISKY TO PUT THIS IN WRITING. THEY MIGHT USE IT AGAINST ME. I'M SURE YOU WON'T. YOU'LL SEE IT'S IMPORTANT TO KEEP ALL THIS BETWEEN US. SORRY IF IT SOUNDS LIKE I'M PRESSURING YOU. I HAVE FOUND—"

And there the message ended. Had he been interrupted? Had he sent it incomplete by mistake? I texted back: "IN A MEETING. HAD TO STEP OUT TO READ. GOTTA GO BACK SOON. PLEASE FINISH." Right away I felt I hadn't been encouraging enough. I added: "I REALLY WANT TO HEAR."

I waited a full minute. No message arrived. I couldn't keep waiting, so I left the fire stairs and returned to the meeting room, where amid the tapping of windblown rain against the windows, I heard Nicole on speakerphone. "I'm serious, Mel. Come visit. I have an idea. We'll do a TV show on the internet. *Rich Sisters with a Bastard Father. And They're Beautiful.* It's bound to go viral. To loosen up, we'll do some weed first. Coke if you like."

I didn't want to be suspicious, but I wondered: With me out of the room, do they have no agenda?

I looked at my cell as I sat back down. Nothing more from Benjamin.

"Let's cut to the chase," Nicole said. "Charlie's shenanigans are too much. The time has come to push him out. Six votes is all we need. Three of us are already pledged. If we get all four sisters, we can probably get Tessa."

"Isn't it cruel to make her choose between her husband and her children?" I said, feeling the pressure.

"The whole situation is cruel," Vivian said. "But it's where we are. Charlie's acting weird, and Tessa knows it. So what about you, Ann? You're the only one of us who doesn't need much support. Would you vote with us? Would you cooperate?"

"I don't know."

"You need to see it from our point of view," Vivian said. "We have needs. Me, I have charities to support. And my riding. Other things. Now that Charlie's cut back, what I'm getting from Cantling Market Research is just not enough."

My sisters might have been spoiled, but their worry was real. For most of their lives, they'd assumed they were heirs to a fortune, and they thought and were thought of accordingly. And they needed to be that way. I understood: it's hard to give up a lifestyle.

"You know me," I said. "Sisters first. But this is asking a lot. I wish I knew more about what's happening with Charlie."

"That's precisely what we want," Vivian said.

"Charlie only needs one vote," I said. "And he's got Theo."

"Our brother may think Charlie walks on water," Nicole said. "But if we can get five, that will put pressure on him. He always needs funding. Who knows? He might join up."

A new message from Benjamin popped up on my phone. Citing the return of the computer glitch, I again hurried out of the meeting room. Before I reached the fire stairs, I was reading.

"Sorry for the interruption," Benjamin had written.

Al Byrne came into my office. I felt I was in for a long lecture, and I was afraid if I waited any longer to press send, I might chicken out. So I went ahead and sent it. Al was tough. Gould, he said, this was a big opportunity for you, a chance to show what you're made of. So what's the first thing you come up with? A so-called confession from Cantling's wife. Like you walked into the room and solved everything. Do you expect me to believe that? What the hell did you do to her?

I hoped Al would take me off the case. Unfortunately, Ann, it didn't happen. I got no traction with Al. I'm still screwed. But I can take a few steps on my own behalf.

When I got this assignment I wondered if it might somehow cure me of you. In fact, it's done the opposite. It's made me think constantly about you, about talking to you, about what I should say. So here goes: I'm in love with you and maybe I have been for a long time. I respect you, I desire you, I adore you. I know we're very different and there are obstacles: background, family, you name it. I refuse to let that stop me. One other thing: I don't care what you did with my brother way back when. So you went out together. Lots of people go out. It doesn't mean that much. You are you, and I love you, and that's the only thing that matters. We could be closer still, we could protect each other—and that's what counts. If we do that, if we care for each other, and if you feel anything like what I feel, we can get past whatever gets in the way.

If you're interested, even if it's just enough to explore some of this, I'm ready when you are. The next time we're together, we could talk about you and me and the rest of it. If you'd rather not, I understand. And this never happened and nothing has changed.

Wow! Dear, sweet Benjamin. How long had he been carrying this? Yes, I'd had glimpses of his feelings. Yes, I was interested, though not in the wholehearted way he was. For me it had been a slow-growing thing, so slow I almost hadn't noticed. But I had felt something. In the spring, when I stopped seeing Jody. At the Early Fourth. Other times. A week or two ago, at the boat pond with Jody, I'd wondered if I was with the wrong brother. I thought: After all that's happened in both of our families, how can I be honest with Benjamin? How much truth is enough?

I couldn't leave him hanging. "Very very nice," I wrote back. "Can't talk now. Will think. Soon!" It wasn't inspired, but it was all I could give him at the moment.

When I returned to my sisters, I must have seemed distracted. "Everything okay?" Melanie asked me. "Computers behaving?"

I nodded.

"We've been talking about you," Vivian said. "It occurs to us there's one person with a pretty good idea of what's on Charlie's mind. I mean, someone who's been given instructions based on Charlie's thinking. It's your old friend Benjamin. The question is, how do we get him talking?"

I'd been afraid of this. "I doubt he can help much," I said. "I'm sure Charlie's as opaque with him as he is with everybody else."

"Don't you think that's something to find out?" Vivian said.

"How? By grilling him?" I said.

"There are ways," Nicole said.

All these years of trying to maintain family relationships during feuds and fights and rehabs, dismal romances, other disappointments, all the time hoping the wilder ones didn't self-destruct—had it come to the three of them ganging up on me to betray a friend at the very moment he wanted more?

"Benjamin never gets much going with women," Vivian said. "Then there's all his panting after you, Ann."

"What panting?"

"Don't deny it. We all saw it. I used to wonder if he did it to dodge the fact that he's gay."

"He wasn't gay on the Early Fourth," Melanie said.

"You know that because?" I said.

"He made a run at me."

"Is that a fact? Then you might be the one to get information out of him."

"No," Melanie said. "Things didn't turn out well. He'd be suspicious."

"If Benjamin was interested in me," I said, "I always thought it was finished a long time ago."

"We don't think so," Vivian said.

"He's my friend," I said. "He trusts me. Even if I could learn something useful about our father, it would be wrong to try to turn him. Aren't we better than that?"

"No," Vivian said. "The people in this family are not good. Our parents saw to that. They were selfish. There was work for Daddy, travel for both, parties. We all came to know there were affairs. We were witnesses and victims. We struggle. We follow their example. Ask any shrink who's seen us, and they'll tell you: we look out for ourselves and not much else. Except you, Ann. You have the bigger heart. You don't play to the crowd or the camera. You look out for us. It's time to do that again."

"It's not robbery," Nicole said. "It's not murder. We're talking about sex. It's not that big a deal."

"You want me to have sex with Benjamin? That's your plan?"

"With horny guys like Benjamin, have a good session underneath them, and they'll tell you anything you want to know," Melanie said.

"A blowjob wouldn't hurt," Nicole said.

"Sex is not a strategy," I said. "And it's not a tool."

"Grow up," Nicole said. "It wouldn't be a huge leap. You always liked him."

"Which is good reason not to take advantage," I said.

"You have a lot of history with Jody," Melanie said. "Maybe you could talk to him instead. He might know what's going on with Benjamin."

Suddenly angry, I said, "You guys have history with Jody too. Why not invite him to the vegetarian benefit and take turns making a run at him?"

"It's a long shot," Vivian said, taking me seriously. "I'm not Jody's biggest fan. But we need to try everything. Unless anybody objects, I'll do it."

It was all coming into focus. I pictured the family dynamic: Vivian had organized them. Nicole had supplied the energy, probably drug aided. Melanie had gone along.

"You're way ahead of me," I said. "What sisters you are!"

"Ann, you're different from the rest of us." Nicole's was an unlikely calming voice. "But not as different as you think. You're still a Cantling. You present a certain way. You have advantages, which you use. Really, you'd be a fool not to. So step up."

"You might not need to have sex with him," Melanie said. "You might just string him along. Show interest, not too much, and some guys follow you around like a lapdog. Come to think of it, maybe that's been happening between you two the whole time."

"It's so nice to see all three of you agreeing," I said. "Harmony comes to the Cantlings. But don't count on me."

"We know you," Vivian said. "It's like you tell us: sisters first. You'll do it."

CHAPTER TEN

BENJAMIN

Ann's words troubled me all morning. "Very very nice" felt condescending. "Can't talk now" and "Will think" were ambiguous. "Soon" was deflating. If those nine words had formed the entire message, I might have felt like a fool for opening up to her. But then came the exclamation point, an indicator of hope. "Soon!" The word itself sounded like the rush of time.

Byrne had told me our website needed "punch," and to keep my mind off Ann, I pondered revisions to it. Byrne had volunteered some text and titles: "With Cybercrime, the Best Defense Is the Best Defense." And then: "Don't Expose Yourself to Exposure." While I wondered how to sidetrack Byrne's ideas, my wretched timidity returned. I kept thinking I'd presented Ann with a dilemma: how best to let me down easy.

I texted a simple reply to her: "Whenever you're ready." Then I waited. And kept waiting. All I seemed to do was wait.

Before noon, I did receive a message from a Cantling—Theo, with an invite to his farm in Western Connecticut. His text sounded jaunty, as if nothing untoward had happened on the Early Fourth and shotguns were irrelevant. I forwarded the message to Byrne. Citing the tensions between me and Theo and the presence of a million bees, I told him I assumed he'd want me to stay home. He wrote back: "WEBSITE REVISIONS LATER. DO VISIT NOW."

I had a backup plan. I wrote: "I HAD A COUPLE OF BEE STINGS AS A KID. I THINK I'M ALLERGIC."

Byrne's reply: "STOP. MAN UP. GO."

Two mornings later, with my silent cell phone on the seat beside me, I drove north. I had still not heard from Ann, who was certainly taking her time. Had I written too much? Had I already wrecked it? I realized that I, who'd always been so guarded, had no practice opening up.

Theo owned 180 acres of medium-productive farmland in a slowly suburbanizing area near New Milford. Visions of his antics at the Early Fourth enlivened the bouncy approach on his entrance road, where my tires spat stones and crunched gravel. By my reckoning, it was doubtful that he'd risk prison and shoot me, but he might arrange a mishap at the hives. Luckily, I already had a plan to keep me from his bees.

An antique farmhouse updated with large picture windows awaited. Fields of corn and hay surrounded the house, yielding to woodland at the western edge. Closer in was a sad white barn in need of painting, an equipment shed, a parked SUV, and a pickup truck. Because I wouldn't take a call from Ann in her brother's presence, I switched my cell phone off and left it in the car. I opened the door to a nearly windless morning that verged on hot and was glad I'd worn light clothes.

Jaunty in jeans, a work shirt, and improbably red sneakers, Theo trotted down the porch steps and through the yard and gate to meet me in the parking area. He shook my hand with vigor subbing for warmth and guided me toward the house. A droopy white fence enclosed the house and a yard containing beat-up Adirondack chairs, a stone grill, and a rusty swing set.

"I'm starting to fix up the place," he said, following my gaze. "Before now, the beehives got most of my attention."

I tried a compliment. "It seems you have time for your fields. They look good."

"The farm's a complex operation," he mumbled. I seemed to have unnerved him. "I strike a balance."

The front door opened into an air-conditioned living room whose contemporary furniture—metallic chairs, a narrow couch, elongated lamps—somehow struck me as ungainly. Some surfaces showed a thin layer of dust, and particles floated in the sunlight. Amid the attempt at chic modernity, the antlered head of a buck overhung a fireplace, and a shotgun stood barrel-down in a corner. Two matching bongs in purple glass rested on a table.

"So, you noticed the shotgun," Theo said. "It seems we have raccoons out here, too. They're like you, Gould. They follow me around. Maybe you deserve the same treatment." He was grinning at me. "By the way, I really was shooting blanks."

Theo, the heat, the trip, frustrations with Ann, my predicament with Byrne—they conspired at this very moment to make me lose all patience with the Cantling attitude toward danger. With Jody I coped with it because I had to. Here, since I'd never wanted to visit the hives with Theo, it was time to draw a line. "Where are the bees?" I said.

"Way out in the fields. Why?"

"If you're armed, Theo, I won't go. I'll wait at the house."

"If we do that, you could have stayed in the city and nursed your grudge about the Early Fourth."

"So, it's a grudge?"

"Gould, you need to see the bees. They go about their work like they have for millions of years, and they completely understand each other. Close up, I find it soothing. If it makes you feel better, I'll leave the gun here. The raccoons can have a day off."

Before I could answer, Theo's karate-loving girlfriend strode out of the kitchen. I hadn't expected her. In gray slacks and a frilly white blouse, Whitney wore a look of cheery expectation more extreme than I remembered from New York City.

"I believe you two met in my parents' apartment," Theo said.

"We did," she replied without embarrassment. "We have a lot of catching up to do."

"There's a problem with the truck," Theo announced as if on cue. "A fan belt needs replacing. It'll be a couple of minutes." He sauntered out, swaying confidently.

My hostess invited me onto the couch. I eased down, raising the dust cloud I'd hoped to avoid. While I sneezed, straight-backed Whitney sat beside me without respiratory incident. A vase of drooping Queen Anne's lace on a stand beyond her promised more dust to come.

"The place could use some cleaning," Whitney said. "I might try to talk him into it."

"How long are you here for?"

"I have a few days off. Good timing, isn't it? We can clear up what happened in New York. I may have said things, done things, that confused you."

"You don't need to explain."

"But I do. I might have made it sound like Theo had been too aggressive. But you saw us together, so you know I don't really believe that." Her smile was thin. "Games," she said. "Just games."

"Rough behavior isn't just games with Theo."

"It's the drinking. He's promised to stop, and I believe him. Theo really wants to do the right thing."

"Your karate was part of a game?"

"Exactly. But Theo and I have stopped all games. We need to look to our future."

"Your future?"

"We can have one. I'm not some airhead they hired to clean the house. I have a college degree. I've managed a small store. But my father's been sick for years, my family's run out of money, and the Cantlings offered a lot. I bet Charlie is a great judge of character. I hope he understands I'm nothing to be afraid of. I would never take advantage of Theo."

It seemed that her purpose this afternoon was to manage the flow of information to Charlie. That assumed a big role for her in Theo's future.

We heard footsteps on the porch, and Theo returned without so much as a smear of grease on him. "Things okay with you two?" he asked, full of affability.

Whitney's nod was minimal.

"We had a fine discussion," I said.

"I knew you two could get along. Gould, are you ready to look at some hives?"

"There's one more thing," I said, playing a long shot. "I was stung a few times as a kid. I had a bad reaction once. It seems I'm allergic."

"Then you probably know," he said, "anybody can have a reaction. It's hard to predict."

"But it's serious. Possibly fatal. If you've had one reaction, you're at higher risk of another. What with the cost of insurance and all, if you don't want me out there, I'd understand."

"Stop worrying. Tessa insisted I get state-of-the-art protective equipment. Really, she's a royal pain in the ass about it. You'll be safer than in your own backyard."

"Is there much to look at?"

"We had some mites. It's pretty common. I sprayed. Now I want to weigh the hives. We'll see if the bees have bounced back."

"Why not take pictures and show me later?"

"Photos only tell you so much. Every hive has a different feel. It can be agitated, hostile, calm, you name it. Due diligence. That's the word these days, right? Isn't it what you came for? Don't be so difficult."

I remained leery of Theo. It occurred to me, too late, that by faking an allergy, I'd given him extra incentive to set bees on me. But after his assurances, if I refused to join him, it might be adios to employment. I hoped that Tessa had truly committed him to safety.

"Theo, let's go."

"Do you want to hit the bong first?" he said. "We have some strong stuff."

"That won't be necessary."

As we left, he grabbed a walking stick that had been leaning against the side of the house.

Under a hazy sky, on a rutted track through a cornfield, we started westward toward the woods. The rows of plants, with plentiful silks and tassels, seemed to promise a bumper crop. When we reached a hayfield, Theo's fat Lab appeared and loped ahead as if to guide us.

"Whitney's something else, isn't she?" Theo said.

"Yes, she is."

"When I want her, I want her bad. I don't understand how she gets to me. The games are only part of it. I'm hooked. If you can, pass this along to Tessa: if she fires Whitney, I will be pissed off for fucking forever."

Theo's vulgarity, at first an adolescent affectation, had become endemic.

"Tessa hopes it will go away," Theo said, "but she's wrong. When I heard about Dad's accident, I was totally fucked up. I thought: I can't go on. I mean, who am I without him? But then, very quickly, I was okay. Having Whitney there, it was huge. Que será. Life goes on. The woman's changed my life. We have things to work out, nothing's a slam dunk, but right now it looks like the sky's the limit. Rembrandt!" Theo waved his stick to menace the Lab. "Damn dog, he's always in a hurry for those bees. It's a fucking lovefest. Slow down, you fat slob!"

The dog slouched and cut his pace.

"Cards on the table," Theo said as we continued through the field. "My sisters think Charlie's gone off the deep end. I don't buy it for a minute. My father is the greatest man I've ever known. He's a fucking genius. He's made this family what it is because he's always five steps ahead of everybody else. We need him to keep helping family and company for as long as possible, until it's time for me to take over."

"You're taking over? Is there agreement on that?"

"More or less. Some of them don't like me, maybe one or two can't stand me, but they understand: if anybody can keep this company moving forward, it's me. The age of the network is coming. I've gotta keep preparing for that. This bee operation isn't some expensive hobby. Bees are all about signaling. Communication. They're an information network. Well, every day the human race is more like a beehive. It's happening faster and faster. We're all getting plugged in. There's so much to learn from bees. Not to mention the feel I'm getting for running a business."

Unsurprisingly, I found myself thinking of Ann. I wished I'd brought my phone so I could at least know whether she'd called. I said, "How's the bee thing going?"

"I'm glad you asked. It's going great. We've got fifty hives now. Fifty! It gives us economies of scale. Visibility. Market penetration. Those damn losses are going to disappear. I just need a little more help to get there. I wish Dad understood that. It's like he forgets how start-ups can be very expensive. Eventually, he'll see it my way. He always gets it right in the end."

"What losses?" I said.

"Wait a minute." He stopped and faced me. Ahead of us, the dog slumped on the trail. "Is that why Dad cut us back? He thinks I'm failing?"

Cantlings weren't used to pushback from anyone outside the family.

"Yeah, I had that problem with the honey bureaucrats. One of them came and took samples of crops and honey. Weeks later another guy shows up with the test results. Now, I'm honest. I don't buy bulk honey from Walmart and repackage. I don't feed my bees sugar water. So I ask the guy: what's so awful about a hint of beet sugar in the honey? It's an accent. 'Rules are rules,' he tells me. 'Your label says pure honey. I have to fine you.'

"Okay, a few thousand dollars. Where do I send the check? 'Wait,' he says. 'There's more. You rent out your fields, right? Well, the guy you rent to sprayed pesticide close to the hives, and he's unlicensed. Well, there's no spraying around hives without a license. Under the law, you're responsible. At the levels we found, we had to assume multiple incidents. It adds up to three hundred thousand dollars!' This is fucking harassment, I say. 'If you believe that, Mr. Cantling, there are remedies. You can take this to court.' Right, like I don't know the cost of lawyers? Bottom line, Gould, the fines are brutal."

"Have you explained it to Charlie?"

"Not in so many words. I suppose this makes you think I tried to smother Dad. Like I snuck into his room when things were slow and grabbed a pillow. Never in a million years! You might bear in mind I'm not the only one who needs help from him. Talk about expensive hobbies! What about my sisters? They're up to something. Lately, I don't hear from any of them. In this family, you learn to shut out the tantrums and read the silences. What are they up to? I don't believe for a minute they're sitting on their hands."

With a grunt from Theo and a growl from the dog, the walk resumed. The path through the hay opened to a mowed area near the woods where the fifty beehives stood—stacks of rectangular boxes, each resting on a pair of two-by-fours. On a slight rise behind them was a pile of outsized rocks, probably dumped there when the fields were cleared.

Theo raised the cover of a large bin flanking the hives. "We'll go with the full regalia," he said, lifting out a body-length white suit of thin synthetic. "You still need to be careful. If you die, it's bad for the brand." Chuckling, he lifted out a helmet and veil, a pair of gloves, and large rubber boots. "Put everything on," he said, handing them to me. "Don't forget to clip the veil to the suit."

I followed his instructions while he lifted out a second set of protective gear. Next he brought out a bee smoker—a spouted can attached to a small bellows—as well as a small, flat bathroom scale. He pulled matches from his pocket, lit the smoker, and suited up.

"Want to look inside a hive?" he asked.

"You said you'd keep me a nice distance away."

"You were panicking. I needed to calm you down. You'll be fine. The protection is full body. State of the art."

Theo's adherence to safe procedure seemed genuine. "Why not?" I said, feeling Byrne would be proud. "Due diligence."

Carrying scale and smoker, Theo led me to the hives. Rembrandt followed, apparently beloved by bees, several of whom buzzed above him. We stopped at a hive, where dozens of bees were flying in and out through a gap at the bottom. Theo pried open the lid and lifted out a wooden frame covered with wax and honey and a bustling mass of insects.

"Beautiful, isn't it?" he said.

I nodded.

"The hive," he said. "The network."

Theo reformed the hive and placed the scale alongside on the two-by-fours. He tilted the hive back and, balancing it on its edge, used his foot to slide most of the scale beneath it. When he repositioned the hive vertically, it rested on the scale. The window showing the weight peeked up at us.

"A hundred and forty pounds," he said. "Excellent."

"Are congratulations called for?"

"One hive doesn't prove much. Let's check some others."

He retrieved the scale, walked to the next hive, and positioned the scale beside it. I was impatient. I could foresee the results—he had to have checked before inviting me—and I was hot and sweaty under the layers of clothing.

"I'll leave it to you," I said. "I'll take a break."

"Whatever. You're the guest."

I walked to the rock pile and climbed to a flat spot to sit and watch. I removed gloves, helmet, and veil. The air, so warm inside the helmet, felt cooler.

Theo tilted back a second hive to weigh it. I relaxed to watch the show. I had seen the hives, I'd extracted a few of Theo's secrets, and now I longed for the end of the visit and the drive home. And there was the possibility that Ann had tried to reach me.

Hearing Rembrandt behind and above me on the rocks, I turned and saw him lift a leg to pee. The urine trickled down one stone to another, part of which formed a rough bowl just below me. A dozen bees appeared and landed to drink from the spreading puddle. I wondered: Can bees turn urine into honey?

It seemed they'd been doing it.

I pieced together what was happening. I became disgusted. Without thinking, I waved my helmet above the puddle to shoo the bees away. Most of them remained atop the liquid. Two or three rose and glided toward me. Network strategy, I thought. A neat division of labor. Then came the sting on my neck. Damn! Another on my cheek. Goddamn!

With both stings burning, I scrambled off the rocks and back onto flat ground, where I probed my skin for the poison needles. One remained in my neck—I plucked it out. To protect my lie about my allergic reaction, I was tempted to not inform Theo about the stings, but I expected he'd see the welts. I reset the helmet on my head, reattached the veil, and walked to him.

"You two distinguished yourselves," he said after I told him about the pee and the bees and the stings. "I knew you were dumb, Gould. But this? You took your helmet off. Why?"

"I was hot."

"You'd better not have a fucking reaction. Come with me. I've got some cortisone."

At the bin, he smeared ointment on the stings. It seemed to help. "They tell me a bad reaction can happen quickly—or not," he said. "We'd better get back."

We returned our suits and other gear to the bin. When we started toward the farmhouse, Rembrandt showed up ahead of us on the path. "You fucking idiot!" Theo shouted. He brandished his walking stick. "You like to show off for the bees? You can't piss somewhere else?" With no look back, Rembrandt trotted on.

We had nearly reached the yard and farmhouse, and the stings were itching. Heat and exertion seemed to have worn me out.

Theo stopped. "Gould, maybe I need to be clearer. Let me put some cards on the table. There's a number, the most important number in the world. The number everything depends on. What do you think it is?"

"I don't know," I said, annoyed.

"Think. Think hard."

"I don't know. I give up."

"Okay. The number is six."

"Six? Why six?"

"Four sisters, Tessa, and me. Six votes. And the way things look, it may come down to me."

"You could vote against your father?"

"Never in a million years. But he needs to help me, just a little. The bee thing looks great, but it's still cash-flow negative. Meanwhile, the rental income from the fields is weak, and there's a mortgage on the farm I can just about keep up with. There was some extra cash coming in—might have been from my mother, might not have been—but it looks like that's over. When you add it all up, I can't afford children now. There's no way Whitney could keep working, for my mother or anybody else. Do you see what I'm getting at? Has Charlie ever talked to you about grandchildren?"

This was unexpected. "You want to get married? Have children?"

"I don't have to tell you, but I'm no saint. I banged somebody else a few weeks ago. It was damn good, by the way. Give that up? What they don't know can't hurt you. But I like fucking Whitney, too."

"What are you trying to say?"

"She really didn't want me to tell you. Why create an issue that might go away, she says. Okay. I get it. But talking to you, I see we need to start preparing the ground. People need time to think."

"About what?"

"You and me, we've never been what you'd call tight. But I trust you. Plus, you're a guy. You get the pros and cons. Bottom line: Whitney's pregnant. Twins, she tells me. Goddam. Do I look like the father of twins?"

"Whoa. You just found out?"

"A few days ago. She showed me a picture from the ultrasound—two tiny little blobs in there. I know what you're thinking. Some girls might make it up to catch a Cantling. I mean, anybody can borrow an ultrasound. Well, I talked to the doctor. He confirmed. She was supposed to be using an IUD. She wouldn't have lied about that, would she? I guess they can fail."

"How early is it?" I asked.

"Two months, she says. Way too early. Why stir things up? With twins, there's a one in five chance of a miscarriage. She wants us to wait until she's further along."

"She wants to have the kids? She doesn't want to terminate?"

"'I think I'm an old-fashioned girl,' she tells me. 'It's a tough world to bring kids into. But I don't have the heart to kill babies.' Gould, she's making me crazy. Sometimes I admire her principles. Sometimes I think she doesn't have any. She thinks stuff through like you can't believe. The minute I saw her, I realized: this girl won't be anybody's assistant for long. Mostly, I want to keep fucking her before she gets too fat. She came here a few days ago, and we've been at it like there's no tomorrow. If she wasn't already pregnant, you'd think she was trying to get there."

"You haven't told your parents?"

"Whitney's practical. She says, why stir things up?"

"You need to tell them soon," I said. "I can't keep your secret for long. I was hired to develop information for Charlie."

"Don't be such a hard-ass. I've got all kinds of expenses with the hives—and now two kids! I'm at the end of my rope. How much time will you give me?"

"I don't know. Just tell him as soon as you can."

"Will Charlie help us?"

I shrugged.

Theo had surprised me. He'd maintained deniability but suggested his vote might be up for grabs. That much subtlety seemed beyond him. Whitney had probably helped him prepare. In spite of our history, I felt sorry for him. "What do you really want?" I said. "Are you ready for a family?"

"How the hell would I know? She's got that fresh face. That innocent look. But then she says stuff with this double edge. Like there's this other thing going on inside her that I can't get to. It drives me up the wall. The only other woman who did that was that awful bitch I married."

I recalled the episode: a ten-month marital boomerang after college. Everyone else knew it made no sense, but Theo on a binge was not to be denied. Not now, either. "I can't help much with Charlie and Whitney," I said. "But I can tell you something about honey."

"Don't push it. I don't need help with honey."

"Then call it an observation about Rembrandt. For a while, my mother had a big dog who never liked to exercise. He'd lie around, do nothing, and gain weight. She got worried about him and took him to a vet."

"Your point?"

"It turned out the dog had sugar in his urine, from diabetes. Well, I think there's sugar in your dog's pee. That's why the bees collect it and use it to make honey. There's other stuff in pee, and I think that's where the ammonia smell comes from."

"Vivian mentioned ammonia one time. I thought she was just being bitchy."

"Exercise your dog. He needs to burn off the sugar. Then he can pee all week near the hives, and the bees won't go near it. Your honey might taste a lot better."

"I suppose there's a chance you're right." Rembrandt had settled near his master's feet. "Goddamn dog!" Theo shouted. He swung his stick hard at the Lab, who sprang up ahead of it and scampered off. Ten feet away, Rembrandt turned to watch. "If you fucked up my honey, you're gonna pay!" Theo said. "What an asshole!"

"Don't blame him. He was just being a dog."

"You had a moment, Gould. Now you sound like Vivian. She tells me how I am with the dog proves I'm a sadist. Do you know what makes Vivian an animal expert? Riding pants. That no one wants to get inside of. Vivian wants me to vote with her? Forget it. Rembrandt! Stay where you are!"

Returning to the farmhouse and Whitney, I praised bees, drank ice water, and tried to cool off. Then I gave my empty glass to Theo and stood to say goodbye.

"Reactions to stings can take a while," he told me. "You might wait and see. We could give you lunch." He seemed unenthusiastic.

"The doctors felt I shouldn't worry. I wasn't very allergic. I'll pick up a sandwich on the way home."

"What do you mean, not very allergic? I'm sensing something. When you told me about the reaction, did you make it up? Were you just afraid to go out there?"

I've never been a nitpicker about truth—a guy who, because he can't think of better alternatives, settles cravenly on not telling lies. Is there not a higher truth, the truth of passing around the lies that get us through the day? Love the dress, Mrs. Cantling. How are those wonderful daughters, that kindly son?

Yes, I'd had a few stings. No, I'd never had a reaction.

"I wouldn't make up something like that," I said. "The doctors weren't a hundred percent sure. They thought an antibiotic I'd been taking might have caused the reaction."

"Slick," Theo said. "I didn't think you had it in you. I hope you didn't lie about your mother's dog. That felt like the real thing."

"Count on it."

With the stings still smarting, I said my farewells and returned to the car. Before I started the engine, I checked my cell phone. At last, a message from Ann: "I'M GLAD YOU WROTE WHAT YOU WROTE. IT'S A LITTLE WEIRD. BUT MAYBE NOT TOO WEIRD. CALL ME TONIGHT."

I sat in the car to gather my thoughts. She was glad, but about what? That I'd spoken up? Or what I'd said? Why had she created yet another delay? Tonight seemed a month away. I felt lightheaded. Ann. I may have said her name out loud: Ann, I don't understand your indecision. Have you connected to tell me to forget it? Will you see me in order not to?

Calm down, Benjamin.

I couldn't. I felt dizzy. The bee stings and a strange red bump on my arm itched furiously. I thought: Can a text message, a completely decent one, do this to me? What kind of reaction is this? I've been drugged. What the hell was in the water Theo gave me?

"Was the point of the visit to drug me?" I might have said out loud. Did they hope I would die in an accident on the way home? But Theo had warned me, had tried to get me to stay at the farm, said it was risky to leave. It wasn't a drug—it was the stings! I was having a reaction! The thing I'd tried to lie about was true.

I stepped out of the car and stumbled toward the house, dizzy and out of breath.

I thought: Ann, this may be it. The last day of Benjamin Gould! We never got our chance, did we?

I wobbled through the yard and up the steps. Theo was already at the door. I must have looked like a ghost.

"Wait for me!" he shouted. "Go in and lie down!" I heard him hurry past me and down the steps while Whitney guided me to the couch. I fell onto it. I wondered if Theo was waiting for me to die. Suddenly, he returned and yanked me to my feet. I leaned on him and Whitney as they walked me through the yard. He had parked the SUV just beyond the gate. They shoved me into the back seat, where I slumped against a door. Then they climbed into the front seats and drove.

Where were they taking me? I thought as the bouncing of the SUV enhanced my dizziness and pain. "Benjamin, can you hear me?" Theo said.

I mumbled, "I can hear you."

"Who'd have thought you were such an idiot? You took your fucking helmet off! If you die, do you know what will happen? They'll blame me."

"Benjamin made a mistake," Whitney said. "We'll just have to live with it. Benjamin, are you listening?"

I must have nodded.

"I don't want it to look like we're pressuring Theo's parents," she said. "You won't tell anybody about the twins, right?"

In no position to oppose them, I said, "Right."

"Whitney, look on the bright side," Theo said. "If he croaks, he can't poke around anymore. Let's dump him in the woods. Hey, Benjamin," he called out. "Sorry, buddy. I didn't mean it. Except I did . . ."

I must have passed out, because everything faded to black. When I woke up, I was lying on my back, immersed in an intense quiet. I thought: Where am I? What does it matter? I'm alive!

I began to shed tears of gratitude, then thought: Wait! You can't trust Cantlings. Not Theo, not any of them, except Ann. Did he dump me somewhere to let me die? He wouldn't. He might.

I started to tear up again. How would my tombstone read?

Benjamin Gould
Saw too much. Did too little.
Died alone.

At least I'd opened my heart to the woman I love . . .

———•———

I woke up again and recognized a hospital room, with a beeping monitor behind me and an IV drip in my arm. A young doctor was explaining that the epinephrine could make me fearful, the IV cortisone could cause mood changes, and other polysyllabic meds might do wretched things she'd rather not go into. I asked if I could expect to survive.

"I've been trying to tell you," she said. "You should be okay in a couple of days."

For much of the afternoon, I slept. During a waking interlude, I developed enough coherence to text Al Byrne and Jody and Ann. When Byrne called back, my head was clearer.

"After all your troubles," he said after I explained about the stings. "Did you learn anything useful?"

"Theo's money problems are getting more serious." I remembered my promise to let Theo tell his father about the pregnancy. "Bees are expensive."

"Expensive enough to make him try to smother Charlie?"

"I doubt Theo would ever do that. But if he wanted to, it should have been easy. Really, any of them should have been able to."

"Maybe they got interrupted. Or maybe, with their hands on the pillow, they changed their mind." It was apparent that Byrne and I had been thinking alike. "Let me know if you'll need a ride to the city. We'll send a car."

Jody called, jabbed at me in something like commiseration, and offered to visit. I told him it wasn't necessary. I'd be out of the hospital soon.

Finally, Ann's name flashed on my cell phone.

"I'm embarrassed," I told her.

"Don't be. I hope allergies are the worst thing about you." I was too drugged to feel more than a modest lift. "When you're ready, I'll drive out and pick you up."

"It's three hours round trip."

"You don't want me to come?"

"Of course I do."

Theo and Whitney returned after dinner, bringing my rental car. "Isn't it weird?" Theo said, dropping the car keys onto the bedside table. "I thought you lied about reacting to bee stings. If you weren't such a jerk, I'd owe you an apology."

"You came through for me," I said, dodging further explanations. "How can I thank you?"

"Easy. Don't let Charlie know about the pregnancy. I shouldn't have told you. Whitney wants to wait until the babies are further along."

"I'll wait as long as I can, but you need to tell him soon."

"How long is that?"

"A week," I said, preparing to bargain. I was learning.

"A week! That's nothing. For God's sake, make it two!"

"Okay. Two weeks. It's the absolute limit."

Whitney, who had mostly remained silent, had been sitting in the room's lone chair. I watched her pull a phone from her pocketbook, tap at it, and set it on the window ledge beside her.

"I thought you hated me," I said to Theo.

"Not enough to let you die. Plus, you helped me with the ammonia situation. This afternoon, I sniffed a couple of jars. You may be right. It's an easy fix. I'll run the fat off that mutt. I don't care if it kills him. But you and me are not friends. You have no business poking into our affairs. If you want to make me happy, go away."

They left a few moments later. Far from feeling weak and maudlin, I felt vaguely angry. I thought: These people, with their wounds and their scheming and their furies. And me in the middle getting whipsawed. Can I fight back? How do I do it?

I dozed off. When I opened my eyes, Whitney was standing over the bed.

"I came back for this," she said, waving her phone. "Silly me. I can forget anything." Her chirping unsettled me.

Feeling bolder, I said, "You left your phone on purpose. You told Theo you needed to go back for it."

"If I did that, it was so I could be open with you. I don't blame you if you doubt my connection with Theo. I told you about my own doubts in New York. With your help, I've put them aside."

"How's that?"

"You've shown me what kind of man Theo is—how valuable he can be in a crisis. I think: Here's a man I could marry and spend my life with, a man who could help raise my children."

"One incident doesn't make a man," I said, rather loose at the tongue. "Are you sure you want to move forward with him?"

"It's my nature to be optimistic. I try to get through the day with a smile on my face." She produced a grin to back her words.

I wondered how much of what I'd heard from her was true. Was her father really sick? Her family out of money?

I said, "If Theo doesn't get a promise of extra money, what then?"

"Theo and I need to feel secure. I know Mrs. Cantling well. She's involved with her children. I expect the help will come promptly. Do you?"

I shrugged, and she turned and walked out.

I didn't know why Whitney wanted to delay telling Theo's parents about the twins. Surely she'd want to get them involved right away. But everything else made harrowing sense. She didn't want to rely solely on payments from the trust. She wanted cash in the bank. It seemed clear: had the Cantling fortune not existed, there'd have been no flirtation with Theo, no sex games, no IUD flimflam, no threat. When Cantlings screw up, they can usually gloss over the consequences: Whoops. Another mess. Time for a trip to Paris.

But Theo had seen the ultrasound, had talked to the doctor. There would be no retreat to bankrolled unreality. Another schemer, far more effective than Theo, lay beside him at night. And there were babies.

CHAPTER ELEVEN

ANN

Many people look at me as the Cantling who makes good decisions, with a job, a healthy attitude, and a plan for a career in psychology. But they don't know about my driving.

The small BMW I keep in a garage near my apartment is my indulgence. On the road, I love the feel of the metal beast unleashed, moving at the speed it wants. I refuse to be too careful. It has cost me. Unlike my mother and sisters, I've never had the charm to talk my way out of things, and when policemen stop me, I bluster pathetically. I've had my share of tickets, all deserved.

Late in the afternoon, I drove up I-684, on course to bring Benjamin back from New Milford. His messages had brought me doubt and confusion. It was sad that he'd bottled up his feelings for so long. We might have had a very different history—because I did have some feeling for him. I always had. After the Early Fourth debacle, I sort of expected him to declare himself. But now that it had finally happened, it worried me. For the more glamorous Cantlings, relationships were difficult, and people got hurt. I wasn't quite so glamorous, but there were so many reasons not to take a chance with Benjamin, and on the way to the hospital, I reviewed them all: my sisters, my father, money, status, religion, Jody.

I'd even learned that Benjamin had tried to have sex with Melanie. How could he?

Who was I to talk?

My cell rang on the passenger seat. I turned the radio down and took the call. I knew the folly of talking on the phone while speeding, especially today and to my mother, but I stayed to the left and kept passing cars.

"Your sisters told me about your trip," Tessa began. "I guess the whole family should be grateful to you."

"For what?"

"For trying to get to the bottom of this Benjamin business."

"Let's be clear, Mother. To get information out of Benjamin, my sisters want me to have sex with him. It's ugly."

"I suppose they mean well."

"They want me to be a hooker!"

"That's an exaggeration," she said.

"I'm not going to use sex to get information from Benjamin."

"I want you to do what's best for you." Her resort to mother-speak tripped an alarm. I passed a truck at high speed.

"You don't want me to go?" I said.

"It seems your sisters don't understand the risk. Luckily, there's time to call off the trip."

"Why should I do that? What's the risk?"

"The spy thing can work both ways," she said. "Are you going to tell Benjamin what your sisters put you up to? It could tip their hand. It might help Charlie figure out that people are moving against him."

"Do you take my sisters seriously? As long as Charlie has Theo, he's in control. Why start a fight when they're going to lose?"

I glanced at the speedometer and discovered I was at eighty-five and heading upward. I slowed slightly.

"You could help them," I said. "You could tell Theo you're going to stop the extra support unless he agrees to vote Charlie out."

"So, there's a schemer in you after all. I wasn't sure. Of course, you're assuming I give Theo extra help."

"Do you deny it?"

"Theo tries so hard these days. If I was helping him, would you want me to cut him off at the knees?" She had all but dropped the pretense. "What kind of mother would agree to something like that? What kind of sisters would ask for it?"

"What kind of mother asks a daughter to be a manipulative whore and betray a friend, someone I've known my entire life?"

"I'm trying to focus on the family, to find the solution that hurts the least. It's no time to be concerned about the feelings of an outsider."

"Maybe it's precisely that time. Because this family is hopeless." I had caught up to a pickup truck and started to tailgate. I was too close. I didn't care. "You people and your self-absorption! Does it occur to any of you that I might have goals that have nothing to do with you?" Shouting hands-free to the phone felt liberating. "My sisters want to think I'm even-tempered, reliable, always on top of things. That way, they can keep acting out, and I can keep helping them. None of you have any idea how much I hold in."

"You're not holding in now."

"Mother, your main concern is always Theo. You do have other children."

"Won't these ancient grievances go away?" she said. "I worry about each of you in different ways. God doesn't make all your children alike. To treat every one of them the same is to ignore their differences." It didn't comport with my view of my mother that, amid Tessa's seemingly arrested development, she had dispensed a modicum of wisdom.

The pickup driver flashed his brake lights to warn me off. I backed away.

"Tell me," I said. "With no bullshit. Why did you call me?"

"I'm trying to find out where you stand," she said with surprising directness. "Are you with your sisters? Or are you with Benjamin, which puts you in Charlie's camp? It seems that your father, in his current mental state, has created a crisis. It may be time to do something formal about his role."

"So, my sisters have been talking to you. Whatever they hope to accomplish, they still need Theo's vote. How would you get that? Pray for a miracle?"

"I know my son. Something's going on with him. If we can get him, do we have you?"

"We? We? Poor Dad. There has to be a better way."

"When you think of one, call me. Do we have your vote?" I had never heard my mother so assertive.

"It would be hard for me to go against my sisters," I said.

"You won't tell Benjamin about this discussion? It would get right back to Charlie."

"I won't tell him."

"And you won't tell Charlie?"

"And break his heart? Start a war?"

"Good," she said. "We'll call that cooperation. I'll mark you down as probable."

A few minutes later, Jody called, and I slowed down. I was not going to talk to Jody while speeding.

"My brother tells me you're on your way to see him," he said. "I wish you'd mentioned it to me. Let's talk. What's going on?"

"Nothing for you to hear about."

"Ann, we've been too close for you to stonewall me."

"Have we?"

"I bet he told you the old torch is still burning. You and my brother. It's gross."

"I'm just taking a friend home from the hospital."

"Have you told him we were more or less together for longer than he knew?"

"More or less together. Lovely. No, Benjamin and I haven't discussed it."

"If Benjamin's still in the dark, it's because he wants to be. That's how he kept the peace. Don't mess with it. Whatever you're planning when you pick him up, don't tell him about us."

"Would that be honest? Or fair?"

"It would be helpful."

I was still trying to understand the code that let Jody lie to get out of the trouble his impulses created and yet think of himself as honest. I hoped some of the lies were meant to spare other people's feelings, especially mine.

"Let's say there's something between me and Benjamin. You're good at it—help me with my story. In the past couple of years, how often have you and me seen each other? How much sex have we had?"

"You want actual numbers?"

"I want to know how many lies you'd have me tell him, and how much truth, and what I should leave out," I told him. "I need to know the secrets I'd have to live with."

"I can't help you," he said, seemingly subdued by my tone.

"Okay. When I see how he reacts, I'll decide how much to tell him."

"Afterwards you'll tell me what you said?"

"Some of it."

"Here's the big question," he said. "When did we break up?"

"Good question. Just a couple of weeks ago, something almost happened, didn't it?"

"You mean after the boat pond? That was an almost?"
"Don't be coy," I said. "I turned you away at the door."
"Almost doesn't count."
"Not to you. It might to Benjamin."
"What are you going to tell him?" Jody asked.
"I'll see what feels right. You'll be the third to know."

CHAPTER TWELVE

BENJAMIN

Late afternoon on the next day, I was dressed and ready to leave when my fifty-something Jamaican nurse arrived with discharge papers on a clipboard.

"Have you arranged for someone to pick you up?" she said as she checked off boxes.

"She'll be here soon."

She raised an eyebrow. "She?"

I gave her Ann's name.

"That one," she said, writing.

"What about her?"

"You don't remember? You and the drugs. What a talker. Okay, we'll call her 'friend,'" she said, writing. "Whatever that means."

A half hour later, Ann arrived in sneakers and jeans and a lavender blouse, looking more attractive for the seeming lack of effort. I saw no hint of her response to my text messages—she was full of smiles and politeness—but then, my nurse had walked in with her.

The nurse handed me a large envelope full of paperwork. "Okay, friend," she said to Ann. "If you want to kick it up tonight and do things friends don't usually do, remember he's had trauma. There's drugs in him. He'll get tired. You can try if you want, but go easy."

Ann nodded.

I was unsure of my driving because of the drugs, so I was grateful that Ann drove slowly ahead of me to the rental-car dealership. With the car deposited, I slid in beside her in her BMW, and we headed south. It didn't help that she looked so appealing, her brown hair flecked with the gold of the bright afternoon, her sunglasses lending a trace of glamour.

As we sped onto the interstate, my impatience won out. "Ann, did what I wrote offend you? Was it off the wall?"

"A little. But you didn't offend me."

"We need to talk."

"Okay."

"You say you want to talk, but you don't do it."

She sighed. To my surprise, she settled below the speed limit and in the right-hand lane.

She said, "Let's start with the family, to get it out of the way. Ask your questions."

"All right. When you raised the payout while Charlie was in the hospital, who led the charge? Vivian? Nicole?"

"Nobody led. It was a consensus."

"So you and Melanie were as strong as Vivian and Nicole?"

"Since you think you know the answers," she said, "why ask the questions?"

"Are you stonewalling?"

"I guess it might seem that way."

The family discussion seemed to be finished. She switched on the radio. Like the one in her father's helicopter on the Early Fourth, it was tuned to hip-hop. I assumed Ann had played disc jockey both times.

The male singer's baritone was husky and defiant, the drum-drowned words something like "No more won'ts, no more can'ts. Booty don't like underpants. Bring it out, bitch, bring it out."

This drollery had unexpected appeal to Ann, who tapped a finger in rhythm on the steering wheel. I recalled Charlie rapping the controls of his helicopter.

With a twist of the dial, she softened the noise. "I have things to say. You may not like them, but I won't be comfortable if I don't do it."

"It's about you and me?"

"About me."

"Bring it out, bitch, bring it out" kept repeating as if the radio were stuck.

"Are you letting me down easy?" I asked. "If you're not interested, just tell me."

"For once in your life, Benjamin Gould, don't overthink it. Haven't you realized I'm sort of a spy? And so are you? Charlie says he's developing information. Everybody's on edge. What do you know about it?"

"If I knew anything—I'm not saying I do, I'm not saying I don't—I couldn't pass it along."

"I expected that. Another question: if the sibs tell our father what we want from him, are we supposed to believe he'll give it to us?"

"No comment."

"Is he testing us to see who fights him?"

"No comment."

"Is Theo still backing him?"

"No comment."

"Very helpful," she said. "My sisters told me to have sex with you to get you to talk. Would that be a good idea?"

"It could work."

She laughed. "Benjamin, just because I admit they want me to spy doesn't mean I'm not spying. It makes our situation very difficult. We may have too much history. Now we might have too much present."

"You could drop me off at the train station. I'd understand."

"For God's sake, don't give up so easily! I came all the way up here. I want to take you to dinner."

"Dinner," I said. "Fabulous."

"I made a reservation at an inn—for the night. I packed a bag. It's in the trunk."

"We have a room? You and me?"

"We'll eat dinner. We'll talk. Then we'll use the room. Or not, depending."

I was thrilled. I was worried. "Depending?"

"There's a lot more to talk about. Plus, the nurse said go easy."

From forbidden zone to what, I thought. Confusion?

At the wheel, Ann seemed to study the scenery. What was so fascinating about farms and forests, fields and barns?

"Fuck the nurse," I said.

Ann switched to public radio, where an obscure injustice was being broadcast sotto voce. Yet again I waited. Twenty minutes later, a modest sign bearing the Many Comforts logo of two cradling arms marked the entrance road to the inn. It curved through a sprawling property with several structures before leading to a main house that looked to be from the early nineteenth century.

After Ann parked the car and retrieved her overnight bag, we walked inside and followed a narrow corridor to the registration desk, where a young woman smiled forcefully and used our first names too often. When Ann reached for her credit card, I objected, but she rolled her eyes and paid. Kept man for a night. A first.

We climbed creaky old stairs carpeted top to bottom with a dusty runner. On the third and final floor, an oversized key admitted us to an ample room with angled ceilings under the gabled roof. The décor mixed vestigial quaintness with extensive remodeling. Most of the furnishings were fresh and up to date, except for tiny landscapes and framed cartoons dotting the pale-pink walls. A freestanding wooden beam braced a slanted segment of ceiling and gave me a moment of doubt about structural integrity.

Ann tossed her bag onto the four-poster bed, the gesture saying, "Not yet." We retreated to the large alcove that qualified the room as a suite. I sat beside her on the couch, close enough to touch. Thanks perhaps to drug residual, and with mild resistance from my light summer pants, I became aroused. How could I not? This was Ann, the best of the Cantlings. Ann of my fruitless hope. Ann of my waking dreams. Feeling red in the face—didn't she notice?—I said, "I only have the clothes I wore to Theo's. You might get tired of them."

"We'll be in New York by midmorning."

Thinking it couldn't be this easy but why the hell not, I reached out to rub her arm. She pushed my hand away and said, "Sorry. I'm tired and hungry—and not done talking. Be patient."

Part of the first floor had been renovated to form a dining room with pale-yellow plaster walls and a series of wide beams traversing the ceiling. At the far end, a row of handsome mullioned windows offered framed views of the property. All the tables were round, draped with white cloth, and crowned with a burning candle. The décor seemed to call for a genteel hush, and in any case, the dark carpet muted any upstart noise. Now and then came the muffled clatter of dish against dish. At this early hour, the place was largely empty.

While Ann drank wine, I sipped water per hospital instructions. Hungry and leery of being overheard in the quiet room, we sailed politely through appetizers and the main course. When the restaurant was full and noisier and dessert was on the way, she said, "Benjamin, I rehearsed so much. I hope I get this right. Whatever happens, I want us to still be friends and maybe more. I mean, I did reserve the room."

A waitress arrived, cupping a bowl of ice cream in each hand. After she set the ice cream down and left us, Ann spooned up a mouthful, swallowed, and said, "What Jody and I had, it never amounted to much. It only happened now and then and mainly because it was convenient."

"But why the big secret? You kept everybody guessing."

"At the start I wanted it secret because these things are usually over quickly, and I didn't want to explain. And yes, soon there was an ending. It looked like it was all behind us. But that ending, and the next, turned out to be interruptions."

"And you still kept it to yourselves."

"I didn't want my family to find out. You know how difficult they can be. If I'd been more open with them, they'd have never let me forget. Plus, I think one or two of my sisters would have been miserable."

"You kept me in the dark too."

She plunged her spoon deep into her ice cream, lifted it halfway to her lips, and held it there. "A couple of times, I came close to telling you. I guess I was afraid you'd disapprove. And I worried you'd be hurt or upset with Jody. I told myself you might know anyhow and you might want it this way, as a sort of open secret. But when I got your text messages the other day, I knew I had to tell you."

I was relieved. The only genuine surprise had been to hear it out loud, the only real change the loss of the last uncertainty. "Jody's an appealing guy," I said. "Lots of people are drawn to him. I don't like you tricking me, but I don't blame you that you two were together."

"Thank you for understanding." With her free hand, she brushed what might have been a tear from her eye. She said, "It lasted longer than it should have, longer than people think. I'm glad it's finally in the open."

I was excited.

"Let's finish here," I said. "We have business upstairs."

"Finally."

We paid—I insisted on using my credit card—and returned to the room. Beyond the small twin windows by the bed, the sun had set, leaving a faint orange glow in the sky. In wordless harmony, we pulled the curtains shut. She flung her overnight bag onto a chair, sat on the quilted comforter that covered the sheets, and motioned for me to sit alongside. I did as instructed. She leaned against me and looked at me with longing.

I should have been bursting with desire, ready to wrap her in my arms. But the moment felt perfunctory, like I was being called to do what was expected. All of a sudden, I was angry. There's nothing like truth to distract from a lie. Ann the straightforward? "It lasted longer than people think," she'd said. I told myself: Don't be a fool. Don't go there.

But I did.

"Tell me: exactly when did it end?"

She sighed. "I don't even know. There's no date you could mark in your calendar."

"I'll accept approximately."

"Okay, it probably ended a couple of years ago."

"Good. Great." My relief was genuine. "That's earlier than I expected. Why would Jody object to us? He can't rule out all the girls he's been with."

"Can we please stop talking about Jody?"

"You did trick me. It will take some getting used to."

"I think you tricked yourself," she said. "If you didn't sort of know already, why didn't you declare yourself? What was holding you back?"

"I guess, as long as I didn't ask how you felt about me, I could hope. I feel like I need to ask: why did it end when it did?"

"I was growing out of it. I was working, I had started graduate school. The charm of the perpetual adolescent wasn't good enough anymore."

"Two years," I said, unable to dispel my anger. "Far enough in the past so the slate is clean. Recent enough so it looks like you're admitting something. Two years."

"Ask Jody if you like."

"Jody? He can stare you in the eye and lie like a champion. You were supposed to be different."

"Benjamin, someday your brain will kill you."

"I'm just trying to understand. At the Early Fourth it looked like you and Jody were still close. Which means it's possible you might go back to him—or worse, start bouncing between us."

"If I were you, I wouldn't talk about the Early Fourth. Something happened between you and Melanie. Unlike you, I don't want the details. All that matters is I'm here."

For how long had I yearned to stop being Ann's intimate without being her lover? It was as if I had stood wobbling on a tightrope but never made it across—until now, when Ann slipped a hand between my thighs and rubbed my leg. But I felt no quickening of my breath, no stirring in the loins. Idiot. Loser. I pulled her toward me and with imitation passion kissed her lips.

Nothing. I thought: Keep going. The rest will follow.

I tried to unbutton her blouse. She brushed away my fumbling fingers, replaced them with hers, and motioned for me to undress. I had my polo shirt off when, incapable of much else, I stood up.

In a bra and unbuttoned jeans, she looked just right—and untouchable. "Benjamin, what's the matter?"

I shook my head. This had never happened to me before.

"Is it something I did?" she said.

"Maybe we shouldn't try this."

"You don't want to?"

"Of course I want to. But something—the drugs, I guess—is making it weird. And it's against the rules where I work."

"It's not the rules. You're upset about me and Jody."

"It's not that." Maybe it's the lies, I wanted to say: the new ones.

"Is there something I can do?" she said. "Like with my mouth?"

It seemed she'd been visiting my dreams. But I knew, with absolute certainty I knew, that she'd fail and leave me more humiliated.

"Not tonight, Ann."

"It happens," she said. "You just got out of the hospital. You need rest. Let's go to sleep."

I was angry again. "Ann, I don't believe it ended when you said. I believe it continued."

"Damn you! Whatever we hid, it wasn't to hurt you."

"Tonight's story, that it ended two years ago? That was to help me?"

"Would this be better? I don't know if I ever broke up with Jody, because you have to be together to break up. You wrote me that you loved me. With Jody, I'd have laughed if he said that. With you, it doesn't seem crazy. I came here to be with you. Don't use whatever you think I've done as an excuse to not try."

"There are excuses," I said, "and then there are reasons."

"This is your idea of love? I wish you'd never sent those messages. By the way, you're right. I had a date with Jody when he visited in the winter. It amounted to nothing. Then I played tennis with him on the Early Fourth. A couple of weeks ago, we had dinner."

"Every time you pull back the curtain, guess what? Another curtain."

"Damn you! It doesn't have to be like this. You're ruining everything. No! I shouldn't talk like that. I shouldn't get you more worked up. You're recovering. We're better than this. You need rest. We'll sort it out later." She reached for her overnight bag. "I saw a blanket in the closet. I'll be on the couch."

She stood and hurried to the closet. I wanted her to turn around and come back. And I wanted her not to—because I couldn't perform. Had I really never had this problem? Maybe once, a few years ago, when the girl started accusing me of things, and I changed my mind. Would I ever know why it had happened tonight? I lay down, rolled over, and eventually fell asleep.

At 1 a.m., I was awake. A night-light near the bathroom door supplied the sole illumination. Amid the darkness and quiet, my thoughts seemed to shout: It's one episode among hundreds. Well, maybe fifties. I can't let it happen again—but Ann's in the room, and she wants you. You feel something down there now. Wake her. Declare. No! You can't risk more arguing. Or more failure. Not now. Not yet.

Minutes later, I was asleep.

CHAPTER THIRTEEN

ANN

When I was much younger, I saw the Gould family as a refreshing antidote to mine: two ordinary boys with reasonable parents and destined to grow up nicely, though there were doubts about Jody. Then I came to admire them when they lost their parents and still kept it together. I believed they were very different from me, who lived in the cocoon of Cantling success and glamour and resented it. I felt different from my sisters, too. I couldn't toy with life the way they did, couldn't skate along the surface of things. I had seen too much, remembered too much, knew too much. It was weird that I, who seemed to get along with all the Cantlings and Goulds, felt outside of it all.

Now, of course, much of what I'd believed about Cantlings and Goulds might have flown out the tiny window that brought morning light onto the quaint and silent scene of our debacle. The Goulds, the neighbors who met the world on equal terms, who didn't condescend and didn't need to, might be just as screwed up as the Cantlings.

Benjamin was asleep. Good. He needed it, and it gave me the opportunity I'd been looking for. In my pajamas, I rose carefully from the couch and lifted my phone from a tiny table nearby. As I tiptoed by the bed, he stirred but stayed asleep. In the closet I found and donned a bathrobe embroidered with the Many Comforts logo. When I reached the bathroom, I locked the door and sent Jody a short message.

"I TOLD HIM: ONE REAL DATE IN THE WINTER. THEN TENNIS. THEN DINNER AT THE BOAT POND."

I didn't expect to hear back for hours. Instead he answered immediately. "YOU LEFT OUT THE ALMOST AFTER THE DINNER?"

I thought: Is this a new Jody, who wants precision, who'd lie awake tonight and worry?

I muted the ringer so Benjamin wouldn't hear and wrote back: "YES. NO MENTION OF ALMOST. BTW I HATE INTRIGUE."

He persisted: "I HATE IT 2, BUT HERE WE ARE. YOU TOLD HIM THERE'S NO HOPE FOR YOU AND ME?"

"RIGHT. NO HOPE."

He replied: "HAVE WE BEEN IN TOUCH THIS MORNING?"

"No."

"ARE WE GOING 2 B SOON?"

"No," I replied.

"GENERALLY, HOW DID IT GO?"

"NONE OF YOUR BUSINESS. DELETE THIS STRING."

CHAPTER FOURTEEN

BENJAMIN

When I woke up in the morning, Ann was robed in inn-supplied terry cloth. Leaning over the couch she'd slept on, she clasped an arm to her chest so that the thick lapels didn't flop open and expose the firm breasts I'd pictured too many times. A sloganeering seamstress had stitched into a couch throw pillow MANY COMFORTS. FEW INTRUSIONS. Irony was everywhere. I would try again, but not this morning.

Her overnight bag rested on the couch. She lifted out a folded white material that, after a flick of her wrist, unraveled as a blouse. Without looking up, she said, "Are you okay? Did you sleep well?"

How did she know I was awake? "Good enough."

She turned to me, hugging the robe tighter to her chest. "I want to say, I think last night was my fault."

"Your fault?"

"The nurse was right. You need time to recover. I shouldn't have pushed it."

"Ann, you didn't do anything wrong."

"I'm not sure. Why don't we see what happens? Let's get together again in a few days—if you'd like."

"Of course I want to see you. It will get better between us," I said.

"Good. This is nowhere near over."

It was clear that her priority, and mine, was to drive back to New York without further damage. In the room, she kept moving. She soon had her hair combed, her teeth brushed, and her clothes in a bag and was ready to walk downstairs. As I closed the door behind us, my humiliation was complete. Even if my other relationships had reliably self-destructed, at least there'd been sex. Had last night's failure transformed Ann, once the girl of choice, into the option least likely? What would I be without the dream of Ann? It was the meds. The fucking meds.

She kept chatting all the way to the dining room, which had been rearranged for breakfast. A lavish buffet promised to spare us server delays. A pair of waitresses glided through, wielding coffee pots. Ann avoided silences and kept the talk innocuous. Thirty minutes later, with the latest flag of truce still flying, we started toward New York. Ann's driving seemed too aggressive, but in my discouraged state I lacked the will to try to slow her down. For further diversion, she turned again to radio music.

Impatient with the unreal mood, eager to stop revolving on last night's nonevent, I tapped out a text message to Al Byrne: "SORRY. CANNOT IN GOOD CONSCIENCE STAY ON CASE. WANTED TO LET YOU KNOW ASAP SO U CAN LOOK FOR REPLACEMENT. DEEP APOLOGIES. WILL EXPLAIN LATER."

Byrne replied instantly with a phone call I couldn't accept. Then came the text message.

"NO TO YOUR REQUEST. CALL ME. EXPLAIN."

"NOT ALONE," I wrote back. "CANTLING DAUGHTER ANN WITH ME."

Ding. Another text. "UNDERSTOOD. KEEP TEXTING. WHAT HAPPENED?"

Feeling sheepish, as if I were gossiping about Ann in her presence, I wrote: "Something came over me. Broke rules. Made move on Ann. Sorry . . ." I'd aimed for "generation text-me" ellipsis and a buddy-buddy tone.

Moments later, another ding. "Was move successful?"

"No."

"Anything close? Hand job? Oral either way?"

Ann interrupted. "That's a lot of texting. What's going on?"

"Office stuff. I have reports to edit."

"You just got out of the hospital. They won't leave you alone?"

"Tell that to my boss."

"You can talk on the phone if you like. I'll turn the music off."

"I can't let you hear," I said. "Client confidentiality."

I wrote to Al. "No hand job. No oral. Nothing."

He wrote back: "IOW dumb move no payoff."

"Yup."

A minute passed without dings from Byrne. I had made my pitch to him. Was he pondering it? A reassignment to old tasks would be welcome. There'd be no more apologizing to Cantlings and no more failing with sisters. I'd revel in cutting and revising, in clarifying ambiguities. I'd scrimp and save and somehow keep the house.

Ding. "Seems like u sabotage project and ask for your old job back. Not a good look. B careful. U may be hanging by thread."

Now it was I who pondered, rather panicky, the lack of a paying job. I tapped out a reply that didn't quite read like begging: "No sabotage. Just horny." Too flip, I decided—and deleted it.

Ding. An unusually expansive message spread down the screen. "If you had fucked her, you'd have an airtight case. But the rules say no sexual contact, they don't say no trying. A loophole. Needs tightening. A job for a stickler—who might that be? FTR what is sexual contact these days? A kiss on the forehead? A slap on the butt? Worth thinking about. In sum: EYHO."

Essentially You Have Outmaneuvered? Eagerly You Head Offstage? I tapped, "EYHO?"

"Eat Your Heart Out. You're still on the case."

I wrote, "Is there in fact a rule against sex with a principal in an investigation?"

"Of course there's a rule. Our clients need to know we have standards. But who the hell follows the rule? Point him out. I'll give him a medal."

I wrote from the last ditch, "Very awkward if CC learns I made move."

"No. Slight misunderstanding between u and girl. To b clear, did current sister tell u anything about what might have happened in hospital?"

"She claims to know nothing."

"We believe her?"

I glanced at Ann driving, muttered a curse, and answered carefully. "I think she's too attached to her sisters to let herself know nothing. If you ask me, she's heard things. Suspects things. No one's being very honest."

"Including sister M? She called the office again. Still trying to see me. Other than family money, what does she want?"

"I don't know."

"Will she tell us the truth?"

"I doubt it. No one else is."

"Welcome to the human race. You, Benjamin, will talk to Ann again. Eventually. Stay away for a while. Try a different sister. Make no move. In future, learn women. Ciao."

I looked up from the phone and asked Ann, "What are you going to tell your sisters about our trip?"

"I didn't get anything out of you. You were too tired to go to dinner. I drove you straight home."

"Shouldn't you offer them something—a tidbit?"

"Benjamin, I always thought you were a straight arrow. What turned you into Machiavelli?"

"Cantlings," I wanted to say.

After we agreed not to talk again for a few days while I recuperated, Ann dropped me off at my apartment. It was midmorning, but I was exhausted and fell into bed with all my clothes on. When I awoke an hour later from deep sleep, the phone in my pants pocket was ringing with a call from Vivian Cantling. I left her for voicemail. I thought: Of course I'd hear from Vivian.

Jody and I used to call her "the bothered princess," for she seemed to be near the center of every Cantling fray. She recorded no message for me. After I changed clothes and showered, I took calming breaths and called her back.

"I already spoke with Ann," she said. "I hear you two had quite an experience."

I didn't believe Ann would tell Vivian anything useful about last night. "It was stimulating," I said.

"Would you do it again?"

"You bet."

"What part?"

"All of it."

"Benjamin, are you trying to not tell me what happened?"

"Yes."

"Have you ever thought about this?" she said. "Are you sure you had the right sister?"

The purr in Vivian's voice suggested she sensed a weakness. I wondered if she was stepping in as fallback seducer after Ann had told her nothing. Vivian imagined herself, by reason of brains and seniority, the future head of the family.

"Why are you calling me?" I said.

"It's simple. If we're going to avoid power plays and make the right decisions, this family needs information. Get on board. Help us, and we can help you—any number of ways."

"How would I help you?"

"First, you need to talk to me. Which you're supposed to do anyhow. Come see me in Bedford. It's only an hour's drive. Do you have hiking boots?"

"I think so." I recalled a dusty pair deep in my closet, the residue of some doomed clinches with a lover of trails.

"Bring them. And wear long pants. Jeans will be fine."

Ann and I kept our agreement for a time-out, so Vivian was the next Cantling I saw. Three days later and fully recovered, donning a baseball cap and polo shirt and the recommended boots and jeans, I drove north to meet her at the New Age Eatery in Bedford. The restaurant interior proved to be shiny white, its lighting bright and vivid and its seating spacious. A hostess led me to a table and handed me a menu printed on typing paper, featuring exotic vegetables precisely cooked—the word "artisanal" preceded most of the nouns—and several varieties of fish. An anemic selection of meats was strictly back page.

Vivian arrived in riding clothes and carrying a crop, which she leaned against the table as she sat. Apart from the mini backpack she hung from her chair, her choice of clothes seemed odd for a hike. "I'm calm about it," she told me. "But something weird happened yesterday. Can I trust you with it?"

"I don't know. I work for Charlie."

"Just so you understand: if I tell you and you pass it along to him, I'll deny everything. You won't look good. The point is, Theo called me. Theo! We've never gotten along. He's too mean and pretentious. Why did he call? Do you know anything about it?"

"Not really. I couldn't discuss it if I did."

"He told me that because he saved you, you'd given him time to sort things out and explain himself to Charlie. Very decent of you. Even Charlie might understand." Despite her attempt at self-control, sarcasm had leaked out. "When Theo called, he started out friendly. He reminisced about old times, like they were so wonderful. In the interest of family harmony, I tried to remember that some of it was okay. Then he launched. 'Viv, would you go against Charlie? The other sisters, Viv. What do they think about the family trust?' I couldn't tell him what I really believed—which was that a twisted version of everything I say will go right back to Charlie. So I told him, very carefully, that I'd be willing to keep talking to Charlie about raising the payouts, but Charlie made us what we are, and I'd never vote to remove him. And if something other than that got to Charlie, I knew who to blame.

"He said, 'I'm not running to Charlie with anything. But nothing is forever, not even Charlie. Maybe, Viv, we should all be open to changes in how the family trust is run.' I mean, he was Vivving me like I've never been Vivved before. 'Viv, I'm not saying I'd vote against Dad. That would be very hard. But, Viv, I could discuss with him what it means to be an adult and how our responsibilities are going up. Viv, with Charlie about to do a big deal, maybe the trust should make special distributions now to help us out. Then we could take some time to think about the long term.' He even mumbled something about half-shares for kids. I was thinking: Out of the blue, Theo dangles stuff that could affect our whole family's future? Tell me, Benjamin, what is going on?"

"I don't know."

"Yes, I forgot. You know nothing. I told myself it's possible that Theo has turned, though not very likely. I didn't encourage him. I mean, it would take an awful lot for me to sign on with him. He told me he'd get back to me in a day or two. So I'm waiting. And the more I wait, the madder I get. I've learned you can never count on anything with this family. As weird as it seems, it's possible he might be willing to vote Charlie out. More likely, he's trying to find ammunition to use against me with Charlie."

"Even if I knew what Theo was doing, I couldn't tell you."

She picked up the riding crop. "Tell me, isn't cooperation supposed to be a two-way thing? If you want information for Charlie, don't you need to give me something in return?" She waved the crop. "Theo might have saved your life, but that's old news. I could give you sex. Now."

"Are you making an offer?"

"Do you want me to? Ann isn't talking, but it seems like it didn't happen between you two. Which, if I was serious, which I am, would make you fair game."

"Please stop the teasing," I said, losing patience.

"I'm not teasing."

I focused on my menu. Vivian said, "It's not a choice for me. I can't eat flesh. That's why I like United Vegetarians so much. I could give them every penny I have. Charlie and Tessa want to live like royalty. Me, I want to relieve the pain and suffering of living things. Check out the rutabaga. Mashed to perfection, they promise. I just love the taste of roots," she said, restarting the tease.

I ignored it. A waitress arrived to take our orders. Vivian ordered the day's vegetarian special, and I chose a hamburger. No plate of vegetables had ever filled me up.

With the waitress gone, Vivian said. "My mother, Ann, Theo—they tell me they can't get anything from you. It's like you're rubbing our noses in your knowledge and our ignorance. I'm just proposing a simple exchange: bodily fluids for information."

If proof of manhood has to come through Vivian, I told myself, would that be so terrible? Byrne would figure out how to not fire me.

But I didn't believe her.

I said, "I'll think about it."

"Poor boy. I frightened you. Sorry."

Vivian's vegetables arrived looking fresh. My hamburger proved to be nicely charred, and the side of ketchup appeared artisanal. I took a bite, swallowed, and said, "Where are we hiking?"

"I asked you to bring hiking boots. I didn't say how we'd use them. You helicoptered with Charlie, you did bees with Theo. If you want to learn about me, you need to discover riding."

"Me? Riding?" The bite of hamburger dried up in my mouth. "I've never done any."

"Of course you haven't. But if we're to develop some understanding, if you're going to learn what I'm about, you can feel what it's like to sit on a moving horse, to hold a large animal between your thighs, and why it means so much to me. Otherwise you can finish your disgusting meal, get in your car, and go back to New York. I'll tell Charlie you were snotty and rude and I refused to cooperate."

"How safe is riding?"

"Calm down. Everybody has to start somewhere. These horses know their job. And they're too worn out to pose a threat to your delicate bones. Are you ready to ride?" she said. "A horse, that is. And then riding of another kind."

I'd never been much drawn to Vivian. She was nearly four years older and had never shown interest. Yes, I wanted sex with someone. Anyone, really. But Vivian would tell Ann, and it would hurt her.

"Sorry," I said. "Sex with a principal in an investigation would get me fired."

"Or promoted, if it helped you learn a lot."

"Vivian, stop teasing."

"Okay. I promise."

"I'll ride, but only the horse."

We drove separately to the riding academy, where the gravel parking lot was nearly empty on the weekday afternoon. Vivian emerged from her car with her helmet and backpack in hand and her crop jammed under her arm. In the warm afternoon, we headed toward a red barn, beyond which long white fences outlined grassy fields. With the tang of horse manure in the air, Vivian began to amble along like a cowboy, loosening her shoulders, rolling her hips. It passed for relaxation.

The barn proved to be dark, gloomy, humid, and fetid. Immediately inside the entrance were shovels, saddles, harnesses, and other implements hanging from the walls and several long wooden shelves supporting rows of helmets. When Vivian reached up to a shelf to find me a helmet, her clothes stretched tighter against her body. She was trimmer than Ann, possibly in better shape, with fewer curves.

I replaced my baseball cap with the helmet she'd chosen. After I signed a waiver, we proceeded down an aisle extending nave-like through the middle of the barn. On each flank were stalls containing lugubrious horses that eyed us with minimal interest. We turned at what would have been the transept, which led us out to a corral where a lone stable hand gripped the reins of a saddled, sleek-looking horse. In a field beyond, two riders aimed a pair of sluggish chargers toward the motionless woods.

Vivian stopped and breathed deep. "I love horses. I'm good with them, and they respond accordingly," she said. "People tell me if I practiced jumping, I could turn professional."

"There are professionals? There's money in it?"

"I don't care about money."

She handed me her backpack. It seemed to be nearly empty. Then she approached the saddled horse, nodded toward the stable hand, and with one hand took the reins from him. With the other she gripped the front of the saddle, shoved her left foot into the stirrup, and boosted herself up. Straight backed and balanced, she led the horse away at a slow walk that gradually increased to what might have been a trot. Soon after came a canter. In a minute or two, Vivian and steed were skimming in harmony along the edges of the corral.

She slowed the horse down, stopped where I stood, and dismounted with ease. It was difficult to reconcile her explosive nature with her skilled and disciplined riding. I wondered if she did indeed need the riding. It seemed to soothe her.

"Are you starting to get it?" she said, taking her backpack from me. She slid her arms into the straps and threw it over her back again. "I've worked hard. I've practiced."

"I believe you."

"Tim," she told the stable hand, "saddle up Prancer and bring him out. My friend wants to ride." Tim nodded and led Vivian's horse into the barn.

"Are you ready?" she said.

"Tell me about Prancer?"

"Stop worrying. You can do this. He's a gelding. He's the most docile horse you'll ever see." She was impatient again. "You'll feel like you're sitting on a pillow."

A few minutes later, Tim approached with a gray gelding in tow. Because of his altered anatomy, I felt some sorry kinship. Like me, he'd been pressed into Cantling service. Like me, his essentials weren't working. I thought I saw in him a horrid vision of my future: numbness in his eyes, weariness beyond measure, nonexistence. At least he might be safe to ride.

Vivian motioned for me to stand beside her, to the left of the gelding and near his head. "Take these with your left hand," she said, passing the reins to me. "Now boost yourself up like I did."

I managed it and in moments sat in the saddle. Too nervous to celebrate, I brushed sweat from my eyes.

Vivian walked ahead, guide rope in hand, and slow-walked us just inside the corral fence. In every direction I sensed motion. Pitch. Yaw. Bounce. Shake.

"You need to sit up and stay relaxed," she said. "It will keep Prancer relaxed—so he won't bolt."

I straightened my back. "Prancer might bolt?"

"Even Prancer has his breaking point."

"You could control him, couldn't you?"

"That's a big animal beneath you. He may have slowed down, but he was born to run. If he tried to speed away, you'd be on your own."

"You're holding the rope," I said. "What would happen to you?"

"A hard pull from me releases it. There's a panic hook. Don't worry. It's very unlikely."

Prancer snorted and shook his head. "Loved the ride," I said. "Now get me down."

"For God's sake, Benjamin, where's your sense of humor? And use a soothing tone."

I was sweating more and more. I took deep breaths.

"I'll let you down right now," she said, "if you'll explain something. You went to see Theo, and a day or two later he called me about the trust. That's no coincidence. You still won't tell me what's going on?"

"I wish I could help."

"Damn you! You have some guts after all. I like it. Do you see the gate in the next section of fence? We could pass through and take a short walk in the woods. There's an old shed nobody ever goes to. You might enjoy what would happen there."

I was losing patience. "Stop the teasing. I'm happy in the corral."

"When you think about it, all I have to do is open the gate, hit Prancer a couple of times, and off you go. How long would you last in the saddle?"

"That's not funny."

"Are you sure you don't want to go to the shed? You're red in the face. You're breathing hard."

"From the ride."

"Right. You're having so much sex that you don't need me."

"Vivian, if it means so much to you, I'll do it."

"Go to hell. Even if you don't do anything with me, I could still tell my sisters you did. You might as well get something out of it."

I realized that because of who they are, Cantlings feel entitled to tease, to flirt with sex and other adventures. To them it's all largely meaningless. On the other hand, if Vivian's offer were somehow genuine, was I in any position to turn it down?

It seemed I communicated my weakening to the horse, who snorted and flicked his ears.

"I forgot," Vivian said. "You're not interested."

We had passed the gate and continued around the next corner when a cell phone rang. I was startled more so than the horse, who seemed not to notice. Passing the lead rope from one hand to the other, Vivian managed to wriggle out of the backpack straps and extract a phone. The ringing stopped.

"Theo again," she said, looking at the screen. "Why can't he go away? I'm never going to trust him." The ringing stopped. She had routed the call to voicemail.

She let Theo's message play out loud. "Viv, we need to talk. Call me."

"God, he's annoying," she said as she returned the phone to the bag, which she slung over one shoulder. "That's what he's good at—that and wasting money. It seems my brother wants more now. Either he gets it by getting tighter with Charlie, or he helps us vote Charlie out."

Walking ahead, she seemed to have half forgotten I was sitting on Prancer behind her. The horse had to be aware of Vivian's agitation. He snorted.

"Maybe my brother's showing his true colors. If he wants money so much, maybe he actually tried to smother Charlie. Whoever did it will never admit it—they don't know how Charlie will react. My father may look at the perp as a hero, a villain, or whatever. The situation reminds Charlie of his weakness every day. He hates that.

"Think about this," she said, suddenly talking to me. "Maybe I was the one who tried to smother Charlie. There's nothing worse than cheap rich parents. The fruit's hanging there on the tree, but you try and try and can't quite reach it. That makes you a wealthy beggar. How do you think that feels? Thanks to Charlie, I now have money issues. Me! A Cantling! If I could get just a tiny bit of support from him, I'd be fine. Do you think there's a chance?"

"I don't know."

"Right. For years I did stuff for everybody and never got anything for it. At trustee meetings, when one of my sisters or Theo said something stupid, I was the one who shut them down and rallied the family. Without me, Charlie couldn't have done half the things he did. Then, all of a sudden he was dying. I had to think seriously about my future. I wasn't twenty-three anymore. I needed stability, a decent house. The perfect property came on the market, with a lot of land and a horse barn already there. They were asking too much for it, but you don't see properties like that very often. I thought: Fuck it. I'm buying."

Although her right hand still gripped the guide rope, her left kept jabbing at the sky. Prancer's ears twitched. I thought: Is it my imagination, or has our pace picked up?

"I signed the contract," she said. "The down payment cost me everything I had, but my income from the company qualified me for a mortgage. Then Charlie came back, and the first thing he does is cut our eight hundred thousand to six. And then to four. And he blusters about cutting the rest."

"Does Charlie know how much you need?"

"I explained it to him very calmly. His answer? 'It's for your own good. You have to learn to fend for yourself.' You can't treat people like that—unless, of course, you're my father. The bank told me if the payout stays where it is, even with all my other expenses pared way down, I'll no longer qualify for the mortgage. I'll lose the down payment. Flushed down the toilet by Charlie Cantling! I'm too grown up to be treated like an irresponsible child. It's not decent! It's not fair! I want what's mine from the trust and from Cantling Market Research. So yes, I'm ready to vote him out."

For the first time, I felt real affinity for Vivian. Her vulnerability about simply wanting a house reminded me that I, too, wanted a house—the one I already had. Had we bonded? Were we heading for the shed?

Her phone rang again. She lifted it from her backpack. "Theo again," she said. "I guess, as long as he has a vote, I have to be nice to him. Benjamin, I want you to listen. You should hear what I'm up against."

With the hand holding the lead rope, she tapped the phone. Theo's voice rang out. "Come on, Viv. Stop ducking me. It's important. Take the call!"

"He's so damn self-centered!" Vivian said, growing more agitated. "Like I have to be ducking? Like I can't be legitimately busy? I shouldn't have talked to him the last time. It will all go right to Charlie."

"Vivian! Answer the phone!" Theo said.

"Listen to him—the prince of idiots!"

"Maybe now isn't the time," I said. "We don't want to rattle Prancer."

"Nothing rattles this horse. I want you to hear this. I want you to see what I'm up against." She dialed, held the phone in front of her, and said, "Theo, I'm in the middle of something, but okay. Family comes first. Let's talk."

"Great," Theo said. "Communication is everything."

"Here's my question," Vivian said to him. "How am I supposed to trust you, how can I not tell you to go fuck yourself, when it's abundantly clear you've been ripping us off for years?"

"What's this about?" he said.

"It's about you being a pig! For years Tessa's been shoveling family money out the door to prop you up, money that belongs to everybody. It's a disgrace!"

"It's not true!"

"Go ahead. Keep denying it. Nobody believes you. How else could you keep making all that horrible honey?"

"How do you know I'm not making a profit?"

"Making a profit? You and Tessa are flushing money down a huge toilet!"

"All right," he said. "Full disclosure. There may have been some problems with the honey, every start-up has its issues, but I've solved them. It's smooth sailing from here. And yes, Tessa's lent me capital now and then. But it's not propping me up. I've started a business. She's invested to help me build it."

"Why did you keep her so-called investment secret?"

"We didn't want to complicate things. We thought people might misunderstand."

"Do you have paperwork? Does Tessa get a percentage?"

"We have a handshake agreement. Tessa insisted that the whole family will share in the future profits."

"Fuck your future profits! That money belongs to the family. You've been stealing!"

"It's Tessa's money. She can do with it what she likes. Don't you do what you want with your money? What about your horses?"

"Am I tricking anybody? Am I stealing? Fuck you!"

Prancer seemed to shudder. I said, "Vivian, please get off the phone!"

"Did I hear somebody?" Theo said. "Who's there?"

"Nobody. A stable hand. I'm at the barn." She looked up at me and mouthed, "Shut the fuck up!"

I'd had enough of the Cantlings. I thought: Skimming along the surface of things, they might imagine their little games are innocuous.

I mouthed back, "Get me off this horse!"

She stopped walking but otherwise ignored me. "You're a businessman?" she shouted into the phone. "Your honey operation's gonna make money? Fuck you!"

"What about Charlie and all the sisters?" Theo said. "What about the jewels he bought for you? Graduation presents. Birthdays. Every now and then a sports car. Was that stealing? Did I bellyache about it?"

"Once he bought me a car! Once!"

"Vivian! Get me off this horse!"

"I've been trying to do something productive," Theo said. "With you people it's just spend, spend, spend."

"How can you compare Charlie's little gifts to what Tessa's given you? It's gotta be millions!"

"You know this because . . . ?"

"I know what a loser you are."

"Fuck you, Vivian!"

"Fuck you!"

They disconnected. Still holding the phone, Vivian started to lead the horse again in a slow walk. Prancer settled down and seemed to be the calmest among us. We were approaching the gate that would take us to the woods. As Vivian reached for the metal latch holding the gate in place, I saw her cheek muscles twitching. What it might lack in passion, it would make up for in symmetry. Ann and my brother. Ann's sister and me.

Her hand gripped the latch but didn't flip it. "I must be out of my mind," she muttered. "Why fuck the brother when he just wouldn't care?"

"Whose brother?" I said.

"Are you really that thick?" She glared up at me, and I realized her rage at Theo was bursting in other directions. Her eyes were moist.

"This spring, after three years, out of the blue he calls me. He must have been in a dry period. He asks me how I am. Like I didn't know what he wants! That boy is about one thing and one thing only. I called him every name I could think of. He took it, he's like that, and by the time I was done, I was tempted. Damn if he doesn't know his effect on women. Listen to me. He's a waste of effort, an overgrown child, and I can't get over him."

"You're talking about Jody. You lied to me. You two did have something. Did you want to get back at him through me?" I remembered the Early Fourth and Vivian pointing her flashlight away from Jody and toward me.

"It's sex, Benjamin. Does it really need reasons? Okay, yes, I wanted to compromise you with Charlie. Yes, I wanted to get back at your brother! So what?" She started to cry. One of her hands still gripped the latch.

I was amazed to see Vivian brought low, her face streaked with tears. Had she encouraged Ann with me to steer her sister away from Jody? That would mean Vivian believed there was still something between Ann and my brother. Were the Cantling sisters cunning enough for that? I felt way out of my depth.

Vivian's phone dinged with a text message. She looked down at the screen. "I don't believe this. It's from Theo."

"What does it say?"

She read: "Vivian, now that we've cleared the air, I think we can work together." She looked up. "That's not Theo! It doesn't sound anything like him. It's much too clever. What is going on?"

I thought: Whitney. I said: "I don't know."

She released the latch on the gate. A sniff and a shrug seemed to signal she'd regained a scrap of composure. "You and I will not be fucking today," she said. She started to lead Prancer across the corral and toward the barn. "I was never going to let it happen."

Cantlings, I realized, acted as if their license to flirt with sex and danger was a sign of their status, a perk. But their attraction to risk came with a cost. The joke was on them.

I said, "Neither was I."

CHAPTER FIFTEEN

BENJAMIN

Phil Weller had sent me more emails from Cantling Market Research, but once again they'd been of little use. I had made barely any progress. A week went by before Charlie Cantling called me at the office.

"Benjamin, are you going to your house this weekend?"

"I planned to."

"Will your brother be there?"

"He usually is."

"Did you know I heard from him?" Cantling asked.

"No. What did he want?"

"Let's say it was Christmas in August. I'll explain when I see you. There's a meeting on Saturday, 10 a.m. You should be there."

"It works for me," I said, suggesting I had a choice.

"We'll put everything we've learned on the table. Theo will be there. Tessa. Whitney. Phil Weller. We can sort out all sorts of things."

This seemed unlikely, but I said, "Have you told Al Byrne?"

"We will—when the time is right."

As soon as we disconnected, I called my brother. "Cantling says you got in touch with him. Why would you do that?"

"I haven't said two words to Charlie Cantling."

"Have you said one?"

"Not really."

"He told me something about you and Christmas. What's he talking about?"

"Beats me. The guy used to be half-crazy," Jody said. "Now he's full-on."

When I stepped off the train in Stonefield on Friday evening, the sun was already spreading orange light in the western sky. I was hungry, and knowing Jody's knack for emptying a kitchen, I took a cab to our local food store and loaded up with as much as I could carry. I reached our house, found I was alone, and ate a late dinner.

My brother arrived at eleven, smelling of taverns.

"You'll be happy to know," I said, "Cantling tells me he's sorted out all kinds of things. I might be able to get out of this soon."

"Don't count on it. If Cantling says to look up, you should look down. If he says something's ending, it's just beginning. Deal with an asshole, get shat on." From the refrigerator, Jody took some of the food I'd bought and the beer he'd stocked and sat down to eat.

Minutes later, he lifted a forefinger to his lips. "Shhh! Listen!" I heard the faint grind of a distant engine. "The helicopter! He'll be on top of us any minute. I guess he didn't get the message last week."

"What message?"

"You'll see."

Jody ran to the front door, flipped a switch for the patio electricity, and hurried outside. Baffled, I followed and found him gazing west into the night sky, where the low-flying helicopter floated toward us. Spread out before us on a section of our lawn, strings of vivacious little lights blinked bright yellow.

"Why Christmas lights?" I shouted above the din. "It's August! We're Jews!"

"They were easy to get hold of!" Jody shouted back. "Cantling's on a charm offensive. He's been spreading the donations. The churches are thrilled. And the hospital. Even the baseball team! He doesn't want anybody to stop him from flying. The cops won't let me shoot flares. Well, I have other tricks!"

Cantling's helicopter approached, the whoosh of blades mixing with the hum of the engine. When the chopper reached our property, it hovered and pivoted to examine Jody's display.

My brother shouted to the sky, "You getting the message, Charlie?"

"What message?" I asked Jody.

"You're the editor! Figure it out!"

I stepped off the patio and walked along the strings of lights, trying to read them. Jody had tapped thirty gardening stakes into our lawn and wound the lights among them so that the installation flashed, in four-foot letters, the word "Asshole." It was just like Jody to be deft in his pranking. The doubled "S" struck me as especially challenging.

"Where'd you get the lights?" I shouted.

"I borrowed them! From a good Christian!"

"Did he know your plan?"

"Not in detail."

"Hey, moron, I have your handiwork on video," Cantling's voice boomed from the helicopter. "There are laws against profanity. And harassment. You'll love prison."

Jody waved toward the helicopter. It started to rise and nose over toward the Cantling house. I told my brother, "You're awfully casual about being on video."

"He won't show it to anybody. It's not consistent with the Cantling brand." With the helicopter moving away, light from the installation pulsed on Jody's face.

The helicopter settled onto the Cantling property, a soft plume of light arising where the machine had disappeared. For several minutes, we listened to crickets while we waited for Cantling to walk over for a visit. There was no sign of him.

"He just doesn't give a shit," Jody said gloomily. "He'll just keep flying."

Jody switched off the Christmas lights, and we returned to the living room, locking the patio door behind us. "The more he annoys us, the happier he gets," Jody said.

"So don't fight him. It's a waste of energy. Do something constructive."

"For once in your life, you may be right," Jody said. "We're going downhill, and I'm not helping much."

I took a chance. "Are you broke again?"

"You could say that. My Taurus died last week. I picked out a replacement, something six years old so I wouldn't need another one next summer. When the dealer rated me for a loan, they practically threw me out. So now I'm driving a borrowed piece of junk. What am I gonna do? Ask you for more money? Swear one more time I'll pay you back so you can tell me not to worry? I'm not happy, bro. I'm not pulling my weight."

"Are you selling any houses?"

"Not really. I don't have patience. I want to scream at the clients: 'Buy a house already. I need the cash.' And the deals don't close."

I'd heard some of this before from Jody. I wondered if it would stick.

He said, "I ask myself what women see in me. I don't make a living. I don't have much of what they call prospects. I live off my brother."

I took a chance. "Is that what ruined things with Ann?"

"Everything ruined things with Ann."

"Why did you lie about it for so long?"

"We didn't lie," he said. "You didn't ask."

I pressed on into uncharted territory. "Tell me, when did it stop?"

"It stopped, bro. That's all that counts. It's over."

"How over?"

"I get it: you're finally making your move. Fair enough. It was over whenever you want it to be. Last week. Last month. Last year. Take your pick. Do what you want—but don't expect anything from me. I don't want to talk about it!"

With long, angry strides, he rushed out of the house. His borrowed car managed to start, followed by an angry spew of gravel. Back to the bars and the chase, I thought. Will he ever get tired of it?

I'd been firm with Vivian, and I had dared to probe my brother. It seemed that neither was used to me asserting myself. They'd expected my usual caution, my adjusting nature. I couldn't claim any great success thus far. My efforts had mainly yielded pushback. But I was resolved to keep trying.

I awoke Saturday morning to rain blowing against the windows that faced north and east. I dressed with care in gray trousers and a white shirt and blazer. Downstairs, I immediately encountered a drip from the top of a dining room window often caulked and due to be replaced. I found a bucket to catch the drip and old towels to wipe the floor, and I wondered if our effort to hang on to the house was a perversion of common sense—a sweet impossibility.

The Cantling assignment wasn't a total loss. I had learned what I could, withstood onslaughts, and developed facts as instructed. I had a plan for handling Charlie today. If he told me he didn't think much of what I'd accomplished, I'd accept his comments without rancor and move on. Overall I believed Byrne would agree that I had acquitted myself well on unfamiliar turf. If Charlie couldn't appreciate that, it would be his failing, not mine.

I found another leak, wiped the floor beneath the drip, and positioned a large pot to catch it. Then I ate breakfast and headed to the Cantlings' via the tennis court path. Wherever the wind found an opening to blow through, I fought to hold my umbrella upright—for

I had underestimated the strength of the rain, which soaked my black trousers from the knees down. Low points on the path accumulated water and muddied my shoes. When the Cantling property opened up ahead, I saw wind pushing waves onshore. Sheets of water splashed into the slate-gray sea. I swung around to the front where, shielded from the worst of the wind, the helicopter looked marooned in the pelting rain. Three cars sat in a parking area around the side of the house.

Theo opened the front door for me and summoned me in. I steeled myself for his jousting and insults as I closed my umbrella and left it outside. Reluctant to sully the floors, I knelt in the foyer to remove my muddy shoes. Above me, Theo cocked his head and strained to hear a dialogue from another room, but echoes in the minimally furnished house blurred the words.

In a low voice he said, "Whitney's holding her own and then some." I wrestled one shoe off, set it near the door, and started on the other. "Amazing, isn't she? She's in there with my parents, firm and strong and not scared at all. Doesn't kowtow, doesn't fall apart. It's a fact, Gould. When you insisted we tell Charlie about the pregnancy, you helped us." He slapped me affectionately on the shoulder, then led me shoeless down a hallway and through open double doors to the living room.

With a lifetime of reasons to doubt the likelihood of Cantling peace, I wished I were at home coping with leaks. Subdued voices briefly softened my suspicion and gave me hope that we all might escape unscathed. Soon the voices outdueled the patter of rain and made themselves distinct.

The first word I detected was Charlie saying, "Pistol."

CHAPTER SIXTEEN

TESSA

Charlie and I faced Whitney across our coffee table, the room illuminated by lamps in the darkness of the storm. To one side, Phil spilled out of a small stuffed armchair. I tried to look at Phil neither too much nor too little, but it felt impossible to get right. Why had Charlie invited him?

Though I had tried long and hard to learn my husband's moods and never quite managed it, today he frightened me. His lips were pulled back in the tense and gritty smile that no one who knew him well would trust. He was a lion hidden in the bush, hungry for blood, crouched, ready. Who was the prey? Me and Phil? Theo? Everybody? It was another sign of his recovery that he had returned to the hunt. I supposed I should be grateful.

When Benjamin arrived with Theo and saw the four of us in the room, he said, "If you're busy, I can come back later. I don't want to intrude."

"How like you to offer," I said.

"Benjamin, don't be ridiculous," said Charlie beside me on the couch. "You're here for a reason. Take a chair. There's nothing but goodwill in this room—nothing to be afraid of."

Charlie pulled up a pant leg to display his calf, which bulged above his long black sock.

"Like I've been saying: no pistol anymore, no holster. I've seen the light. If I was paranoid for a while, I have an excuse. They were giving me drugs. Too many, if you ask me. They still are—but less."

"We're glad to have you, darling, no matter what," I said.

"Amen," Theo said.

"Benjamin, doesn't this weather remind you of a Caribbean storm?" Charlie said. "There's a lot of wind. There's warm rain and a churned-up sea. For all I know, there are lizards on the lawn. Didn't your family go to the Caribbean?"

"We went to Jamaica," Benjamin said. "And Puerto Rico."

"Jamaica," Charlie said. "That's not too far from Cuba—and the Caymans. Have you been to the Caymans?"

"I don't think so."

"I bet you liked the Caribbean."

"I don't remember much," Benjamin said.

"Do you wish you were there now?"

"Sure. If it's sunny and not too hot."

My husband's Caribbean detour seemed as puzzling to Benjamin as it was to me. Since the crash, Charlie's mind wandered more. It would fix on something, like the smothering or now the Caribbean. I wondered: Is this what dementia looks like—a mix of complexity, simplicity, and confusion? Or is it just that he's as irritable and mean as ever, a little older, and a step slower? What to do?

I stole a glance at Phil and clasped my hands, afraid they might start to shake.

"I think you know Phil Weller," Charlie told Benjamin as if he'd followed my gaze.

"He introduced me around the company," Benjamin said, nodding to Phil. "He showed me some of the systems. Thanks, Phil. You gave me a good start."

Phil hadn't spoken to me ahead of today's visit, nor, except for painful pleasantries, since he'd arrived in Stonefield the night before. If he knew why Charlie had invited him to what seemed to be a family occasion, he hadn't told me. It hurt that Phil was so careful to keep me at arm's length, but I tried to see it like he did—that the best way to not seem intimate was to not be intimate. I understood Phil could straddle and not seem terribly weak, and he could step in at the right moment to assert himself. I suspected that was what he was doing with me. But last night, with Phil nearby and me in bed with Charlie, I'd spent hours awake and afraid.

"In case anybody's wondering," Charlie told us, "Phil's here because he's been working with the family. That gives him valuable perspective. Does everybody realize how much he stood in for me generally? He kept customers happy, employees in line, and Cantlings from battling each other. Theo versus the girls. The girls versus each other. Anybody versus anybody else. Phil kept such a firm hand on the tiller I'd have to say me returning might be a comedown for him and everybody else. Right, Phil?"

"Let's not kid ourselves," Phil said, managing not to sound too much like a toady. "We're much better off with you than without you."

"Some would disagree," Charlie said. "Hell, I might disagree myself."

When Charlie was on his game, his ability to convince himself, to bend facts to his will if he had to, was a source of power. Those of us in Charlie's orbit accepted his version of events or got slammed. But now his self-belief was troubling. If he was truly in the dark about me and Phil, it might be a sign of his decline. Charlie had returned far more like himself than anyone believed possible, but with both of them in the room, the nuances of Charlie's condition didn't matter much to me anymore. It became clear to me—it cried out, it shouted—which of these men I wanted.

"Life sure has twists and turns," Charlie said. "A few months ago, I was a goner. Now I'm back at work and soon to be a grandfather. Twice. It's a new world. There are new decisions to make. Theo, how much do you want?"

"How much what?" Theo said.

"Money. That's what this is about, isn't it? Money."

I winced. It was crude of Charlie to dwell on that word. Of course, though I hoped Whitney and Theo had more than that in mind, Charlie wasn't necessarily wrong.

"Whitney and I have been talking a lot," Theo said. "Obviously, we have decisions to make. Where to live? How big is the wedding and when? What to name the babies? But the more we discuss it, the clearer it gets: We want no more financial help from you. We'll stand on our own two feet."

"Did you memorize that?" Charlie said. "If so, congratulations. But you can't come to my house and just lie to me. How much do you want?"

"This is so insulting!" Whitney said.

"Phil and Benjamin," Charlie said. "I hear you both play a mean game of Ping-Pong. There's a table in the basement. My money says Phil's the better player. Why don't you let us know?"

Phil rose. "Benjamin, let's see what you've got. How do we get down there?"

"Follow me," Benjamin said.

"Phil, watch out for spins," Charlie said as the pair headed toward the basement stairs. "The guy's tricky."

Typical of Charlie, I thought, to know they both play Ping-Pong and to use it.

Once the family and Whitney were alone in the living room, I still hoped for peace. I said, "Theo, Whitney, I'm very excited. What's happened to you could be wonderful—or a big burden. It will take a major commitment from both of you to make it work. Charlie and I want to be involved. And we want to be sure you're as prepared as possible."

"We're very committed," Theo said, "to each other and to the twins. In the last few weeks, we've been better than ever. I can honestly say I've never been happier."

"If I want euphoria, I'll take drugs," Charlie said.

"Charlie," I said. "Give him a chance."

"What chance? His marriage lasted twelve seconds. He's never earned a living. His honey stinks of ammonia. And he drinks too much."

"That's not fair," Theo said, stricken. "Can't a guy change? I'm older. I've learned. I know where I'm going. I see great things ahead for Theo's Aromatic. Benjamin helped us. Dad, you deserve some credit. You sent him."

"Cut the suck-up. How much money do you want?"

"Mr. Cantling, I understand why you're so skeptical," Whitney said, steady and calm in the face of Charlie's glare. "If I were in your position, I might feel the same way—because money's always a consideration, and it would be irresponsible to ignore it completely. But it only plays a small role with me and Theo. You and your family have given me a fine job. It's been a special opportunity. I did my best, and I never broke your trust.

"I didn't plan to fall in love, but you know what Theo's like. He's unique. It just sort of happened. And I did use protection. The last thing I wanted was to get pregnant. Twins? I never saw that coming. I would love to bring them into the world. I think Theo and I could be good parents. But I don't want to if it's going to create suffering all around. Because of that, because we really don't want to hurt anyone, yes, we need help. But it's not the kind you think."

"What kind, then?" Charlie said.

From the basement came the tap of a ball being knocked back and forth. If Phil and Benjamin were talking, they kept their voices low.

"I don't have much experience," Whitney said. "But I know a young family needs backup. There's babysitting, access to doctors, legal stuff. Plus emotional support. With twins, everything we'd need would be so much greater. If there's a termination and treatment after, and pain and suffering, we would need help with that, too."

"What termination?" Theo said. "What pain and suffering? We didn't talk about that."

"We haven't discussed these sorts of things very much," Whitney said, her gaze fixed on Charlie. "But we need to be realistic."

"Whitney, we seem to understand each other very well," Charlie said. "So let's focus on areas of common interest and build from that." Charlie seemed to be mocking Whitney's saleswoman tone, which, though she had worked for me, seemed new. "We can all agree you should have the best prenatal care in the world. They tell me with twins the risk of miscarriage is high, like twenty percent. We'll get you tested regularly. These days doctors find all kinds of things they can fix. We can improve your odds. I've already contacted a top woman at New York Hospital. She'll see you next week."

"That's very generous," Whitney said. "And don't think I'm not grateful. But we have a doctor. We can handle that part on our own."

"Interesting. Can we see the test results? We can get you a second opinion."

"There's no need. Everything looks good."

"If you give me the name, I'll ask around about your doctor," Charlie said. "I've come to know a lot of people in medicine. I can get you feedback in twenty minutes."

"That won't be necessary," Whitney replied, her smile tight and wide.

"We're ready to help, but we need information," Charlie told her.

"And you'll get it," Whitney said.

"What else do you need to know?" Theo said to his father. "Whitney's having twins. I've seen the ultrasound."

"When?"

"Three or four weeks ago," Theo said.

"But not lately."

"What are you suggesting?" Theo said.

"Nothing. I just think we should be up to date."

"I'll get a new ultrasound at my next appointment," Whitney said. "And I'll get a paternity test. I don't want there to be any doubts. In the meantime, we can talk about other things."

"There is no meantime," Charlie said. "I'm getting a funny feeling. Is there something you don't want to tell us?"

"We've told you everything we know," Theo said.

"Everything," Whitney said.

"Why do I have doubts?" Charlie asked them. I recognized the sharp look. Charlie felt he'd found a weak spot. "Whitney, I think you might be here for one last play. If you are, Theo doesn't know about it."

"I know everything," Theo said.

"Whitney, do you know what I hear in all your fancy talk? I hear there's been a setback. I wonder: have you already miscarried?" Charlie said.

"That's insulting. You believe I would lie about that?"

"It's easy to prove me wrong. Let me talk to your doctor."

"I'll see what I can do."

"Nice. A good salesman always says yes. But I think you miscarried and didn't want to tell Theo. You're here because if you could make sure Cantling money was available for child support, you'd try to get pregnant again. Hell, I think you were already at it in your big week of love. It was a lousy hand to play, compared to carrying twins. In the end, even Theo would have figured something out. But you'd soften him up, you'd tell him all you wanted was to have his children and you had to keep trying. He'd crumble. And you'd be set: the wife of a Cantling, at least for a while. That's some very cold calculating. You're a scary young woman."

I watched in horror as my hopes unraveled. Theo looked pale and bewildered.

"You're wrong about me," Whitney said to Charlie. "I'm just trying to get by. You people have no idea what that's like. You've been handed everything, and you think life revolves around you. That means everybody might be out to get something from you, especially me. But you don't know anything about me."

"I know enough."

"Do you? As far as you're concerned, I didn't exist before and I won't after. I paid your bills, made your appointments, organized your parties, cleaned a few of your bathrooms after Theo threw up in them. I've never taken anything from you that you don't know about, not a nickel, not a scarf. And trust me, there were opportunities."

"Why take a chance for nickels," Charlie said, "when you can go for something big?"

"Think what you want. You will anyhow. I would fake a pregnancy? You people, you still don't know what I had to cope with while I worked for you. Your beloved son forced himself on me!"

"What?!" Theo shouted.

"Forced himself?" I said. "My son forced himself?"

"If I had turned him down, what would have happened?" Whitney said. "Do you think his ego would have allowed rejection by a mere employee, a servant? He'd have gone to you with a tale that made me a villain. Even if you didn't believe him, you'd have thrown me out in a second. Think about this: I have a case for sexual harassment and sexual assault. And pretty soon, if I'm not mistaken, wrongful termination."

"First the big bluff," Charlie said. "Now this. You did get the termination right, though it won't be wrongful. Have you been to a lawyer? Worked on your story? Or does all this come naturally?"

"What the fuck is happening?" Theo said. "Is this some kind of game?"

"Yes, I have a lawyer," Whitney said. "That's a name I'll be happy to share."

"Did you really expect to get away with this? Not that you care very much, but what kind of life would a pair of your twins have?" Charlie asked.

"They'd be well looked after."

"The best care my money could buy," Charlie said. "You came here to see how far you could get with the pregnancy thing. It was a long shot, so you had a fallback. Assault. Harassment. Wrongful termination. All right, I'll give you fifty thousand dollars, not a penny more, to sign a release and go away forever. If you fight us instead, believe me, we'll fight back. You might end up with nothing."

"Here's an idea," Whitney said. "Go fuck yourself!" She stood up.

"What the fuck?" Theo said, rising to face Whitney—but she was fixed on Charlie. "What the hell is going on?"

"Wake up, Theo!" Charlie said. "For once in your life, face the truth! She lost the babies. She's been playing for time so she can get pregnant again."

"You lost the babies?" Theo said. "And you didn't tell me?"

Whitney turned to Theo. "Are the keys still in the car?"

"Why do you need them? Where are you going?" Theo said.

"Are the keys in the car?" she repeated.

"Yes. Why do you need them? What are you doing?"

"My stuff's upstairs. I'll leave the car at the train station. Mr. Cantling, my lawyer will be in touch."

"I've been here before, with employees at the company," Charlie said, sounding bored. "Your lawyer gave you a number. Let's see. Assault? Iffy. You kept at it with Theo. Harassment? Easier, but technically you didn't work for Theo. Unlawful termination? You'd have a hard time with that. There was no contract. But you could play for sympathy: a forced relationship, an unwanted pregnancy you refused to terminate because babies are sacred, and then you lost them. So here's what I'll do. You sign a full release, and I'll give you two hundred and fifty thousand dollars. That's close to your lawyer's number, right? If you want more, we might as well take our chances in court."

"Two hundred and fifty thousand!" Theo said. Benjamin reappeared with Phil. If Theo spotted either of them, it didn't register. To him, it was as though he and Whitney were alone.

"When would I get the money?" Whitney said to Charlie.

"For God's sake, you don't want this!" Theo said.

"Half now," Charlie said. "The other half a year from now—if you've had nothing more to do with Theo. Remember: if you fight me, you might end up with less. And it will take you forever to collect."

"This is crazy!" Theo said. "We're not in a negotiation!"

"Is that right?" Charlie said.

"Whitney and me will see each other if we want. We make our own rules."

"Theo, get real," Whitney said. "There's enormous feeling between us. There always will be. But it's not going to work. Not after today."

"You are good," Charlie told her with a grin both vicious and admiring.

"What?" Theo said. "You accept his terms? You'll walk away from me?"

"I need to look out for myself. I'm not a Cantling."

Theo and Whitney were talking as if they were alone.

"Don't I have a say in this?" Theo asked her. "I thought we had something real. That week at the farm—it was great. You said so yourself."

"You haven't figured it out, have you?" she said.

"Of course I figured it out," Theo told Whitney. "Goodbye to the IUD, you said. It didn't work anyhow. Let's smoke and go to bed. And all the time, you were trying to get pregnant again. You could have just told me. Did you think the twins were the only hold you had on me? I care about you."

"You care? How many times have you come to me when everything about you screamed of other women? That hangdog look. That extra attention you'd suddenly show me. I knew. What could I do about it? If I broke up with you, I'd lose my job. I was on constant alert. If I've been a monster, you turned me into one. Were you ever loyal? Were you faithful?"

"I was faithful that week."

"Exit Whitney racing for the train," Whitney announced with a furious smile. She hurried toward the stairs past Phil and Benjamin and called over her shoulder as she took a step up, "Goodbye, Theo. Goodbye, parents. I'm not stealing your car. It will be at the station."

"You can't leave!" Theo said. "The car's way around the side of the house. You'll get soaked just walking to it."

"I'll take an umbrella." She ran up the stairs.

"I don't believe this," Theo said, flopping back onto the couch. "That fucking bitch!"

I went to him as he hunched forward in molten fury. I put an arm on his shoulder to comfort him. I thought: What a horrible turn of events! Theo deserves so much better. He'll blossom someday. He's much too talented not to. I wanted to shout at Charlie: Couldn't you have eased up on them? Did you have to be so rough?

Theo wasn't the only one suffering. I could have used a hug. Charlie had never been one for that. Phil was different—Phil, who on several very different occasions had wrapped me in his arms and told me things would work out, even if both of us understood they wouldn't.

Phil stood at the edge of the room, grim and stoic, no doubt wishing he could help. Charlie doesn't comfort anybody, I thought. He creates the need.

CHAPTER SEVENTEEN

BENJAMIN

I hadn't seen the Cantlings' finished basement in years, and as we listened to the turmoil upstairs, the cheeriness of the freshly painted yellow walls seemed preposterous. Toys abounded. There was a dartboard, a video console, long wooden shelves filled with games, and the Ping-Pong table. A gun cabinet with a combination lock and glass windows was large enough to hold several standing shotguns, but it contained only two. A third shotgun leaned against the cabinet from the outside. Two small cardboard boxes of cartridges had been tossed on a table nearby.

I'd been wondering why Charlie had sent Weller and me down here, but now I thought I understood: we were meant to somehow keep Theo from arming himself.

Weller and I found paddles and Ping-Pong balls and deployed to opposite ends of the table. Remembering that Weller had been approachable at Cantling Market Research, I said, "Will they be all right up there?"

"I don't know. All we can do is hope."

Weller was adept with a paddle. As we started to rally, he returned nearly all my twists and spins and showed flashes of latent power. Neither of us tried very hard. It would have been absurd to keep score. I wondered whether the upstairs shouters could hear the sound of the ball.

Not long into the game, Weller set his paddle down. "You're not dumb, right? You've seen the problem?"

"Theo doesn't lock things up."

"Right."

Weller walked to the cartridges and held the boxes up for me to read the printed labels. One read: SHOTGUN SHELLS. The other: BLANKS. Each box could hold about two dozen shells.

"It's a family matter," he said, returning the boxes to the table. "I don't like to get involved. After all, Theo Cantling may be running the business someday. He'll certainly have a say. And the risk that he'll race down here and grab his shotgun is tiny. I have to insist you don't get in the middle."

"Really?" There was another burst of shouting. "We should leave a shotgun and shells out in the open?"

"I'm encouraging you, in the strongest possible terms, not to get involved. It's tricky down here with these weapons and ammunition. Something could go very wrong. I don't want you to figure out the best safeguard against disaster. In the meantime, I'm heading upstairs, where I might be useful. Is there a bathroom down here?"

"Yes."

"Do you want to stay and use it?"

Taken aback, I began to understand. I said, "I guess I do."

Weller walked out. A lull in the ruckus above gave me hope the worst was over, and I heard Weller's measured footsteps on the stairs. Before he reached the top, the fight resumed. Once again, a Cantling misadventure had placed me in a difficult position. But I was getting used to it and already calculating.

I couldn't simply lock up the shotgun and cartridge boxes sitting on the table. Theo would know the combination to the gun cabinet and retrieve whatever he wanted. I studied the two boxes and found that each contained about eight shells. Both cartridge types were red, with very similar shapes, except that the blanks were more recessed at the front.

I wondered whether Theo, in an agitated state, would remember how many shells were in each box and recognize which was which. I told myself: Benjamin Gould, you may be over your head, but you need to make up your mind.

After rearranging the cartridges, I returned upstairs and stood alongside Weller at the entrance to the living room.

"It's a family matter," Weller said quietly. "You didn't meddle, did you?"

"Why would I do anything remotely like that? You told me not to."

"You're learning," he said.

Tessa sat next to Theo, who was slumped forward on the couch, miserable and seething. She awkwardly patted his shoulder.

Charlie said, "Call it a life lesson, Theo. You'll get over it. Maybe it will make you tougher. You need some of that. Too much has been handed to you."

"You bring all that up now?" Tessa said. "Can't you leave him alone?"

"What a bitch!" Theo said. "I wanted to marry her! What a goddamn greedy bitch!"

"Next time be more careful," Charlie said. "How often can your parents save you?"

"Charlie, enough!" Tessa said.

There were footsteps above the living room. Seconds later, Whitney appeared on the stairway, carrying a small roller bag.

Theo stood up. "Whitney! What the fuck is going on?"

She didn't answer, didn't turn to look at him as she continued down the last steps.

"How did you pack so fast?" Theo said. "Talk to me!"

With her eyes focused straight ahead, Whitney marched out of the house.

"She knew she was playing a long shot, so she was ready to bolt," Charlie said. "Theo, you sure can pick 'em."

"For God's sake, leave him alone!" Tessa said.

"She can't go! I won't let her!" He raced past me and Weller and toward the basement stairs.

"Phil!" Tessa cried out when we heard Theo on the stairs. "He's getting one of the guns. Stop him!"

Without a glance at me, Weller said, "We need to let it play out."

"That's crazy! Phil!"

Theo reappeared from the basement, both hands holding a shotgun not cracked open. He was furious, determined, frightening. No one moved to stand in his way.

Tessa screamed, "Theo! What are you doing?"

Theo ran out the front door.

"Is everybody useless?" Tessa shouted. "This family and its guns! This was bound to happen! Charlie, stop him!"

Charlie sent a puzzled glance at Phil, who must have seemed too calm. Charlie said, "Tell me how, Tessa. I'm a gimpy old man."

"Not when you don't want to be. Look on your handiwork, Charlie Cantling! Couldn't you have been easier on them? You made it happen."

"Bullshit!"

The four of us hurried out the front door and stared into the rain, where Theo stood waiting for Whitney in the parking area. Suddenly, she appeared from around the side of the house, driving a gray SUV fast on the gravel. Theo waved the shotgun high in the air and ran to block the car. Whitney swerved around him. When she passed him, he fired both barrels at the rear of the SUV. Tessa screamed! The vehicle sped away and disappeared toward the town road.

Theo approached us, rainwater dripping from his hair. "What the fuck? I tried to shoot one of her back tires. It's a huge target. I was ten feet away. How could I miss? I can't even do that right." Disgusted, he tossed the shotgun onto the ground. "Charlie Cantling. The way you treated Whitney, you humiliated me!"

"No," Charlie said, "you did that to yourself."

"Whitney and me, we're not infants. You could have shown us a little bit of respect."

"Respect? You fell in love with a con artist."

"Fuck you!" This was the first time I'd ever heard Theo Cantling raise his voice to his father. "Fuck you!" Theo stalked past us and into the house. His parents followed.

Weller bent down and retrieved the wet shotgun from the gravel. "Didn't you hear what I told you about not interfering?" he said. "But you did something, didn't you?"

"Yup." I pulled out a cartridge from my blazer and held it up. "I split the blanks between the boxes and took the real shells."

"I don't get involved in family matters," Phil said with the faintest of grins. "I don't even comment. But some people might think what you did was clever."

The Cantlings, confirmed in their status and prerogatives, didn't do as others might and send me home with apologies and a false promise of another visit soon. Tessa and Theo huddled on a living room sofa and seemed to forget about me. Charlie approached me in the hallway with a triumphant glimmer in his eyes.

"My son the buffoon," he said. "What will we do with him?"

I thought, charitably, that after his hospital ordeal, Charlie needed every taste of power he could find. I shrugged.

"Don't leave us," Charlie said. "Today's the day for settling up. I'll see you upstairs in fifteen minutes."

I returned to the living room and walked quietly past Tessa and Theo, who continued to seethe while his mother tried to comfort him. It was eerie to move like an unnoticed ghost through someone else's house. I wondered: Has it always been like this? Did they just not see me?

I continued out a door and up a back stairway, where I found a bedroom and, with time on my hands, walked in. Three colorful blouses dangled from the doorknob on hangers, and a makeup kit topped a bureau over which a large mirror held sway. When I saw seven pairs of dressy shoes lined up beside the bed, I assumed Melanie had been using the room.

Sitting in a stuffed chair with a teddy bear balanced on one of its arms, I had an extended view down the lawn and toward the sea. The gray ceiling of the sky had begun to lift, the lashing wind had slowed, and the ocean churn had quieted. Beyond the breakers, a few intrepid gulls wheeled and dove at swells.

I was deep in Cantlingland, deeper than I'd ever been, and I was learning. For Theo to have become so entwined with Whitney seemed ghastly. I was observing the Cantlings in an ever less-appealing light. Their failures seemed too pervasive, and too substantial, to merely be mistakes. The sibs were anointed and proud—and clueless. Except for Ann, what happy, productive future could they expect? Would their talents be squandered in a lifelong orgy of privilege? Would inherited money and substance abuse shield them from the pain? I was old enough to know this wouldn't be the last time one of them would be tested. Their chances to fail would take a thousand obliging shapes. They wouldn't need to seek flattery and exploitation. It would find them. The Cantlings might not be ready for the world, but the world was ready for them.

Minutes later, I walked the upstairs corridor toward Charlie's office. I felt I had contributed to the "settling up" he had promised. I had forced the issue and helped them unmask Whitney. I had demonstrated that further inquiries about the smothering were probably useless. There was no real evidence, and fear of Charlie meant that no one, except bluffing Tessa, would ever confess. I hoped Charlie would acknowledge my contribution and we'd part on decent terms.

Near the office, I heard familiar music and wondered if someone had told Charlie of my musical taste, however unlikely. This nod to it was consistent with the decent outcome I expected. I opened the office door to the overture to *Figaro* blasting from a tiny speaker on a shelf.

"Are you ready for me?" I asked loud enough to be heard.

"Sure. Come on in," Charlie called from his desk. "I found this music on my playlist. I'm no opera lover. My assistant must have set it up. He's a highbrow like you. Do you know what it is?"

"Yes. Mozart."

Charlie tapped at his keyboard, and the music fell to medium volume, and I realized Charlie was masking our words with music. I assumed his assistant had chosen only highlights. Charlie wouldn't be keen on the full opera.

Charlie's claim to have given up his pistol wasn't entirely accurate. Holstered not far from his right arm, it rested like a paperweight atop sheets of typing paper. The pistol's handle was visible outside the holster.

"Charlie, is the gun loaded?"

"Why would I need a loaded gun? Were you planning to attack me?"

I managed to laugh.

"You need to relax," he said. "Despite what people think, I'm not crazy enough to play with a loaded gun. Oh, I see how they treat me. They agree to anything I say—the sky is made of tissue, the earth's made of cheese—like I'm some idiot child. 'Charlie's had a major trauma,' they tell themselves. 'And multiple operations. And drugs. Guys his age don't bounce right back. Do we believe he's the same guy?' Fuck them! This business with Whitney should put that crap to rest. The crazy old fool saw right through her. Sooner or later,

Theo will have to get over it. He might learn something from the experience. The occasional miracle does happen. Whoops. I should be discreet. Have I upset you?"

"Not at all."

"Let there be no doubt. I am what I was before the accident and wiser for the experience. When you get down to where you're fighting for life and limb, you realize there's not a whole lot that's pretty about life. People like us have to protect ourselves, no matter what it costs. Nobody messes with me or my family, not while I'm still around. I will destroy them all. The pistol isn't loaded—but it ought to be."

I half expected him to pat his metal ally. Mozart chimed in with an act 1 aria. We were definitely hearing the highlights.

"Everybody understood you were high IQ," Charlie said. "But a lot of them told me I shouldn't have hired you. You looked down on us, you and your mother. Like we were brainless WASPs who got lucky and inherited a business. Which, by the way, was an empty shell when I got hold of it. You know who was lucky? Your father. Feckless guy with no sense marries a smart cookie."

"I don't think my father would agree," I said, irritated.

"What I saw in you was a young guy with potential. You just needed the right circumstances. With the Cantling family, you understood the players, you knew where they came from, you probably had stuff on them I didn't have. They'd have trouble bullshitting you. And I needed answers. The memory of somebody stuffing a pillow into my face was making me kind of edgy. I expected you'd find out a few things, nothing earth shattering, I would decide it was all in my head, and that would be the end of it. Then Tessa stuck her nose in, trying to protect somebody, and it got messy. You must have pressed her too hard."

"I didn't press. We were in the living room. Talking."

"You can look at Tessa and think all she does is buy clothes, so you imagine you can push her around. Except she has an independent streak. Sometimes an extra necklace works, sometimes it doesn't. She can nurse a grudge. There was that time five years ago when she left me. Okay, that really is indiscreet. You didn't know, did you?"

I shook my head.

"Why should you? Smiling Tessa. Takes her lumps and still looks good. One time, with no warning, she said she'd had it. She got it in her mind about me and one of her friends, blew everything out of proportion, and then, boom. It was nothing that hadn't happened before—though, let's face it, I couldn't use that as a defense. She moved out. It took weeks to get her back. There was begging and pleading and half a day with her at Cartier. Even so, she was never the same. 'From now on,' she said, 'I live my own life. It's my Declaration of Independence.' I never got a clear idea what that meant, but it was a big deal to her.

"So, how does all this lead to a false confession? Was she just throwing it in my face? I kept thinking she was covering up for Theo, except it was hard to believe he had the guts. Let's hope, if he did, it was because he couldn't stand to see me the way I was. To the authorities, it could look like something else. There are laws. They like to enforce them against people like us. It makes for great publicity. Son tries to kill wealthy father. Cable news, here we come."

This was the first I'd heard that the rich were disadvantaged at law. Charlie's meanderings made me uncomfortable. Had I been too stoned in the helicopter on the Early Fourth to notice the extent of his decline? I recalled from years ago an old, mumbling woman wandering disheveled on a Stonefield beach. Was that in Charlie's future? I'd heard the other Cantlings wonder about him. A sharp mind partway failing could be a menace.

"Let's agree," I said. "The confession was false. And apart from the fact that the kids want more money, which we could have guessed, I haven't found anything useful about the smothering. Are you actually happy with that outcome?"

"Let's say I accept it."

"The authorities haven't contacted you?" I asked.

"No. And after so many months have gone by, it looks like they won't. The case isn't even closed. It was never opened."

"Does that mean we're finished? I don't have to do this anymore?"

"Right." From his speaker, a raucous "Non più andrai" had my attention. I silently translated: "No more bed-hopping, you horny butterfly."

"But something else has come up," Charlie said. "It's lucky you were around when it did. You can help."

"Help with what?"

"You've probably heard we've been trying to buy a software company called Celestial Intelligence. Well, there have been some bumps along the way."

"Sorry to hear it. What does it have to do with me?"

"Bear with me. Celestial assured us they were the best around. We investigated, of course, and we believed them. But a couple of weeks after we signed the contract, a different company contacted us with better software that does the same job as Celestial's. The new guys are just starting, they've only got a handful of customers, and they were keen to sell to us for half of what Celestial would get. Our customers would have loved what they have. But we're honorable people—and we were doing a deal with Celestial."

Charlie continued to stare at me. Mozart played on.

"It came time for due diligence. Celestial sent their auditors in, and we told them we were confident they'd find no problems. But lo and behold, within a few days, they discovered someone had very recently stolen two hundred thousand dollars from us. Trust me, the news was devastating!"

"Somebody stole from you? How?"

"I've asked you about the Caymans. Are you sure you've never been there?"

"If I have, I don't remember."

"Our family has history with the Caymans. The company pays one of its software consultants through a Caymans account. And my wife has transferred money from a personal account to an account down there belonging to Theo. Well, it seems this two hundred thousand had been wired direct from our company to a new Caymans account. It looked like Theo and Tessa had started up again, this time with company money."

"They had access?"

"They're insiders. Somehow they might have gotten the passwords. When I told Celestial about it, they were understandably upset about what looked like embezzlement and lack of financial controls. It seemed they might crater the deal. But before they'd make that decision, they wanted to know more. They said a sophisticated hacker might have broken into our system and stolen the funds. That wouldn't bother them so much, they said. Cyberattacks can happen to almost any company. They wanted to know who the account belongs to. I told them it's not easy to peek into foreign banks, but we'd see what we could find out."

From Mozart I heard: "L'ho perduta." I translated: Charlie's lost it.

"Cantling Market Research has a terrific IT guy," Charlie was saying. "I asked him if it was possible to do what Celestial asked. He looked into it—didn't take him long—and found whose account it was. I shouldn't have been so surprised. I've always said smart guys with shaky personalities are the most dangerous. They don't have the backbone to stand up to their own bad ideas. Arrogance gets them every time. Benjamin, you're a little man in a dead-end job, and you went for something bigger. Who'd have believed you had it in you?"

"Me? You're talking about me?"

"I trusted you. I let you into our systems. The access went to your head. If we ever found the theft, you figured because of the Caymans angle, Theo would take the fall."

"That's not what happened, and you know it!"

"Somebody stole that two hundred thousand—unless you think we stole it from ourselves."

"I see what's going on! You never liked the Goulds. So you decided to frame me for something. Well, you won't get away with it!"

"Don't get all worked up. If you cooperate, we won't even go to the authorities."

"In that case, just take back the money, wherever it came from."

"I wish it was that simple."

"I don't understand. For one thing, why are you telling me all this?"

"Because in case Celestial gets in touch with you, you need to know what I told them."

"You've already told them?"

"I had to. And the next step? You need to confess."

"Confess? I didn't do it!"

"Really? You're telling me somebody at our company put your name on the account and wired the money? Come on. Who'd believe that?" With his free hand, Cantling reached for the papers under his pistol and pushed them toward me. "This is a very difficult situation. It's embarrassing for my family and yours. Let's not drag it out. Do us both a favor and sign this."

"What is it?"

"A full confession explaining what you did."

I glanced at the papers and frantically tried to read.

"Let's not dwell on details," Charlie said. "Basically, the document says you admit what you did and give us permission to recover the funds. After all, I can't let you enjoy the fruits of your crime. I promise I'll use this document just once. With Celestial. Then I'll bury it. It will be our secret."

"I can't confess to a crime I didn't commit!"

"If my wife can, so can you. In fact, I'm going to insist." He slid the pistol from the holster on the desk and aimed it at my face.

I stared at the weapon, frozen. "I thought you said it wasn't loaded."

"I lied. Stress of the moment. Now, let's put this nasty business behind us."

"Why are you doing this? It's crazy!"

"I agree. My accident left me traumatized. And volatile. With impaired judgment. See what I mean? For your own safety, sign the paper. Admit what you did, and it will vanish like a bad dream."

"If I don't sign?"

"The story might go like this: I confronted you with your crimes, you saw the gun and grabbed for it. We struggled. It was an accident. No, a tragedy. I'll never keep a gun around again."

"You're bluffing."

"It's possible. Do you want to take that chance?"

"If I sign, I'll contact Celestial. I'll tell them you forced me."

"Your word against mine," Cantling said. "There'd be scandal, court cases, all sorts of trouble. Sounds good to me."

"I don't understand."

"I don't care. Sign the fucking paper!"

"Mozart won't drown out a gunshot," I said, desperate. "They'd all hear!"

"Fuck Mozart! What are you gonna do?"

CHAPTER EIGHTEEN

MELANIE

My sisters make fun of me because I can be very nervous about what I wear, but dressing is important—not just for how people see me and how I feel but also for how I want to be seen. People who don't pay attention to clothes, who don't know or care about styles and trends and how an outfit can be put together, what does that say about them?

That night, I saw a real chance for fireworks, the awful indoor kind, and because I was extra edgy, I tried on several outfits, searching for the one that seemed right. In the end I came back to the first I'd reached for, a bright-yellow satin blouse and sleek, lightweight navy-blue pants.

Because I didn't want to tower over my sisters, I wore flats.

I took a taxi to the large Midtown restaurant, which was already filling with the eager crowd. All four sisters, even Nicole in from Santa Fe, had signed up for the United Vegetarians bash, my first big benefit after Labor Day. My sisters say that, when it comes to our family, I'm a perpetual optimist. But I had realistic hopes that things would go well and we'd have a night of solidarity. Vivian had even invited Theo and, when she didn't hear from him, held a seat open for him at our table.

I strode up a short stairway to the old stone building with its handsome arched entrance. This took me directly into the event on the ground floor, where one of five gatekeepers—the party was that big—gave me a tag with my name and table number and waved me in. The restaurant, with its enormous five-story ceiling, had been a bank long ago. Dozens and dozens of round dinner tables filled the space, which was very ornate and beautiful, with a tall vase of flowers on every table. At the front was a stage and a lectern, where UNITED VEGETARIANS: COYOTE NIGHT was projected on a large white screen above magnificent color photographs of wild coyotes.

Most of the crowd had already arrived and were clustered around the edges of the party. To one side, movable partitions separated the dining area from a silent auction arranged on a series of long tables. I found my sisters browsing the auction together and right away saw we had a problem. All four of us had dressed in bright outfits. Individually, we looked great. It was the group effect that worried me. We were all in this together, and that was something to celebrate, but was it right to look happy?

I knew that soon we would sit down, and the medley of yellow and orange and pink and red would make us look like a candy-store window. It made me cringe. It was like we were trying to prove we were not in mourning, when really we were—especially Ann, who'd been closest to the Goulds. It was fine to not talk about it, and to try not to think about it, but we knew that terrible things had happened two weeks ago in Stonefield. Even if we got through tonight and the days after without an explosion, we might have lost friends, chances, hopes, and happy memories. Could we ever think of the Goulds and not shudder?

"Have you heard anything from Jody?" Nicole asked me after hugs and greetings. "Is there really a chance he's coming?" The four of us had collected around an amazing silent auction highlight: a famous rock star's torn bandanna. "Wouldn't it be rude if he did?"

"He was invited," Ann said. "How would it be rude for him to show up?"

"Obviously, things have changed since the invitations went out," Vivian said. We had to half shout above the noise. "Still, I couldn't take him off the guest list. He'd confirmed with the benefit committee."

"He confirmed?" Nicole said. "Well, he's gutsy. He doesn't like to back down. You know him best, Ann. Will he show?"

Ann shrugged. "He's Jody. Sometimes he's easy to predict, sometimes he isn't. He might want to confront us. I assume he'd like some of us on his side."

"Are you?" Vivian said to her.

"I don't know." Ann had been very quiet since the Benjamin disaster and hadn't confided much. We tried to not intrude or push her into taking a stand. But Ann—who was maybe the best of us, forever trying to make things right, unlike me, who just went along with stuff—was being pulled hard in opposite directions.

"Have you talked to Jody?" Vivian said to Ann.

"Just for a minute."

"Was he angry?" Vivian said.

"What do you think?"

"If he does come, there's no telling what he might do," Vivian said. "We need to stick together."

After Vivian wrote down a bid for a Yankees cap autographed by someone I'd never heard of, we joined the crowd flowing toward the seating area and found our table. As I'd expected, we were a very colorful foursome—although, like a pair of question marks, two chairs sat empty: one for Theo and one for Jody.

Ann was sitting next to me. "Did you and Al Byrne talk?" she asked, interested even now.

"We had a meeting."

"How did it go?"

"I wanted to discuss the Benjamin situation, but Mr. Byrne made it clear he wasn't ready. I said I'd been trying to see him since before it all happened. It was part of a life plan I was working on. I told him that in acting class a while ago, we did an Agatha Christie play. And it was amazing. Detective work seemed so much like theater. If you need to solve a murder, sometimes you ask questions when you already know the answers. You pretend to know things that you don't. You try to seem sympathetic toward your suspects. Isn't that acting? Aren't the tricks the same? I said: I know it might seem crazy, but maybe I missed my calling. Maybe I was meant to be a detective."

"You want to work for Byrne and Company? Would that be okay with Charlie?"

"I'm trying not to think about that."

"How did Al Byrne respond?"

"He told me he wasn't sure, but if we wait until things settle down, there might be something in sales."

"You'd be great at sales. Would you take the job?"

"I don't know. It's a fascinating place. And Mr. Byrne is interesting."

A woman in a shapeless black dress—why are activists always so homely?—stepped up to the lectern and spoke into the microphone. She introduced herself as the president of United Vegetarians and thanked her "fantastic" board and "wonderful" guests.

She said: "Every year we highlight a member of the animal kingdom, to show the creatures we're trying to save. This year it's the coyote—a marvelous animal. If anyone is surprised that we'd honor a meat eater, we say it's very different when nonhumans eat meat. They have no choice, no moral awareness. They're programmed. Some may say: Why do anything for coyotes? They're doing a great job themselves. Research shows that when someone kills one of the alpha pair in a pack, the other coyotes start to breed more. Wipe out the whole pack, and neighboring coyotes move in and start to breed. They're unstoppable."

"Well now, that sounds like the Cantling way," Jody Gould declared, striding to our table. His jacket and tie sweater showed at least some respect for the occasion and gave me hope he might behave. "It seems Cantlings are not very different from coyotes. Destroy what's left of the Goulds, then take their territory." He sat down in one of the empty chairs. His grin was fierce, his rudeness predicable and disappointing.

"So, Cantlings are destroyers," Nicole said. "That's your idea of hello? Why did you show up? If you had something to tell us, why not call it in?"

"When I say my piece, I want to see the looks on your faces." He glanced around the table. "It's a pretty good turnout. Very colorful. Only Theo is missing."

"He's probably on his way," I said.

"Let's hope not. Your brother's useless, and you all know it. What you don't realize is that the rest of you are useless, too. Some of you grumble, some of you yell, but you take whatever Charlie dishes out. And you keep smiling. Really, you're no different from Theo."

"So good of you to stop by," Vivian said.

"Don't you realize we're unhappy about this too?" Ann said to him. "Nobody here wanted any of this."

"But you got it, didn't you?" Jody, showing none of the charm I knew he had, ripped into us without so much as a polite nod. "Why did your father think he could pull off such a crazy scheme against Benjamin? Because what Charlie wants, the Cantlings do. Don't you think it's time to take responsibility?"

"This is coming from you?" Vivian said.

"I don't bow down to Charlie," Nicole said. "I'm the one who split to Santa Fe."

"So you suck up from a distance. Is there a 'Yes' button on your cell phone? An automatic 'Okay, Charlie' in your email? None of you stand up for anything as long as the cash keeps flowing. Whoa! Slap me—I was rude! Benjamin shipping money to the Caribbean? It's a bad joke! The Benjamin we all know was the last person who'd ever steal a nickel. If a store gave him too much change, he'd return it. He's been so generous with me for years—and he never asked for anything back."

"Jody, there are things you don't understand," Ann said. "Can't you give us a chance?"

"A chance to do what? The nothing you've already done?"

We all knew what Benjamin meant to Jody—and this was the most upset I'd ever seen him. Why couldn't he just trust us?

"By the way," he said, "I fucked every one of you. Tiptoe around that!"

"Bastard!" Vivian said.

"Why would you say something like that?" Ann asked.

"Because I'm pissed off. Everybody, raise your hand if you haven't fucked me. Right. None of you can. Have you ever talked it over? Cursed about it? Giggled about it? That wouldn't be the Cantling way. You'd rather duck and keep on smiling, just like you do with Charlie!"

"Bastard!" Vivian said again.

"So the way to make us honest is to hurt us," Ann said.

"The poor, miserable Cantlings," Jody said. "Some of their secrets have been revealed. Have you thought about what's happened to me? To my brother?"

We were stunned, of course. Me maybe less than the others, because I hadn't really hidden my fling with Jody. And, of course, Ann and Jody were the worst-kept secret ever. But the others? Vivian was blushing and too angry to speak, and the contempt on Nicole's face was like a confession. I didn't know what was more upsetting—that Jody had slept with all of us or that we'd kept so much from each other. I thought: We are Cantlings. We don't just roll over for anybody.

Except it seemed we did.

Of course, Jody had a lot going for him: looks, imagination, whatever. Not to mention energy in bed. I had to smile.

The coyote presentation ended, and the room's hubbub returned. A photo of a vegetable garden filled the screen behind the lectern. Waiters and waitresses fanned out among the tables to serve a large salad.

"Why the rampage?" Nicole said to Jody. "Your brother's not dead. He's not even injured."

"Not injured? He might be scarred for life."

"Why? Word will never get out," Nicole said.

"Wrong! Too many people already know. Pretty soon everybody will. My brother isn't equipped to deal with this sort of thing. He's an innocent, a nerd who can't even do computers. Your family should be ashamed."

"Your brother's got more backbone than you think," Ann said. "The way you worry about each other, it's nice. But it's also like you dump on one another."

"Fuck the psychobabble," Jody said. "Have you actually talked to him?"

"I tried. But he wouldn't say anything. Al Byrne had told him not to discuss it."

"If he didn't steal the money, why did he confess to it?" Vivian said.

"Come on! Your father threatened him."

"That's not what we hear," Vivian told him. "Charlie says he promised Benjamin he wouldn't go after him, wouldn't even ask for the money back, because a story like that might hurt the company's reputation. All Benjamin had to do was admit it and keep quiet. Charlie says Benjamin owned up and it looked like everything was settled, except Byrne and Company and their lawyers got involved. Charlie says they must have decided it was like a ticking time bomb. If word got out that a security company had hired a thief, it could be disastrous. They persuaded Benjamin to deny everything."

"Charlie says this, Charlie says that. And you believe it?"

"Today we believe all sorts of things," Ann said. "Tomorrow we might believe something else. Can't you trust us?"

"No."

"What would you have us do?" Ann said.

"Face the truth. Your father's too far gone to be in charge of Cantling Market Research. You need to throw him out. He can't do what he did to Benjamin and stay. It will look like Benjamin actually stole something, and that story will follow him around forever."

"You need to give us time," Ann said.

"My brother keeps saying the same thing. They're working on something. Who's the they? He won't say. How much time? He shrugs. Enough time for Charlie to ruin him forever? Fuck that!" He slapped the table with both hands and stood up, glaring down at us. Around us, people stared. It was very embarrassing. "Benjamin looks okay, sometimes he talks like he's okay, but he's not. You need to do something! Right away! You owe us."

"I don't know who's more difficult," Vivian said, "you or Charlie. You don't listen."

"To what?" Jody said. "Charlie and his bullshit? Your excuses? We're through, me and your whole family. I'll see you next in hell! Oh wait, you're Cantlings. You're already there!"

He turned and walked out.

CHAPTER NINETEEN

MELANIE

In the taxi to the law firm where Ann worked, I thought: It's like the acting coaches say about auditions. Be positive. Be pleasant. You might think you have no chance to succeed, but anything's possible. You could learn something or make a connection. I understood that no one knew what would happen today. But it was hard to be stay positive.

I walked into the meeting room, saw my mother and all my siblings, and decided my very dark pantsuit was the right choice. I didn't know what Nicole was wearing because she had dialed in from Santa Fe, but my mother and sisters had gone with very little color: a pale-blue cotton blouse and flared pants in deeper gray for Vivian, skirts and blouses that were dark and conservative for our mother and Ann.

When Charlie arrived, I remembered my girlfriends used to say he was very handsome. There was the charisma, that way he carried himself, that look where you might have thought he was sneering but you knew he was in charge and you wouldn't cross him. He and

Theo were in suits. Before they sat down, Charlie took off his jacket and hung it on the back of his chair. Theo immediately did the same, and Vivian glared at him. I knew what Vivian was thinking: did he mirror Charlie from habit, or was he still in Charlie's camp? That was an important question.

"You all wanted a family meeting," Charlie said. "So here I am. Good morning, everyone. Good morning, Nicole."

"Good morning, Father," Nicole said from the speakerphone. I wished things were different, but with those two, formalities always had an edge.

"It's 10 a.m. here," Charlie said. "You're up early. Or is it late?"

"I moved here so I wouldn't have to answer questions like that."

"Cheeky today, aren't we?" Charlie said. "Other than giving Nicole a chance to insult me," he said to the rest of us, "why are we doing this? Because, from a business standpoint, nothing's changed."

"That opinion, Charlie, is why we need this meeting," my mother said from her chair. She was pale and nervous as she tapped at her cell phone.

"I assume this is about Benjamin Gould," Charlie said. "Look, if I could undo what happened, I would. If that's not enough, if you want to get all touchy-feely about it, I'm ready for that, too."

"You? Touchy-feely?" Nicole said.

My mother set her phone on the table and said, "Charlie, there's a guest about to join us."

"This is something new," Charlie said. "You get together, decide who we talk to, and keep me in the dark. I hope the surprise you have for me is pleasant. If not, just remember: I control the company, and I control the trust, and even if you all agree, you can't afford to get rid of me."

"I like to think the family controls the trust," my mother said.

"Pardon me, I forgot," Charlie said.

Al Byrne strode in, leaving the door open behind him. The energy he gave off felt earthy and crude. It occurred to me that he didn't belong in his tailored blue suit, and his wide dark tie didn't seem right. While he introduced himself, he already knew who everyone was. I assumed he'd studied photographs on the internet.

"Always good to see you, Al. But our contract's done. Paid in full," my father said.

"This is a freebie," Mr. Byrne said. "No charge." He sat in one of several empty chairs.

"Let me be clear," Charlie said. "If you people are planning something, you're going to be disappointed. I won't have the company wire you megabucks whenever it suits you. We need cash to run our business, to protect us from downturns, to expand. I won't endanger our future to buy you toys. In the meantime, Al, proceed."

It occurred to me that this was the first time my father seemed like an actor playing the leader—and not the real thing. What was happening? I hated the tension I was feeling. It was so unnecessary! I decided to stay quiet and listen.

Mr. Byrne said: "Charlie, this was a strange assignment for Byrne and Company from the start. You told your family you wanted to find out what they expected in your will. But they know what you're capable of. Right away they assumed you wanted to learn about the attempted mercy killing. Even though they'd seen through the ruse, we're in the business of trying to satisfy clients. We instructed your chosen investigator, Benjamin, to keep poking around."

"And it went right to his head," Charlie said. "I'd brought him close to something he'd only dreamed of. Then he made his move. It's all written in plain English above his signature."

"Benjamin has a different story," Mr. Byrne said.

"I'm not surprised," Charlie said.

"When Byrne and Company learned about the evidence and Benjamin's confession, we were very concerned. We had our reputation to think of, not to mention the possible lapse of judgment in trusting Benjamin. There was a lot of evidence against him. But he just didn't seem to be a guy who would steal. And he insisted he'd been framed and forced to confess."

"Until now, I've given Byrne and Company a pass," Charlie said. "I've kept quiet about the theft. That could change."

"We understood that. We were tempted to do nothing and hope the matter faded away. After all, why would anyone frame one of ours? With all our resources, it seemed crazy to take us on. On the other hand, it might be brilliant. Someone might figure that even if our guy is innocent, we'd need to keep the matter under wraps. A hint of wrongdoing, the mere possibility that one of our employees was corrupt, could hurt us badly."

"Byrne and Company could still get hurt," Charlie said. "So why take the chance? Even now, you could walk away with no hard feelings."

"Very generous of you. But staying silent doesn't seem like a good idea. Too many people in the family and at Cantling Market Research know the story. It's likely to get out. Even if it doesn't, the way things stand, Cantling Market Research has a dagger it could stab into our heart at any time."

"We have no interest in doing that," Charlie said.

"Do you know what clinched the decision? Pride. Cantling Market Research isn't the only business with talented tech people. Ours are up there with the best, and you tried to trick them. You slandered a Byrne employee and by extension everyone in the organization. It guaranteed our people would give you very special attention."

"This is amusing." Charlie sounded sure of himself, but I know something about commanding the stage, and he wasn't doing it.

"You underestimated Benjamin," Mr. Byrne said. "After he signed the confession, he didn't hesitate to come to me. He was forceful and articulate. He laid out everything that had happened. He told me I could talk to other people, like his brother, and confirm that you'd been carrying a pistol around. We did reach out to some of your family members, and they verified that you sometimes kept a pistol in the room where you met with Benjamin. That encouraged us to keep digging."

"Why wouldn't I have a pistol?" Charlie said. "I'd had a brush with the Reaper. I'd felt a pillow in my face. Instead of understanding, you've all been plotting, smiling and plotting, looking for an excuse to get rid of me. Theo, you're okay with this?"

Theo shrugged.

"You're on Benjamin's side?"

"I wouldn't put it that way," Theo said.

"How would you put it?"

"There have been discussions."

"What the fuck does that mean?"

"Melanie?" Charlie said. "Are you part of this?"

It was strange. I couldn't speak. Maybe it was all too much for me. I gave a tiny nod.

Mr. Byrne came to the rescue. "I think, and the family thinks, we should all hear from Benjamin together."

"Of course you do," Charlie said. "Ridiculous!"

Mr. Byrne turned to the door and called, "We're ready!"

Benjamin walked in, wearing a suit. He appeared nervous but also—I saw it in how he carried himself—determined in a way I'd never seen before. He sat next to Mr. Byrne and inched his chair close to the table. There was a jarring squeak. He unfolded two pages of paper from his jacket and spread them in front of him without looking at them.

He said, "Good morning. I haven't spoken to any of you for a while. I needed time and distance. There was a lot to sort out. You can't imagine what happens to you, what goes through your head during and after, when a gun points at you at close range."

"There it is again," Charlie said. "The imaginary gun. What other tales do you have for us today?"

Benjamin didn't seem to hear. "My heart was racing," he said. "I thought: Charlie can pretend to believe this Caymans story. Does that mean he's halfway sane and won't shoot? But there was the gun! I signed."

"Does anybody believe this pack of lies?" Charlie said. "Melanie?"

All I could do was nod.

"There were two separate questions," Benjamin said, reading now. "Why did Charlie Cantling hire Byrne and Company? And why did he turn around and frame me and force me to confess?

"It seems things started to go very wrong when Charlie told the hospital about the attempt on his life. When he was clearer, he knew if he tried to change his story, it could draw attention and make things worse. He decided to use Byrne and Company for cover. He chose the investigator, me, supposedly because I already knew the family but really because he assumed I'd get nowhere. Then, if the authorities showed up, he'd tell them a top-tier investigative firm had looked into it and found nothing. With that working against them, the authorities would be unlikely to spend resources on this."

"Whatever happened," Charlie said, "I did it for the family."

"Of course you did." Benjamin, no longer reading, looked up at Charlie. "And you might have been a hero if you had stopped there. But around the same time, you were making the deal with Celestial Intelligence. Then, within weeks, you wanted to buy a different company. Maybe all that activity showed your judgment was off. In any case, you couldn't just walk away from Celestial, could you?"

"Where did you get this information about the deal?" Charlie said.

"Byrne and Company took a chance," Benjamin said. "We suspected forcing the confession had to do with the Celestial deal. We approached them, and they were interested. They helped us."

"They talked to you? Fuck them! They signed a nondisclosure agreement!"

"It doesn't apply if it's being used to hide a fraud," Benjamin said coolly, as if he'd rehearsed the line. He started to read again. "The contract to buy stipulated you'd pay them an eight percent kill fee, thirty-six million dollars, if Cantling Market Research quit the deal.

But the contract let either party off with no kill fee if they found significant wrongdoing at the other company. You weren't about to part with thirty-six million dollars for what felt like nothing in return. So you invented a phony embezzlement to provoke Celestial into dropping out."

"Some story!" Charlie said. "I wish I was half that smart."

Benjamin kept reading: "Unfortunately for you, when Celestial saw the information about the Caymans account, they weren't convinced. They thought a hacker could have broken into your systems and set up the account using my name and credentials. Then, as soon as banking rules allowed, the hacker would clean out the account. Celestial told you a sophisticated cyberattack against your company wouldn't kill the deal for them. That sort of thing could happen to almost anybody. But they implied that a clear case of embezzlement, with the weak controls and scandal that implied, would scare them away. Essentially, they needed more proof that it was an inside job. You decided to bring them a confession."

"This is world-class crap!" Charlie said.

"You showed everybody who runs things, didn't you?" Tessa said.

"Byrne and Company already told you this crazy theory?" Charlie said.

"Some of it. Enough to know it's true."

"I see. They went around me and got you to believe a fairy tale," Charlie said. "In the real world, the world where a signed confession matters, can anybody tell me how someone at Cantling Market Research created a Caymans account in the name of Benjamin Gould and transferred two hundred thousand dollars into it?"

"Al's people ran that down," Benjamin said. "His tech group broke through the firewalls and into your systems and even into the systems in the Caymans. They traced every keystroke. It's possible your tech guy had been working on his own and planned to pocket the money. More likely, you told him I had a payment due and I wanted it deposited in a new account in the Caymans. Either way, Cantling

Market Research already had my signature on various documents, like an identity card to enter your office building and a nondisclosure agreement. Your IT guy got my other information off the web. From there, he had little trouble opening the Caymans account online and making a deposit. If he did it for you and had doubts about it, his loyalty to you won out."

Charlie snorted. "I knew you people were cunning, but this is another level. I'll tell you what happened: You, Benjamin, set up the account. You transferred the funds. When you got found out, Byrne and Company broke into our systems, jiggered emails and footprints, and made it look like we'd opened the account ourselves. Then you went to Celestial with your stolen and manipulated information. You did it all to protect your reputation and your thieving employee. This is what I get for taking it easy on him. I should have gone right to the authorities when he confessed."

"You'll never do that," Mr. Byrne said. "You won't claim Byrne and Company manipulated the Caymans information to protect Benjamin. We have better relations with police and regulators than you do. We connect with them all the time. They'll believe us. Don't forget you're guilty as charged. And we'll have Celestial on our side. You won't stand a chance."

"You forgot something," Charlie said. "The kill fee worked both ways. Celestial would owe us two percent, nine million, if they backed out. Don't you see what happened here? They used your employee's theft as an excuse to not pay. Did they happen to mention I threatened to sue them for dropping out? They said they'd countersue and expose the appalling way we handle funds. In the end, somebody had to play the grown-up and break up the fight. I told them they were young and foolish, but because I liked their spunk, I'd let them walk away without paying the kill fee."

"Very clever. Do you plan to accept your Oscar in person?" Mr. Byrne said.

"This is no act. If Byrne and Company continues to slander me, I'll sue!"

"Will you now? A bot didn't create that Caymans account. Someone who worked for you set it up, someone who won't be as loyal as you think—not when faced with jail time. Go to the authorities, and your whole scheme will unravel in public."

"Do you really think you have the high ground?" Charlie said. "Your clients would love to hear how you hacked a paying customer."

Mr. Byrne flinched. Charlie might have scored a point. All of us hated what Charlie had done, but even now, after the accident, his energy was scary. I wanted to hide. If I was just a bit player, just a vote for my sisters, I preferred it that way.

"We didn't profit from it," Mr. Byrne said. "We did it to combat a fraud that you committed. Still, we don't need to come to blows. Let's agree that you'll close the Caymans account and restore the funds to your company. Then you'll destroy all copies of Benjamin's confession. Our two companies will work up a nondisclosure agreement about recent events, with substantial penalties for anyone who breaks it. Word will never get out."

"And we'll all live happily ever after," Charlie said, sneering. But he hadn't said no.

"Think it over," Mr. Byrne said. "Everyone in this room should want to keep this among ourselves. Talk to your family."

Mr. Byrne and Benjamin were gone. We had scarcely a moment to absorb what had happened before Tessa said, "Charlie Cantling, how could you? You framed an innocent man. You committed fraud. We can't leave you in charge. If word gets out about what you did, it could be the end of the company. We've decided to remove you. Today."

"That's ridiculous! There's no company without me! Luckily, to move me out, to pull off your suicide pact, you'd all have to get together. Theo, where do you stand?" Charlie said. "Are you really with them?"

My brother stared at his hands.

"Dammit, Theo! Look at me!" Charlie, blustering, seemed like an old train where the engine roars but the railcars don't move. "I don't know what they promised you, but they'll never put you in charge."

"We'll see about all that," Theo said, lifting his gaze at last. "Anyhow, I have my bees."

"After what I did for you with Whitney, you turn on me?"

"You were too hard on her."

"Really? You want to get back together with her?"

"If I can. We're in discussions."

"Unbelievable! On the other hand, there's good news in it. She's violated our agreement. If she'd had no contact with you, she'd have collected another hundred and twenty-five thousand. You two have saved me a bundle."

"For the moment," Vivian muttered.

"It's small change compared to the millions I saved us with Celestial," Charlie said.

"That's nonsense," Tessa said. "You created the problem—and solved it by committing fraud."

"I tried to do an acquisition. It fell apart. It's perfectly normal."

"Charlie, we've had it."

"You're all in this?"

"Yes. We're united."

"The only thing you're united in is greed. That's what this is about. Money. Nothing else!"

"If they're greedy, who made them that way?" Tessa said while the rest of us shrank from Charlie's rage. "Who withheld so much from them? Who treated them like objects? Who knocked them when they weren't perfect, when they didn't look good in a family photo?"

"You're a little late with psychology. They had two parents. Some mother you were! Spent more time on Madison Avenue than with your kids. I know. I have the bills."

"Do we really want to get into all of this now?"

"You're trying to destroy what I've been building for decades, but no, we shouldn't talk about it. All of you, do you have any idea what I've done for you?"

"Actually, we do," Tessa said quietly. "So we've named a new trustee to run things. You're out."

"What? You all signed before you heard my side of the story?"

"There is no side," Tessa said. "There's only what happened."

"Who's your new trustee and chairman?"

"For now, it's me," Tessa said.

"That's loyalty for you! You?"

"For a while. Then we'll find somebody else."

"Listen carefully. If you go ahead with this, it won't be Ladies' Day at the tennis club. Can you handle the responsibility?"

"I can try. And you can stay and help. We'll give you a title. Director of something unimportant. You won't be making decisions."

"What about Phil?" he said. "You'll be nothing without him."

"He's agreed to stay. To spare yourself further embarrassment, you're going to resign today and make it look amicable."

"Amicable? One or two of you tried to end my life. That was a felony! I didn't know who it was, so I tried to protect everybody. Then I managed the Celestial situation brilliantly. Amicable? Go ahead with this, and I'll quit a lot of things I should have quit before. Do I make myself clear?"

"Is that a threat?" Tessa said.

"Are you a wife? Do you want to be? We can fix that."

"Not now, Charlie!"

"Fine. We'll save it. Congratulations, Madam Trustee. Sooner than you can imagine, you'll be hanging by a thread."

"You're dreaming."

"Am I?" Charlie said. "Phil's a good man, but he lacks imagination. There'll be no new products, no new customers. In six months, you'll realize you're stagnating. You'll have no idea how to move forward. You'll beg me to come back."

"Don't count on it."

"Wait till you see what it's like to deal with your beloved offspring. Without me to control them, they'll keep pushing to raise the payout. Up and up and up. Hundreds of thousands a month. The little darlings will have their trips. Their toys. Their marriages. Do you have the stomach to face that every day? I built the company. I grew it to be what it is. Every day, I stood between all of you and disaster. And now you people, my dear, dear family, will run it into the ground!"

CHAPTER TWENTY

BENJAMIN

A few weeks later, on a cool day in September, I took a break from work for lunch in Central Park. I arrived early and found a bench with a view of the low thirty-yard arch of Bow Bridge and the film crew clustered on it.

Echoes of my final report to Al Byrne, completed a week earlier and not too evasive, ran through my head: "Although the acquisition of toys, and of the time and money to play with them, is a primal urge among Cantlings, I don't believe it motive enough for any of them to try to kill their father. If one of them had attempted a mercy killing, I found no evidence for it, other than a fragment from one man's addled brain. What happened? An old man had a bad dream," I'd said, quoting Byrne, who declared the matter finished.

I didn't tell Byrne that, if pressed, the Cantlings sibs could probably have guessed what had occurred in that hospital room. Among themselves, Cantling fights might be fierce, but when the world turns against them, which it does seem to do, they protect their own—usually with blithe denial, but if necessary, outright lies. I assumed the Cantlings had not discussed the matter with each other. Who wants even to whisper that a well-meaning family member might belong in prison?

My brother, taller than nearly everyone around him, emerged at the far end of the bridge.

Looking jaunty in jeans, a polo shirt, and an unzipped leather jacket, Jody took instructions from two young women with headsets and clipboards. Last winter in Colorado, he had taught an assistant director how to ski, and Jody's new friend promised him a role as an extra in his next New York shoot. My brother's Hollywood debut seemed to consist of a stroll across Bow Bridge.

Ann approached the bench, clutching a sandwich. She looked pale and tired and grim.

Jody hadn't seen either of us.

"Have you heard?" she said, sitting down. "My mother's so angry at Charlie that she's moved out. I think she has something going with Phil Weller. Vivian saw them in the lobby of Mom's hotel. Charlie might know about it. He's raging at everybody." She grew teary. "I'm so sorry about what he did to you. I keep wondering: why you?"

"My guess? I was around, and Charlie dislikes Goulds."

She sighed. "We always thought his attitude toward your family was a mask for some admiration."

"It seems to me it was a mask for more dislike."

"At least our family's done with Byrne and Company. That part is over."

"Melanie won't be working there?"

"She feels it would somehow be disloyal to Charlie. And she thinks Al Byrne was stringing her along to have sex with her. Is that possible?"

"No comment."

I sent Jody a text message. He looked up, waved, and crossed the bridge toward us, his eyes focused on Ann. "You don't look so good," he told her when he reached us. "It's still about your father, isn't it? He messed up everything, and you can't move on."

She nodded.

"Charlie was old, mean, and dying," Jody said. "He knows he deserved to be put out of his misery. That's why he can believe somebody tried."

"Jody, he's my father."

"I don't care."

"Maybe somebody did try," I said, wondering what games were being played.

"Benjamin, what do you think?" Ann said. "Would it have been wrong to try to put Charlie out of his misery?"

"Me, I don't blame whoever might have had the pillow. To tell the truth, I think it happened. And I think Charlie pretty much knows who it was."

"I thought this might be coming," Jody said. "Ancient history, bro. Leave it alone."

"I can't."

"Anything you think you know, you don't," Jody said. "Let's move on."

"How do you know I'm wrong?" I said.

"Because you usually are. How about it, Ann? Shouldn't we just drop this?"

"You're leaving it up to me?"

"Who else is there?" he said.

She stared at her hands. "No. No. It's time. Let's hear him out."

I said, "Here's what I believe." I'd planned carefully, like I had another script. "The more Charlie dwelled on what seemed to happen in the hospital, the more convinced he was that it had been real. After all, he hadn't hallucinated anything else. Why would he hallucinate this? He had all kinds of confused feelings about the people who did it: fury, admiration, hope that they might get caught, and, depending on his mood, hope that they wouldn't. The people who did it might be upset about it too. Because it turns out, if it had succeeded, it would have denied Charlie years and years of life."

"A worthy goal," my brother said.

"That's disgusting," Ann said. "You don't even believe it."

"You have no idea what I believe," Jody said.

I said, "Ann, I know your family. Could any of them get out of themselves long enough to try to help Charlie out of his misery? Do any of them have the courage? Charlie says there were two of them. Let's take him at his word. So, who was in the hospital? And who might have been there helping? For the most part Charlie was only pretending to be interested in getting answers, and Al Byrne pretended to believe him. Why? Because now and then at Byrne and Company, a client's real purpose is to erect a defense, but it's no reason to turn the client away. Charlie assumed he'd get his whitewash. Plus, he's a sharp judge of his children. Even if I discovered the perp, he expected I'd keep it to myself.

"Why would Charlie believe that about you and the perp?" Ann said.

"Because I'm close with her."

"This is way out of line. Bro, leave it alone!"

"Ann, should I stop?"

"Yes!" Jody said.

"No," Ann said. "It needs to come out."

"I don't see how this concerns you," I said to Jody. "You couldn't have been there. You've got the arm strength. You could smother Charlie anytime you want. On the other hand," I said, "who else would she trust to help her?"

"Are you accusing me?" Ann said.

"It's not an accusation."

"What is it?"

"It's more like praise. Are you going to deny it?"

"Ann, don't get into this," Jody said.

"But I want to!" she said. "It's too much to carry. Yes, I tried to do it! It haunts me! I can't shake the image of my father writhing in that bed. What was I thinking? How could I take matters into my own hands? I'm not God. I'm not even a strong person. At least we didn't damage him."

"Who's the we?" I said.

"This is what I've been afraid of from the start," Jody said to her. "You beating yourself up forever."

"You? Worrying about me? That's a first."

"You're damn right I worry about you," Jody said.

"Don't you think talking about it, admitting the truth, might help?" Ann said.

"It might," my brother said. "But this is not the truth."

"It isn't?" she said.

"I was never going to let you succeed. You were in no danger of killing your father."

"You were there?" I said to Jody. "And Charlie survived?"

"I saved his fucking life!"

"How did you do that?" Ann said. "And why didn't you tell me?"

"Sometimes I wanted to tell you. But I thought: Why tell you I tricked you about something so important? You might not believe me anyhow. Did we really need another argument? Yeah, you talked a big game, like this was what Charlie would want and somebody had to do it. But look at you. You've been having a hard time just because you think we tried."

"We did try."

"Really? You said I was good at sneaking stuff. Thank you very much. I kept hoping you'd change your mind. I mean, why put yourself at so much risk? Believe me, I know a thing or two about risk. But you were determined. When we got to his room, it looked like you might do it. So I volunteered for the smothering. I wasn't sure you'd let me take your place, but you did."

"You leaned on him! He fought you!"

"You actually believe I wasn't strong enough? He was so weak you probably could have smothered him yourself. If that had happened, well, you're a Cantling. You're entitled to do almost anything. If you got found out, your family's lawyers would make it so you never went to jail. But I knew you'd never get over it—because you're not entitled to live guilt-free. You'd punish yourself forever with stories about miracles and people waking up from comas. I pushed the pillow into him. I rocked his head around like he was fighting me. I left him some air to breathe. It was as phony a fight as you'll ever see. Then I gave up. And nobody broke any laws. And nobody got hurt."

"What would you have done if I'd insisted on doing it myself?"

"I'd have rung the nurse."

"I'd have hated you for that."

"You kind of hate me anyhow."

"You have yourself to thank for that. Now it turns out you've been lying about the most important thing I ever wanted to do."

"It's not just me who's been lying. You've been lying to yourself. Have you thought about why you let me take over? Wasn't it because you wanted your hands as clean as possible? I think, if you'd really wanted it to happen, you'd have tried it yourself."

"Talk about being entitled," Ann said, boiling over. "You're convinced you can read my mind. If you're telling the truth, you made a life-and-death decision about my family, and it was not what I wanted. Everything about this was a bad idea, especially you."

"Gratitude from a Cantling," Jody said. "That would be asking too much!"

I tried to play peacemaker. "Ann, I will never believe what you did was a bad idea."

"Was Jody a good idea?" she asked.

Things had, to say the least, gone awry. "I feel like I'm intruding," I said. "I should leave you two to sort this out."

"Don't be such a chicken!" Ann said. "I'm so confused. I'm not sure he's telling the truth, but he might be. Maybe it was all a mirage. Maybe we didn't try to kill my father after all."

Jody scoffed. "Well now, it took a while, but I got a maybe."

She stared across the water, eyes opened wide in amazement. "And maybe it's better this way," she said.

Ann shook her head. For the first time today, she smiled. At what? At being rescued from a lifetime of punishing herself for smothering her father? At the elusive, unpredictable Jody? Or at the impossibility of knowing what had really happened?

Jody was summoned back to the bridge. While I finished my sandwich, I noticed, below him, the occupants of several rented rowboats watching the slow-motion events above. Unperturbed after the revelations with Ann, Jody leaned over the bridge's stone parapet and started a conversation with a young family in a boat. I thought: Jody's charm and energy, his capacity for live action, are both blessing and curse. His behavior keeps creating problems he's forced to solve, but solve them he often does. It seemed he had intervened with care—almost with sensitivity—and saved Ann Cantling from her conscience and Charlie Cantling from death. Did he really need help from me?

Ann continued to gaze out over the water, focusing on nothing in particular as she took small bites out of her sandwich. I wondered if I'd helped my brother gain the high ground with her. She said, "Did you always suspect it was me in the hospital room?"

"Yes."

She fell silent as she finished her sandwich. Then she said, "Vivian told me you tried to have sex with her."

"I didn't try. She had me on her horse. I needed to keep her happy."

"You didn't go through with it?"

"No way."

"That's what she says. I was upset at first, but I guess I understand. You and I weren't really together, and you were upset with me because of Jody. I suppose we could get past it."

I thought: We could? A mixed message if there ever was one.

Below the bridge, a trio of teenage girls in a boat called something to Jody. He borrowed a clipboard from one of the women shadowing him and scribbled on the top sheet. Then he removed the page, folded it into the shape of a rocket plane, and aimed it down at the girls. The glide path to their eager waiting hands was airborne perfection. My brother had signed an autograph.

Ann said, "If we believe Jody, it's no surprise he's been so angry about what Charlie did to you. He kept Charlie alive, and this was the result."

"Is it really over between you and Jody?"

"If there ever was an 'it' to be over, it's been over since the hospital. It's like when I saw just how serious life could be, I had to end the games. It seems ironic. Maybe the most grown-up thing Jody ever did helped push him and me apart."

"And it's still apart."

"Yes," she said. "And I've begun to understand how we got here. For you and me, separately, Jody was a project. We shouldn't have bothered. It held us back."

We watched him. The trio of fans called up to him again, and Jody flung another airplane toward them. Squeals attended the smooth descent into their hands. A couple in a rowboat waved to Jody and seemed to want an autograph as well. Jody constructed a new airship, which, launched with a sweeping gesture, nose-dived into the pond.

Jody Gould, I thought. Exhibit A in the intricate unknowability of everyone. He's spiteful, he's needy, his talents clash with his impulse to waste them, but he reaches people in ways that I can't. Who's to say his autograph is destined to be worthless?

Snap your pictures, ladies, and keep the paper planes. Only God can see the future, and the King of Puzzles doesn't share.

Exhibit B was the love of my life. I said, "The way we're talking, Ann, does it mean we have a chance?"

"After all this, do you want there to be a chance?"

"I do. But I feel humiliated about what happened at the inn."

"You were exhausted," she said. "Can't you forget about it?"

"I shouldn't have tried. It was too soon. I'm a bumbler."

"You? What about me? I spent all that time with Jody."

"Didn't you just say he's kind of a hero?" I asked her. Even now, I'd risen to my brother's defense. "When it comes to bumbling, I'm the real deal."

Ann smiled. "If that's true, doesn't knowing it make you less of one?"

I wondered whether her generosity was tinged with condescension. After all, I thought, she's a Cantling. Does she assume she's entitled to choose between Jody and me? But she's the Cantling who works, who likes to feel productive, who knows something about the world and will most likely contribute to it. She's the Cantling who took a risk to help her father. The Cantling who cares, with the guts to follow through.

The Cantling I've always loved.

"What's going to happen with us?" I asked.

"We're friends, aren't we? That's already something to work with. People say that can be half the battle."

"I could win the other half right now," I said with sudden confidence.

She smiled. "Here? Now? We'd get arrested."

"It would be worth it. Don't we know the law's an ass? By the way, yours is pretty good."

"Why, Benjamin Gould," Ann said. "What's come over you? Who do you think you are?"

THE END

www.ingramcontent.com/pod-product-compliance
Lightning Source LLC
LaVergne TN
LVHW041906070526
838199LV00051BA/2516